THE AU

Edward Frederic Benson was born at Wellington College, Berkshire, in 1867. He was one of an extraordinary family. His father Edward White Benson – first headmaster of Wellington – later became Chancellor of Lincoln Cathedral, Bishop of Truro and Archbishop of Canterbury. His mother, Mary Sidgwick, was described by Gladstone as 'the cleverest woman in Europe'. Two children died young but the other four, bachelors all, achieved distinction: Arthur Christopher as Master of Magdalene College, Cambridge, and a prolific author; Maggie as an amateur egyptologist; Robert Hugh as a Catholic priest and propagandist novelist; and Fred.

Like his brothers and sisters, Fred was a precocious scribbler. He was still a student at Cambridge when he published his first book, *Sketches from Marlborough*. While he was working as an archaeologist in Athens, his first novel *Dodo* (1893) was published to great success. Thereafter Benson devoted himself to writing, playing sports, watching birds and gadding about. He mixed with the best and brightest of his day: Margot Asquith, Marie Corelli, his mother's friend Ethel Smyth and many other notables found their eccentricities exposed in the shrewd, hilarious world of his fiction.

Around 1918, E. F. Benson moved to Rye, Sussex. He was inaugurated mayor of the town in 1934. There in his garden room, the collie Taffy beside him, Benson wrote many of his comical novels, his sentimental fiction, ghost stories, informal biographies and reminiscences – almost one hundred books in all. Ten days before his death on 29 February 1940, E. F. Benson delivered to his publishers a last autobiography, *Final Edition*.

The Hogarth Press also publishes *Mrs Ames, Paying Guests, Secret Lives, As We Are, As We Were, Dodo – An Omnibus, The Freaks of Mayfair, The Luck of the Vails* and *The Blotting Book*.

AN AUTUMN SOWING

E. F. Benson

New Introduction by
John Julius Norwich

THE HOGARTH PRESS
LONDON

Published in 1987 by
The Hogarth Press
Chatto & Windus Ltd
30 Bedford Square, London WC1B 3RP

First published in Great Britain by William Collins 1917

British Library Cataloguing in Publication Data

1. Benson, E.F.
An autumn sowing.
I. Title
823' 8 PR6003.E66
ISBN 0 7012 0762 0

Printed in Great Britain by
Cox & Wyman Ltd
Reading, Berkshire

INTRODUCTION

Edward Frederic Benson was born in 1867 at, of all places, Wellington College, which had recently been established with his father – a future Archbishop of Canterbury – as its first Master. He was the fifth of six children: a strange family, talented yet somehow tormented, of whom the eldest son and the eldest daughter died young, and the second daughter became permanently insane. Of the three surviving sons all, when they took the trouble, could be brilliant writers: Arthur, the academic and man of letters, generally considered to be one of the best Eton housemasters in the history of the College before going on to be Master of Magdalene College, Cambridge; Monsignor Hugh, a Catholic convert, preacher and missioner who wrote plays, novels and (in collaboration with the unspeakable Fr. Rolfe, 'Baron Corvo') a biography of Thomas Becket, and who was burnt out by his own manic energy at forty-three; and – younger than Arthur but older than Hugh – Edward, invariably known to his family as Fred.

There can be no doubt that all three brothers were basically homosexual – though Arthur and Hugh almost certainly remained virgins till they died. As to Fred, an enthusiastic member of the distinctly ambiguous English colony in Venice before the First World War, Arthur himself expressed his misgivings: 'Charles Williams in his Palazzo, Lady Radnor in her salons – the silliness of it, the idleness, the sentimentality about bronzed gondoliers, etc., with I dare say a nastier background . . . It is this life which Fred leads so mysteriously and of which he says nothing. I wonder what it is all about.' But whatever it was all about, he was wrong about the idleness. By the time Fred died in 1940, a few months before his seventy-fourth birthday, he had written at least one hundred full-length books – not counting those in which he had collaborated with other people – including some seventy novels; and he had acquired a numerous enthusiastic public. If he never quite received the critical acclaim he in a sense deserved, it is because he wrote too easily and too much: he frequently told the same story three and four times over in different novels, changing only the setting, the dialogue and the names of the characters. As a result, despite the liveliness of his style and the deadly accuracy of his social satire, the vast majority of his work is now forgotten; he lives on, above all, in the 'Lucia' series – of which *Queen Lucia* and *Lucia in London* are the best – and, for the true cognoscenti, the 'Dodo' books, based on the celebrated Margot, Countess of Oxford and Asquith.

In his excellent essay on E. F. Benson in the *Dictionary of National Biography*, Michael Sadleir mentions some twenty-five titles, perhaps a quarter of his total output; *An Autumn Sowing* is not among them. The most likely explanation is that he had not read it; he could hardly have ignored, otherwise, a quite remarkable novel that shows us the author at the height of his powers. In 1917, when it was first published, Benson was fifty. His eye was as observant as ever, his insight as penetrating, his ear for dialogue as acute, his wit as merciless; but he had lost the brittle quality that spoils some of his earlier work and he had not yet lapsed into the repetitiousness that was so sorely to try the patience of his later admirers. He was, in other words, still capable of setting himself a challenge, and of meeting it triumphantly.

In doing so, he was enormously assisted by a style which was not only admirable in itself – for he was always a natural writer – but which he had polished and refined to the point where it was ideally suited to his needs. Occasionally – just occasionally – we may come across a faintly purplish patch; but seventy years ago such patches were part of any serious author's stock in trade (just as in seventy years' time they may be again) and we cannot in all fairness blame an artist for accommodating himself to the fashions of his day. More often it is his economy that strikes us, particularly in his delineation of character: for an example, we need go no further than the first half-dozen pages – in which he describes, one by one, the members of the Keeling family as they sit on Sunday morning strung out along their varnished pitch-pine pew. Here he is on Mrs Keeling:

Though she quite believed in the next world, she did not take the smallest interest in it: she regarded it just about as the ordinary citizen of a country town regards Australia. Very likely Dr Inglis was right about it, and we should all know in time. She had pale eyebrows, rather prominent gray eyes, and hair from which the orignal yellow was fast fading. Her general appearance was of a woman who, thirty years ago, had probably been exceedingly pretty in an absolutely meaningless manner.

A little later comes the memorable – and wonderfully characteristic – remark:

She had a good deal of geniality which, so to speak, led nowhere, and a complete absence of physical cowardice, which might be due to a want of imagination.

Little by little, as the story goes on, there emerges a character as beautifully drawn as, let us say, Mrs Bennett in *Pride and Prejudice*; indeed I know of no other novel that reminds me so continually of Jane Austen, or that strikes me so forcibly as being exactly the sort of book that she would have written had she lived a century later than she did. But the creation of the odious Mrs Keeling is only one of several *tours de force* in this remarkable book: there is also her husband, for whom our sympathy steadily increases as the story continues, and whom we find before it ends to have developed into a genuinely tragic figure; her unfortunate daughter Alice, whose tribulations also give her, in the closing pages, a touch of unexpected nobility; and the insufferable Mr Silverdale – who must surely have been modelled on some nightmare cleric of the author's own acquaintance. The subsidiary characters, too, are handled with just as sure a touch: Mrs Keeling's mother, 'a tiny, venomous old lady in a Bath-chair', eating her slice of hot beef in dead silence 'with a circular mill-like motion of her chin' and deliberately making the lunch party as disagreeable as possible for all concerned; or Mrs Fyson, very nearly as unpleasant, who can be trusted to put the worst interpretation on any occurrence – as when she inadvertently comes upon Norah Propert one evening at The Cedars. Mrs Keeling, we read,

> . . . had with some appearance of astonishment merely said that she and Miss Propert had had a very pleasant chat while Mr Keeling was telephoning for a cab to take Miss Propert home. On which Mrs Fyson had looked exactly like a ferret and said, 'Did he bring her into your drawing-room? That was *very* clever!'

Michael Sadleir finds evidence, in much of Benson's work, that he had 'a generalised dislike of women'; and certainly, on the basis of the extracts I have quoted above, it would be difficult to argue the contrary. On the other hand there is the all-important exception of Norah herself, the heroine of the novel, a girl of considerable intelligence, strength of character and wit, well able to hold her own against the bullying of Mr Keeling or the insinuations of his wife, behaving impeccably throughout yet never for a moment sanctimonious or priggish. Her competence and efficiency might occasionally frighten us a little, perhaps; but we are left in no doubt of her femininity and very real charm, and when the story reaches its inevitable conclusion our hearts go out to her.

And so, unquestionably, does the author's – I suspect to his own considerable surprise. Indeed, the more I think about *An Autumn Sowing* the more convinced I become that the book took over from him, and ultimately assumed a shape materially different from the one that he had intended. The opening chapters are, as we should expect them to be, witty, cynical and sophisticated; we are all set for another *Lucia*, or something very like her. Then, as the story progresses, the overall mood changes: the satirical passages become less frequent, the prevailing tone more gentle, and shot through with a strange innocence. It is not mawkish: the characters of the two principal protagonists – and of the author himself – are sufficient guarantees of that. But it is very different from what has gone before.

So, too, is the style. It becomes simple and sincere – and

understated to the point where a memorable simile almost passes unnoticed by the reader, just as an awkward repetition does by the writer:

> The ridge on which he walked declined downwards into a hollow full of sunshine flecked with shadow. A few big oak-trees stood there, still leafless, and the narrow path, with mossy banks on each side, led through a copse of hazel which had been felled the year before. The ground was covered with the fern-like leaves of wood anemones and thickly tufted with the dark green spears, where in May the bluebells would seem like patches of fallen sky. It was sheltered here, and a brimstone butterfly flitted through the patches of sunlight.

If this theory is correct and the novel did indeed take an unexpected turn, it would go a long way towards explaining what seems to me its greatest weakness – the last chapter. Could it be that Benson, realising what had happened, made a final effort to bring the book back on to the original lines and then, having done so, found himself obliged to round off the sub-plot as neatly as he had the main one? The result is certainly tidier; and yet, somehow, it fails to ring true. And how much more dramatic it would have been if the book had ended with Chapter Ten, with Keeling walking back to his cheerless home, alone through the snow . . .

But this is only a personal opinion, which others may not share. And in any case it is a minor cavil when seen against the immense pleasure that the book has given me. Some may find it dated – but then so are most novels except the current best-seller, and quite right too. On the other hand the author's underlying theme is eternal, and the chief target of his satire – social and class snobbery – although not perhaps quite as barefaced as it was seventy years ago, is at least still very much alive; and if, while attacking it, Benson himself never loses his urbanity and detachment – he was, I strongly suspect, on his own level no inconsiderable snob himself – he certainly does not pull his punches.

Make no mistake: *An Autumn Sowing* is not great literature. E. F. Benson was no George Eliot or Charles Dickens; nor, despite the comparison I have made above, was he really a Jane Austen. But he was, at his best, a writer whose sparkling wit concealed a far greater degree of perception than is generally allowed him. For this reason he has been in recent years seriously underestimated; and it is greatly to be hoped that this reissue of one of his most brilliant novels will do at least something towards regaining for him the place he deserves. If that place proves, as I believe it will, to be somewhere quite respectably high up in the second league – well, that should be good enough for most of us.

John Julius Norwich, 1986

CHAPTER I

Mr Keeling had expected an edifying half-hour when Dr Inglis gave out as his text, 'There shall be wailing and gnashing of teeth,' and as the discourse proceeded, he felt that his anticipations were amply justified. Based on this unshakable foundation, and buttressed by other stalwart pronouncements, the doctrine of eternal damnation wore a very safe and solid aspect. It was the justice of it that appealed to Mr Keeling. Mankind had been warned in a perfectly unmistakable manner that if they persisted in certain courses of action and in certain inabilities to believe, they would be punished for ever and ever. That was fair, that was reasonable: rules were made to be obeyed. If you were truly sorry for having disobeyed them, a secondary principle, called mercy, came to the succour of the repentant. But Dr Inglis did not say so much about that. He was concerned with the inflexibility of his text.

It is said that a man's conduct is coloured and inspired by his religion, but it is equally true to say of another and more numerous class that their religion is coloured and inspired by their conduct. Certainly that was the case with Mr Keeling.

His life did not so much spring out of his religion, as his religion out of his life; and what he felt every Sunday morning and evening in church was the fruit, the stern honey distilled, so to speak, from the mental and moral integrity which had pervaded him from Monday till Saturday inclusive. All the week the bees collected that store of provender which was transmuted into the frame of mind which was equivalent in him to religion. It did not in the smallest degree enter into his week-day life: his week-day life secreted it, and he found it very well expressed for him in the sermon of Dr Inglis and the fiercer of King David's psalms. The uprightness, honesty, and industry which he demanded from himself he demanded also from others; but it was not his religion that inspired those excellent qualities. They inspired it.

Mr Keeling sat at one end of the varnished pitch-pine pew with his children in a row between him and their mother at the other end. There were large schedules of commandments on either side of the plain, bare table (miscalled an altar), so that everybody could see what was expected of him, while Dr Inglis told them what they could expect if they were not very careful. Next his father sat John, who, from the unfortunate accident of his being the youngest, went last into the pew, while Mr Keeling stood like an angry shepherd in the aisle to herd his family into the fold, just above which rose the pulpit where Dr Inglis at this moment was speaking in a voice of icy conviction.

John's position was thus a peculiarly depressing one, for his natural instinct in those hours of tedium in church was to edge away as far as possible from his father, but on the other side of him was his sister Alice, who not only sang psalms and canticles and hymns with such piercing resonance that John's left ear sang and buzzed during the prayers afterwards, but had marvellously angular knees and elbows, which with a pious and unconscious air she pressed into John's slim side if he encroached on her due share of the pew. And when we consider that John was just seventeen years old, an age when the young male animal has a tendency to show symptoms of its growth and vigour by jerky, electric movements known as 'fidgets' whenever it has to stop in one position for more than a minute or two, it was reasonable that John should conclude that his share of weeping and gnashing of teeth had begun already. But church time did not last for ever and ever. . . . Beyond the angular Alice, who was twenty-five, came Hugh, whose banns had been given out that day for the first time, just before the sermon, and who was still feeling rather hot and uncomfortable about it. He had hinted at breakfast that perhaps he would not go to church that morning in consequence, but his father had fixed him with so appalling a countenance that the hint developed no further.

Alice's banns had never been given out by anybody, and a physiognomist might hazard the conjecture that they never would be, for she had in her face, with its short-sighted eyes, high cheekbones, and mouth that looked as if it had got unbuttoned, that indescribable air of old-maidishness which fate sometimes imprints on the features of girls still scarcely of marriageable age. They do not, as Alice did not, seem to be of the types from which wives and mothers are developed. A celibacy, tortured it may be, seems the fate inexplicably destined for them by the irony of Nature who decreed that they should be women, and they discharge their hearts in peevishness or in feverish activities. Alice was inclined to the more amiable of these safety-valves, but she could be peevish too.

At the end of the row, large, inane, and comfortable, came Mrs Keeling, listening without appreciation, dissent, or emotion of any kind to this uncompromising view of the future of miserable sinners, for that was not the sort of thing that affected her in the slightest degree, since it concerned not this world but the next. Though she quite believed in the next world, she did not take the smallest interest in it: she regarded it just about as the ordinary citizen of a country town regards Australia. Very likely Dr Inglis was right about it, and we should all know in time. She had pale eyebrows, rather prominent gray eyes, and hair from which the original yellow was fast fading. Her general appearance was of a woman who, thirty years ago, had probably been exceedingly pretty in an absolutely meaningless manner. This, indeed, had been the case, as certain photographs (fast fading too) scattered about her 'boudoir' sufficiently proved. It was reasonable to suppose that her marriage with so obviously dominant a man as Thomas Keeling should have sucked all colour, mental and physical, out of her, but in the process she had developed a certain protective strength of her own, an inertia of dead weight. She did not make up her mind on many topics, but when she did she sank deeply down like a stone, and a great deal of grappling and effort was required to move her. She did not argue, she did not struggle, she just remained. Her power of remaining, indeed, was so remarkable that it was possible that there might be something alive, some power of limpet-like suction that gave her force: on the other hand, it was possible that this sticking was mere brute weight, undirected by any human will. She stopped where she was, obeying the habits of heavy bodies, and it required a great deal of strength to shift her. Even her husband, that notable remover of all obstacles that stood in his way, seldom attempted to do so when he was convinced she meant to abide. In the course of years he had tugged her, or perhaps she had really gone of her own accord, to the sort of place where he wished her to be, somewhere between an easy-chair in the awful drawing-room which she had lately furnished, and the kitchen. In other words, she gave him an extremely comfortable home, and took her place there as hostess. But if he wanted more than that, she was, as he had found out, a millstone round his neck. In common with many women of her type, she had a practically inexhaustible flow of words to her mouth which seemed a disintegration rather than an expression of the fabric of her faculties; but every now and then among this debris there occurred an idea, disconnected from all else, and floating down on its own account, which seemed to suggest that Emmeline had a mind after all, though you would never have thought it. But an idea did appear now and again, a bright, solid, sensible idea, lying there like a jewel in a gutter. She had tastes, too, a marked liking for sweet things, for quantities of cream in her tea, for bright colours, for what we may call Mendelssohnic music and for plush-like decorations. She had a good deal of geniality which, so to speak, led nowhere, and a complete absence of physical cowardice, which might be due to a want of imagination.

Apart from the strenuous matter of Dr Inglis's discourse, a circumstance that added interest to it was the fact that this was the last Sunday on which he would officiate at St Thomas's, Bracebridge, and he had already been the recipient of a silver tea-set, deeply chased with scrolls and vegetables, subscribed for by his parishioners and bought at Mr Keeling's stores, and a framed address in primary colours. He had been appointed to a canonry of the Cathedral that stood in the centre of the cup-shaped hollow on the sides of which Bracebridge so picturesquely clustered, and his successor, a youngish man, with a short, pale beard, now curiously coloured with the light that came through a stained glass window opposite, had read the lessons and the litany.

Mr Silverdale, indeed, in spite of the special interest of Dr Inglis's discourse, was engrossing a good deal of Alice Keeling's attention, and her imagination was very busy. He had spent an assiduous week in calling on his parishioners, but she had not been at home when he paid his visit to her mother, who had formed no ideas about him, and Alice was now looking forward with a good deal of excitement to to-night, when he was going to take supper with them, after evening service, as her mother had expressed it in her note, or after evensong, as he had expressed it in his answer.

His conduct and appearance during the service had aroused her interest, for he wore a richly coloured stole and a very short surplice, had bowed in the direction of the east window as he walked up the chancel, and had made a very deep obeisance somewhere in the middle of the Creed, when everybody else stood upright. Somehow there was a different atmosphere about him from that which surrounded the grim and austere Dr Inglis, something in the pale face and in a rapt expression which she easily read into his eyes, that made her mentally call him priest-like rather than clergyman-like. Like most young women in whom the destiny of old-maid is unrolling itself, Alice had a strong potentiality for furtive romance, and while the pains of hell were being enunciated to her inattentive ears, her short-sighted eyes were fixed on Mr Silverdale, and she began to think of Lord Tennyson's poem of Galahad who was unmarried too. . . . She was so far lost in this that the rustle of the uprising congregation at the end of the sermon, reached her belatedly, and she rose in a considerable hurry, filling up the gap in this tall barrier of Keelings. She and her mother were not less than five feet ten in height, John's inches had already outsoared them both, while her father and Hugh, each a full six feet of solid stuff, completed the substantial row. By one of Nature's unkindest plans the sons were handsome, the daughter plain, but all had the self-reliant quality of size about them. A hymn followed, while the offertory, which Mr Keeling helped to collect in serge-lined open mahogany plates, was in progress, and the blessing, pronounced by Mr Silverdale, who made an odd movement in the air with his right hand, brought the service to a close.

According to custom, Mr Keeling, with his two sons, went for a brisk walk, whatever the weather, before lunch, while Alice and her mother, one of whose habits was to set as few feet to the ground as was humanly possible without incurring the danger of striking root, got into the victoria that waited for them at the church-door, on which the fat horse was roused from his reverie and began heavily lolloping homewards. It was not usual in Bracebridge to have a carriage out on Sunday, and Mrs Keeling, surveying less fortunate pedestrians through her tortoise-shell-handled glass, was Sunday by Sunday a little Lucretian on the subject. The matter of the carriage also was a monument to her own immovableness, for her husband, years ago, had done his utmost to induce her to traverse the half mile on her own feet.

'Ah, there is poor Mrs Etheridge,' she said. 'She will get very hot and dusty before she reaches home. I would offer her a lift, but it would make such a crush for us all. And there is poor Mr Moulton. How he limps! I noticed that when he was handing the other offertory plate. He has a long walk before him too, has he not? But we cannot drive everybody home. It is pleasant driving to-day: the thin rug keeps off the dust, and I want no other covering. It is neither too hot nor too cold, just what I like. But it looks threatening over there. I should not wonder if poor Mrs Etheridge got a drenching before she reaches her little house. Her house is damp too: I have often noticed that, and to get hot and wet and sit in a damp house is the very way to get pneumonia. You are very silent, Alice.'

Alice assumed a slightly nippy look.

'I was waiting till you had finished, Mamma!' she permitted herself to observe.

Here Mrs Keeling's disintegration of mind showed itself. She had but a moment before been critical of Alice's silence.

'Yes, dear, that is what I always tried to teach you,' she said, 'when you were children; just as my mother taught me. I'm sure I told you all every day not to talk with your mouths full or when anybody else is talking. If we all talked together there would be a fine noise, to be sure, and nobody a bit the wiser. I took a great deal of trouble about your manners, and I'm sure it was not thrown away, for I consider you've all got very good manners, even John, when he chooses. Talking of that' (This phrase meant nothing in Mrs Keeling's mouth), 'I noticed Mr Silverdale in church. He seemed to me to have a hungry kind of look. I dare say his housekeeper is very careless about his meals, not having a wife. I hope he will make a good meal this evening. Perhaps it would be safer, dear, if you refused the salmon mayonnaise, as you are not so very fond of it. Mrs Bellaway would have it that there was plenty, but she has such a small appetite herself.'

'I saw nothing hungry about his face,' said Alice, with decision. 'He looked so rapt and far-away as if anything like food was the last subject he would think about.'

'Very likely, my dear; you are wonderful at reading character. All the same the people who don't give a thought to food are just those who do go hungry, so we may both of us be right. Is that a spot of rain or a fly? I felt something on the back of my glove.'

Alice put her clasped hands between her knees and squeezed them. She was perfectly willing to go without her mayonnaise, but she could not bear that her mother should think Mr Silverdale looked hungry.

'I thought his face was so like Jonah preaching at Nineveh in the stained glass window,' she said.

Mrs Keeling suddenly became coherently humorous. An idea (not much of one, but still an idea) floated down the debris from her mind.

'Well, he had had nothing to eat for three days,' she remarked. 'That seems to show that I'm right.'

The street down which they drove from church very soon ceased to be a street in the sense of its being lined on each side by contiguous houses, and became Alfred Road, and was bounded on each side by brick and stucco villas. At first these stood arm-in-arm, semi-detached, but presently they took on an air of greater spaciousness and stood square and singly, while the gardens that sandwiched them before and behind were large enough to contain a grass-plot and six or seven laurels in front, and a full-sized tennis-lawn and a small kitchen garden at the back. But perhaps they scarcely warranted such names as 'Chatsworth,' 'Blenheim,' 'Balmoral,' or 'The Engadine,' which appeared so prominently on their painted gates. 'Blenheim' had once been Mrs Keeling's home, and her mother, a tiny, venomous old lady in a Bath-chair, lived and was likely long to live there still, for she had admirable health, and the keen, spiteful temper which gives its possessor so indignant and absorbing an interest in life.

It was to a far narrower home than Blenheim that Emmeline had gone on her marriage with Mr Keeling, and though the greater part of Alfred Road had shaken their heads over her mating herself with a man so much below her socially, her mother, wife, and now widow of a retired P. & O. captain, had formed a juster estimate of her future son-in-law's chin. A silly, pretty girl like Emmeline, she thought, was very lucky to capture a man who was going to make his way upwards so obviously as that strapping young fellow with the square jaw. He was then but the proprietor of the fishmonger's shop at the end of the High Street, but Mrs Goodford knew very well, without being told so by young Keeling himself, that he was not of the sort which remain a small fishmonger. Events had justified her insight, and it was to a much bigger house than Mrs Goodford's that her daughter was being driven on this Sunday morning.

As the victoria pursued its leisurely way, the spaces between the Blenheims and Chatsworths grew larger, the villas ceased to have but one window on each side of the front door: they stood farther back from the road, and were approached by small carriage drives culminating in what was known as the 'carriage sweep' in front of the house, a gravelled space where a carriage could turn completely round. Two gates led to the carriage sweep, on one of which was painted 'In,' and on the other 'Out,' and the spaces surrounding the houses could justly be called 'grounds' since they embraced tennis lawns and kitchen gardens with 'glass,' and shrubberies with winding paths. Retired colonels must needs have private money of their own in addition to their pensions to live so spaciously, and Mr Keeling, even thus housed, was putting by very considerable sums of money every year. Into one of those carriage drives, advertised to passers-by as the entrance of 'The Cedars' (probably because there were three prosperous larch trees planted near the 'In' gate), Mrs Keeling's carriage turned, and after passing some yards of shrubbery stopped before a wooden Gothic porch. Both ladies appeared unconscious of having reached home till a small boy covered with buttons came out of the house and removed the light carriage-rug that covered their knees.

It was but a few months ago that Mr Keeling, taking advantage of a break in the lease of his own house, and the undoubted bargain that he had secured in this more spacious residence, had bought the freehold of 'The Cedars,' and had given the furnishing and embellishment of it (naming the total sum not to be exceeded) into the hands of his wife and the head of the furnishing department in his stores. The Gothic porch, already there, had suggested a 'scheme' to the artistic Mr Bowman, and from it you walked into a large square hall of an amazing kind. On the floor were red encaustic tiles with blue fleurs-de-lis, and the walls and ceiling were covered with the most expensive and deeply-moulded Lincrusta-Walton paper of Tudor design with alternate crowns and portcullises. It was clearly inconvenient that visitors should be able to look in through the window that opened on the 'carriage-sweep'; so Mr Bowman had arranged that it should not open at all, but be filled with sham bottle-bottoms impervious to the eye. In front of it stood a large pitch-pine table to hold the clothings and impedimenta of out-of-doors, and on each side of it were chairs of Gothic design. The fireplace, also new, had modern Dutch tiles in it, and a high battlemented mantel-shelf, with turrets at the corners. For hats there was a mahogany hat-rack with chamois-horns tipped with brass instead of pegs, and on the Lincrusta-Walton walls were trophies of spears and battle-axes and swords. Mr Bowman would have left the hall thus in classic severity, but his partner in decoration here intervened, and insisted on its being made more home-like. To secure this she added a second table on which stood a small stuffed crocodile rampant holding in his outstretched forelegs a copper tray for visitors' calling cards. Mrs Keeling was very much pleased with this, considering it so quaint, and when her friends called, it often served as the header-board from which they leaped into the sea of conversation. The grate of the fire-place, empty of fuel, in this midsummer weather, was filled with multitudinous strips of polychromatic paper with gilt threads among it, which streamed from some fixed point up in the chimney, and suggested that a lady with a skirt covered with ribbons had stuck in the chimney, her head and body being invisible. By the fire-place Mrs Keeling had placed a painted wheel-barrow with a gilt spade, containing fuchsias in pots, and among the trophies of arms had inserted various Polynesian aprons of shells and leather thongs brought back by her father from his voyages; these the outraged Mr Bowman sarcastically allowed 'added colour' about which there was no doubt whatever. Beyond this hall lay a farther inner one, out of which ascended the main staircase furnished (here again could be traced Mr Bowman's chaste finger) with a grandfather's clock, and reproductions of cane-backed Jacobean chairs. From this opened a big drawing-room giving on the lawn at the back, and communicating at one end with Mrs Keeling's 'boudoir.' These rooms, as being more exclusively feminine, were inspired in the matter of their decoration by Mrs Keeling's unaided taste; about them nothing need be said beyond the fact that it would take any one a considerable time to ascertain whether they contained a greater number of mirrors framed in plush and painted with lilies, or of draped pictures standing at angles on easels. Saddlebag chairs, damask curtains, Landseer prints, and a Brussels carpet were the chief characteristics of the dining-room.

To the left of the Gothic and inner halls, a very large room had been built out to the demolition of a laurel shrubbery. This was Mr Keeling's study, and when he gave his house over to the taste of his decorators, he made the stipulation that they should not exercise their artistic faculties therein, but leave it entirely to him. In fact, there had been a short and violent scene of ejection when the card-holding crocodile had appeared on a table there owing to the inadvertence of a house-maid, for Mr Keeling had thrown it out of the window on to the carriage sweep, and one of its hind legs had to be repaired. Here for furniture he had a gray drugget on the floor, a couple of easy chairs, half a dozen deal ones, an immense table and a step-ladder, while the wall space was entirely taken up with book shelves. These were but as yet half-filled, and stacks of books, some still in the parcels in which they had arrived from dealers and publishers, stood on the floor. This room with its books was Mr Keeling's secret romance: all his life, even from the days of the fish-shop, the collection of fine illustrated books had been his hobby, his *hortus inclusus*, where lay his escape from the eternal pursuit of money-making and from the tedium of domestic life. There he indulged his undeveloped love of the romance of literature, and the untutored joy with which design of line and colour inspired him. As an apostle of thoroughness in business and everything else, his books must be as well equipped as books could be: there must be fine bindings, the best paper and printing, and above all there must be pictures. When that was done you might say you had got a book. For rarity and antiquity he cared nothing at all; a sumptuous edition of a book of nursery rhymes was more desirable in his eyes than any Caxton. Here in his hard, industrious, Puritan life, was Keeling's secret garden, of which none of his family held the key. Few at all entered the room, and into the spirit of it none except perhaps the young man who was at the head of the book department at Keeling's stores. He had often been of use to the proprietor in pointing out to him the publication of some new edition he might wish to possess, and now and then, as on this particular Sunday afternoon, he was invited to spend an hour at the house looking over Mr Keeling's latest purchases. He came, of course, by the back door, and was conducted by the boy in buttons along the servants' passage, for Mrs Keeling would certainly not like to have the front door opened to him. That would have been far from proper, and he might have put his hat on one of the brass-tipped chamois horns. But there was no real danger of that, for it had never occurred to Charles Propert to approach 'The Cedars' by any but the tradesman's entrance.

Mrs Keeling in the passionless and oyster-like conduct of her life very seldom allowed any external circumstance to annoy her, and when she found on her arrival home this morning a note beside the crocodile in the hall saying that her mother proposed to come to lunch, it did not interfere with the few minutes' nap that she always allowed herself on Sunday morning after the pomp and fatigue of public worship. But it was a fact that her husband did not much care for his mother-in-law's presence at his table, for as Mrs Keeling said, they were apt to worry each other, and consequently Mrs Goodford's visits usually took place on week-days when Mr Keeling was at the Stores. But it did not ever so faintly enter her head to send round to say that she would not be at home for lunch, because, in the first place, she did not care sufficiently whether Mamma came or not, and in the second place, because there was not the slightest chance of Mamma's believing her. The most she could do was to intercept any worrying by excessive geniality, and as they all sat down she remarked, pausing before she began to cut the roast beef,—

'Well, I do call this a nice family party! All of us at home, and Mamma too!'

This did not quite seem to break the ice, and Mrs Goodford looked in some contempt at her daughter with her eyes, little and red and wicked like an elephant's. Her face was so deeply wrinkled that her features were almost invisible in the network, but what there was of them was exceedingly sharp. She had taken off her bonnet, a sign that she meant to stop all afternoon, and showed a head very sparsely covered with white hair: at the back of it was fixed on a small bun of bright auburn, which no doubt had been the colour of her hair some forty years ago. This bun always fascinated John: it was impossible to conjecture how it was attached to his grandmother's head.

Mrs Goodford ate a slice of hot beef in dead silence, with a circular mill-like motion of her chin. It disappeared before her daughter had time to begin eating on her own account, which gave her an opportunity for another attempt to thaw the glacial silence that presided over the nice family party.

'Well, and there's Mamma finished her slice of beef already! What a blessing a good appetite is, to be sure! You'll let me give you another slice, Mamma, won't you?'

Mrs Goodford had pointedly taken a place next her daughter, which was as far as she could get from Mr Keeling, and, still without speaking, she advanced her plate up to the edge of the dish. Again she ate in silence, and pushed her Yorkshire pudding to the extreme edge of her plate.

'Nasty, mushy stuff,' she observed. 'I'd as soon eat a poultice.'

John, who had scarcely taken his eyes off the bun, putting his food into his mouth by general sense of locality only, suddenly gave a hiccupy kind of gasp. Mrs Goodford, exhilarated by beef, turned her elephant-eyes on him.

'I don't quite catch what you said, John,' she remarked. 'Perhaps you can tell me what the sermon was about this morning.'

'Hell, Granny,' said John cheerfully.

Mrs Goodford began to grow slightly more bellicose.

'Your father would like that,' she observed.

Hitherto Mr Keeling had devoted his mind to his own immediate concerns which were those of eating. He had no wish to get worried with Mrs Goodford, but it seemed that mere politeness required an answer to this.

'I found it an excellent sermon,' he said, with admirable neutrality; 'I only hope that Mr—Mr Silverdale will give us such good ones.'

Mrs Goodford scrutinised the faces of her grandchildren. Her eye fell on Alice.

'We must find a wife for him,' she said. 'I dare say we shall be able to fit him out with a wife. He seems a polite sort of young man too. I shouldn't wonder if plenty of our Bracebridge young ladies would be willing to become Mrs Silverside, or whatever the man's name is.'

'Dear me, Mamma!' said Mrs Keeling, 'you talk as if the gentleman was a bit of beef.'

'Mostly bones, as far as I could see,' said Mrs Goodford, still not taking her little eyes off Alice. 'There wasn't much beef on them.'

'Well, I hope he'll get a good meal this evening,' said Mrs Keeling. 'He's taking his supper with us.'

'Ah, I dare say he'll find something he likes,' said this dreadful old lady, observing with malicious pleasure that Alice's colour, as she would have phrased it, 'was mounting.'

A certain measure of relief came to poor Alice at this moment, for she observed that everybody had finished the meat-course, and she and Hugh (who had at present escaped the lash of his grandmother's tongue) and John hastily got up and began changing their elders' plates, and removing dishes. This was the custom of Sunday lunch at Mrs Keeling's, and a Sabbatarian design of saving the servants trouble lay at the back of it. The detail of which it took no account was that it gave Hugh and Alice and John three times as much trouble as it would have given the servants, for they made endless collisions with each other as they went round the table; two of them simultaneously tried to drag the roast beef away in opposite directions, and the gravy spoon, tipped up by John's elbow, careered through the air with a comet-tail of congealed meat-juice behind it. Ominous sounds of side-slip from heaped plates and knives came from the dinner wagon, where the used china was piled, and some five minutes of arduous work, filled with bumpings and crashings and occasional spurts of suppressed laughter from John, who, like a true wit, was delighted with his own swift and disconcerting reply to his Granny, were needful to effect the changes required for the discussion of plum tart and that strange form of refreshment known as 'cold shape.' During these resonant minutes further conversation between the elders was impossible, but Mrs Goodford was not wasting her time, but saving up, storing her forces, reviewing her future topics.

It was obvious by this time that the family lunch was going to be rather a stormy sort of passage, and Mrs Keeling had before this caught her husband's eye, and with dumb movements of her lips and querying eyebrows had communicated 'Champagne?' to him, for it was known that when Mrs Goodford was in a worrying mood, a glass of that agreeable beverage often restored her to almost fatuous good humour. But her husband had replied aloud, 'Certainly not,' and assumed his grimmest aspect. This did not look well: as a rule he was content to suffer Mrs Goodford's most disagreeable humours in contemptuous silence. Now and then, however, and his wife was afraid that this was one of those tempestuous occasions, he was in no mind to lie prone under insults levelled at him across his own table.

Mrs Goodford being helped first, poured the greater part of the cream over her tart, and began on Hugh. Hugh would have been judged by a sentimental school-girl to be much the best looking of all the Keelings, for the resemblance between him and the wax types of manly beauty which used to appear in the windows of hairdressers' establishments was so striking as to be almost uncanny. You wondered if there was a strain of hairdresser blood in his ancestors. He had worked himself up from the lowest offices in his father's stores; he had been boy-messenger for the delivery of parcels, he had sold behind the counters, he had been through the accountant's office, he had travelled on behalf of the business, and knew the working of it all from A to Z. In course of time he would become General Manager, and his father felt that in his capable hands it was not likely that the business would deteriorate. He spoke little, and usually paused before he spoke, and when he spoke he seldom made a mistake. The brilliance of his appearance was backed by a solid and sensible mind.

'And they tell me you're going to be married next, Hugh,' said Mrs Goodford.

Hugh considered this.

'I don't know what you mean by "next," Grandmamma,' he said. 'But it is quite true that I am going to be married.'

His mother again tried to introduce a little lightness into this sombre opening.

'Trust Hugh for not agreeing with anything he doesn't understand,' she said.

Mrs Goodford took no notice whatever of this. It is likely that her quick little eye had intercepted the telegraphic suggestion of champagne, and that she was justly irritated at her son-in-law's rejection of it. She laid herself out to be more markedly disagreeable than usual.

'Well, all I can say is, that I hope your Miss Pemberton isn't one of those lively young ladies who are always laughing and joking, or you'll be fit to kill her with your serious airs. I should never have guessed that you were going to be a bridegroom in a few weeks' time.'

'But you haven't got to guess, Grandmamma,' said Hugh. 'You know already.'

'And I'm told she has a nice little fortune of her own,' continued Mrs Goodford. 'Trust a Keeling for that. Ah, dear me, yes: there are some that go up in the world and some that go down, and I never heard that the Keelings were among those that go down.'

Hugh hardly thought about this at all before he answered. It was a perfectly evident proposition.

'I dare say not,' he said, still non-committally.

'Yes; and it was true before you were born or thought of,' continued this terrible old lady. 'Your father didn't marry so much beneath him either. Ah, he was in a precious small way, he was, when he came a-courting your mother.'

Mrs Goodford had now, so to speak, found her range. She had been like a gun, that has made a few trial shots, dropping a shell now on Alice, now on Hugh. But this last one went off right in the centre of the target. She disliked her son-in-law with that peculiar animus which is the privilege of those who are under a thousand obligations to the object of their spite, for since nearly thirty years ago, when he had taken Emmeline off her hands, till last Christmas, when he had given her a new Bath-chair in addition to his usual present of a hundred pounds, Keeling had treated her with consistent and contemptuous liberality. This liberality, naturally, was not the offspring of any affection : the dominant ingredient in it was pride. However Mrs Goodford might behave, he was not to be disturbed from his sense of duty towards his mother-in-law. Nor, at present, was he sufficiently provoked to make any sort of retort, but merely told John to pass him the sugar.

Mrs Goodford finished her plum tart.

'Yes, some do go up in the world,' she went on. 'Who'd have thought thirty years ago that T. Keeling of the fish-shop in the High Street was going to be Mr Thomas Keeling of the Stores?'

A slight smile appeared on Keeling's grim face. He could not resist replying to this.

'Who'd have thought it, do you ask?' he said. 'Why, I thought it; I knew it all along, I may say.'

'And they tell me you're going to be Mayor of Bracebridge next year,' said Mrs Goodford, delighted to have drawn him into conversation with her. If only she could engage him in it she trusted herself to make him lose his temper before many minutes were over.

'Yes, they've told you right there,' said he. 'Or perhaps you've got some fault to find with that, Mrs Goodford.'

Mrs Keeling looked round in a distressed and flurried manner, with her feeble geniality showing like some pale moon behind clouds that were growing rapidly thicker.

'Yes, and me the Lady Mayoress,' she said. 'Why, I'm ever so nervous even now in the thinking of all the grand parties I shall have to give. And the hospital will be finished next year too, and what a to-do we shall have over that. And what do you say now, Mamma, to having your cup of coffee in my boudoir quietly with Alice and me, leaving the gentlemen to have a cigarette.'

Mrs Goodford gave a thin little laugh like a bat's squeak.

'No, I'll sit here a bit longer,' she said, 'and talk to the gentlemen and the Lord Mayor of Bracebridge. Dear me, to think of all the changes we see! And I shouldn't wonder if there was more in store yet. I learned when I was a girl that there was once a King of England who used to like a bit of stale fish——'

Keeling suddenly pointed an awful forefinger at her.

'Now, that's enough!' he said. 'Never in my

life have I sold a bit of bad goods, fish, flesh, or fowl, or whatever you like to name, that I wasn't willing to take it back with humble apologies for its having left my shop. Not one atom of bad stuff did any one buy of me if I knew it. And any one who says different to that speaks a falsehood. If you've got anything to answer me there, Mrs Goodford, let's have it now and have done with it.'

There was not a word in reply, and after having given her good space to answer him, he spoke again.

'So we'll have no more talk of stale fish at my table,' he said.

Mrs Keeling rose.

'Well, then, I'm sure that's all comfortably settled,' she said, 'and pray, Mamma, and you, Thomas, don't go worrying each other any more, when we might be having such a pleasant family party, on Sunday afternoon too. Come along with me, Mamma, and let's have our coffee served in my boudoir, and let's all sit and cool after our lunch.'

This appeal was more successful. Something in the simple dignity of Keeling's reply had silenced her, and she was led away like a wicked little elephant between her daughter and Alice. Not one word did Keeling say till they had left the room, and then, though his usual allowance of port on Sunday was one glass after lunch and two after dinner, he helped himself again and pushed the bottle towards Hugh.

'Join your mother, John,' he said to his other son.

'Oh, mayn't I——' began John, with an eye to cherries.

'You may do as I bid you without more words,' said his father.

For a few minutes he sat glowering and sipping.

'That's why some men take to drink,' he observed. 'They're driven silly by some ill-conditioned woman like your grandmother. Nag, nag, nag: it was Alice first, then you, then me. Does she come to eat her dinner with us on Sunday just to insult us all, do you think?'

Hugh considered this as he helped himself.

'I think that's part of her reason,' he said. 'She also wants to get a good dinner for nothing.'

'I expect that's about it. She may call me a tradesman if she likes, who has been a fishmonger, for that's quite true. But she shan't call me such a rotten bad man of business as to send out stale goods. She wouldn't be getting her hundred pounds regular as clock-work at Christmas time, if I had been that sort of a man.'

'You answered her very properly, I thought,' remarked Hugh.

'Of course I did. I didn't want to do it: never in my life have I wanted to speak like that to any woman, let alone your mother's mother, but she gave me no option. Now I'm off to my books.'

He rose.

'It would be rather a good thing if you went into my mother's room and had your cup of coffee there,' Hugh said, 'it would show you paid no heed to her rude speeches.'

'Maybe it would, but she might treat me to some more, and I've no inclination for them. Stale fish, indeed!'

CHAPTER II

Mr Keeling was accustomed to consider the hour or two after lunch on Sunday as the most enjoyable time in the week, for then he gave himself up to the full and uninterrupted pursuit of his hobby. None of his family ever came into his study without invitation, and since he never gave such invitation, he had no fear about being disturbed. Before now he had tried to establish with one or other of them the communication of his joy in his books: he had asked Alice into his sanctuary one Sunday, but when he had shown her an exquisitely tooled binding by Cameron, she had said, 'Oh, what a pretty cover!' A pretty cover! . . . somehow Alice's appreciation was more hopeless than if she had not admired it at all. Then, opening it, she had come across a slightly compromising picture of Bacchus and Ariadne, and had turned over in such a hurry that she had crumpled the corner of the page. Her father hardly knew whether her maidenly confusion was not worse than the outrage on his adored volume. Stern moralist and Puritan though he was, this sort of prudery seemed to him an affectation that bordered on imbecility. On another occasion he had asked Hugh to look at his books, and Hugh had been much struck by the type of the capital letters in an edition of Omar Khayyam, wondering if it could be enlarged and used in some advertisement of the approaching summer sale at the stores. 'That's the sort of type we want,' he said. 'It hits you in the eye; that does. You can't help reading what is written in it.' Very likely that was quite true, for Hugh had an excellent perception in the matter of attractive type and arrangement in the advertising department, but his father had shut up the book with a snap, feeling that it was in the nature of a profanity to let the aroma of business drift into an atmosphere incense-laden with his books. His wife presented an even more hopeless case, for she was apt to tell her friends how fond her husband was of reading, and how many new editions he had ordered for his library. Clearly, if this temple was to retain its sense of consecration he must permit no more of these infidel intruders.

It is not too much to say that the room was of the nature of a temple, for here a very essential and withdrawn part of himself passed hours of praise and worship. Born in the humblest circumstances, he had, from the days when he slept on a piece of sacking below the counter in his father's most unprofitable shop, devoted all the push, all the activity of his energies to the grappling of business problems and the pursuit of money-making To many this becomes by the period of middle age a passion not less incurable than drug drinking, and not less ruinous than that to the nobler appetites of life. But Keeling had never allowed it thus to usurp and swamp him; he always had guarded his secret garden, fencing it impenetrably off from the clatter of the till. Here, though undeveloped and sundered from the rest of his life, grew the rose of romance, namely the sense of beauty in books; here shone for him the light which never was on sea or land, which inspires every artist's dream. He was not in any degree creative, he had not the desire any more than the skill to write or to draw when he lost himself in reverie over the printed page or the illustrations in his sumptuous editions. But the sense of wonder and admiration which is the oil in the artist's lamp burned steadily for him, and lit with a never-flickering flame the hours he passed among his books. Above all, when he was here he lost completely a certain sense of loneliness which was his constant companion.

To-day he did not at once pass through the doors beyond which lay the garden of enchantment. Mrs Goodford had irritated him beyond endurance, and what irritated him even more than her rudeness was the fact that he had allowed it to upset him. He had thought himself safe from annoyance by virtue of his own contempt, but her gibe about the stale fish had certainly pricked him in spite of its utter falsity. He would have liked to cut off his usual Christmas present which enabled her to live in comfort at Blenheim, and tell her she need not expect more till she had shown herself capable of politeness. But he knew he would not do this, and with an effort dismissed the ill-mannered old lady from his mind.

But other things extraneous to the temple had come in with him as he entered, like flies through an opened door, and still buzzed about him. His wife's want of comprehension was one of them. It was not often that Mrs Goodford had the power to annoy him so thoroughly as she had done to-day, but when she did, all that Emmeline had to contribute to the situation was such a sentence as, 'What a pity you and Mamma worry each other so.' She did not understand, and though he told himself that in thirty years he should have got used to that, he found now and then, and to-day with unusual vividness, that he had not done so. She had never become a companion to him; he had never found in her that for which ultimately a man is seeking, though at the time he may not know it, when he goes a-wooing. A mouth, an eyebrow, the curve of a limb may be his lure, and having attained it he may think for a few years of passion that in gaining it he has gained what he sought, but unless he has indeed got that which unconsciously he desired, he will find some day when the gray ash begins to grow moss-like on his burning coals, that though his children are round him, there is but a phantom opposite to him. The romance of passion has burned itself out, and from the ashes has no phœnix arisen with whom he can soar to the sun. He desired the mouth or the eyebrow: he got them, and now in the changing lineaments he can scarcely remember what that which so strangely moved him was like, while in the fading of its brightness nothing else has emerged.

It was this undoubtedly which had occurred in the domestic history of Keeling's house. He had been infatuated with Emmeline's prettiness at a time when as a young man of sternly moral principles and strong physical needs, the only possible course was to take a wife, while Emmeline, to tell the truth, had no voice in the matter at all. Certainly she had liked him, but of love in any ardent, compelling sense, she had never, in the forty-seven years of her existence, shown the smallest symptom in any direction whatever, and it was not likely that she was going to develop the malady now. She had supposed (and her mother quite certainly had supposed too) that she was going to marry somebody sometime, and when this strong and splendidly handsome young man insisted that she was going to marry him, she had really done little more than conclude that he must be right, especially when her mother agreed with him. Events had proved that as far as her part of the matter was concerned, she had acted extremely wisely, for, since anything which might ever so indulgently be classed under the broad heading of romance, was foreign to her nature, she had secured the highest prize that life conceivably held for her in enjoying years of complete and bovine content. When she wanted a thing very much indeed, such as driving home after church on Sunday morning instead of walking, she generally got it, and probably the acutest of her trials were when John had the measles, or her husband and mother worried each other. But being almost devoid of imagination she had never thought that John was going to die of the measles or that her husband was going to cut off his annual Christmas present to her mother. Things as uncomfortable as that never really came near her; she seemed to be as little liable to either sorrow or joy as if when a baby she had been inoculated with some spiritual serum that rendered her permanently immune. She was fond of her children, her card-bearing crocodile in the hall, her husband, her comfort, and she quite looked forward to being Lady Mayoress next year. There would always be sufficient strawberries and iced coffee at her garden parties; her husband need not be under any apprehension that she would not have proper provision made. Dreadful scenes had occurred this year, when Mrs Alington gave her last garden-party, and two of her guests had been seen almost pulling the last strawberry in half.

Such in outline was the woman whom, nearly thirty years ago, Keeling had carried off by the mere determination of his will, and in her must largely be found the cause of the loneliness which so often beset him. He was too busy a man to waste time over regretting it, but he knew that it was there, and it formed the background in front of which the action of his life took place. His wife had been to him the mother of his children and an excellent housekeeper, but never had a spark of intellectual sympathy passed between them, still less the light invisible of romantic comprehension. Had he been as incapable of it as she their marriage might have been as successful as to all appearance it seemed to be. But he was capable of it; hence he felt alone. Only among his books did he get relief from this secret chronic aching. There he could pursue the quest of that which can never be attained, and thus is both pursuit and quarry in one.

And now in his fiftieth year he was as friendless outside his home as he was companionless there. The years during which friendships can be made, that is to say, from boyhood up till about the age of forty, had passed for him in a practically incessant effort of building up the immense business which was his own property. And even if he had not been so employed, it is doubtful whether he would ever have made friends. Partly a certain stark austerity innate in him would have kept intimacy at a distance, partly he had never penetrated into circles at Bracebridge where he would have met his intellectual equals. Till now Keeling of the fish-shop had but expanded into Mr Keeling, proprietor of the Universal Stores, that reared such lofty terra-cotta cupolas in the High Street, and the men he met, those with whom he habitually came in contact, he met on purely business grounds, and they would have felt as little at ease in the secret atmosphere of his library as he would have been in entertaining them there. They looked up to him as the shrewdest as well as the richest of the prosperous tradesmen of Bracebridge, and his contributions and suggestions at the meetings of the Town Council were received with the respect that their invariable common sense merited. But there their intercourse terminated; he could not conceive what was the pleasure of hitting a golf-ball over four miles of downland, and faced with blank incomprehension the fact that those who had been exercising their brains all day in business should sit up over games of cards to find themselves richer or poorer by a couple of pounds at one o'clock in the morning. He would willingly have drawn a cheque for such a sum in order to be permitted to go to bed at eleven as usual. He had no notion of sport in any form, neither had he the bonhomie, the pleasure in the company of cheerful human beings as such, which really lies at the root of the pursuits which he so frankly despised, nor any zeal for the chatter of social intercourse. To him a glass of whisky and soda was no more than half a pint of effervescing fluid, which you were better without: it had to him no value or existence as a symbol of good fellowship. There was never a man less *clubbable*. But in spite of the bleakness of nature here indicated, and the severity of his aspect towards his fellow men, he had a very considerable fund of kindly impulses towards any who treated him with sincerity. An appeal for help, whether it implied the expenditure of time or money was certainly subjected to a strict scrutiny, but if it passed that, it was as certainly responded to. He was as reticent about such acts of kindness as he was about the pleasures of his secret garden, or the steady increase in his annual receipts from his stores. But all three gave him considerable satisfaction, and the luxury of giving was to him no whit inferior to that of getting.

Charles Propert, who presently arrived from the kitchen-passage in charge of the boy in buttons, was one of those who well knew his employer's generosity, for Keeling in a blunt and shamefaced way had borne all the expense of a long illness which had incapacitated him the previous winter, not only continuing to pay him his salary as head of the book department at the stores during the weeks in which he was invalided, but taking on himself all the charges for medical treatment and sea-side convalescence. He was an exceedingly well-educated man of two or three-and-thirty, and Keeling was far more at ease with him than with any other of his acquaintances, because he frankly enjoyed his society. He could have imagined himself sitting up till midnight talking to young Propert, because he had admitted him into the secret garden: Propert might indeed be described as the head gardener. Keeling nodded as the young man entered, and from under his big eyebrows observed that he was dressed entirely in black.

'Good-afternoon, Propert,' he said. 'I got that edition of the *Morte d'Arthur* you told me of. But they made me pay for it.'

'The Singleton Press edition, sir?' asked Propert.

'Yes; sit down and have a look at it. It's a fine page, you know.'

'Yes, sir, and if you'll excuse me, I really think you got it rather cheap.'

'H'm! I wonder if you'd have thought that if you had been the purchaser.'

Propert laughed.

'I think so. As you said to me the other day, sir, good work is always cheap in comparison with bad work.'

Keeling bent over the book, and with his eyes on the page, just touched the arm of Propert's black coat.

'No trouble, I hope?' he said.

'Yes, sir. I heard yesterday of my mother's death.'

'Very sorry. If you want a couple of days off, just arrange in your department. Then the copy of the *Rape of the Lock* illustrated by Beardsley came yesterday too. I like it better than anything I've seen of his.'

'There's a very fine *Morte d'Arthur* of his which you haven't got, sir,' said Propert.

'Order it for me, please. The man could draw, couldn't he? Look at the design of embroidery on the coat of that fellow kneeling there. There's nothing messy about that. But it doesn't seem much of a poem as far as I can judge. Not my idea of poetry; there's more poetry in the prose of the *Morte d'Arthur*. Take a cigarette and make yourself comfortable.'

He paused a moment.

'Or perhaps you'd sooner not stop and talk to-day after your news,' he said.

Propert shook his head.

'No, sir, I should like to stop. . . . Of course the *Rape of the Lock* is artificial: it belongs to its age: it's got no more reality than a Watteau picture——'

'Watteau?' asked Keeling.

'Yes; you've got a book of reproductions of Watteau drawings. I don't think you cared for it much. Picnics and fêtes, and groups of people under trees.'

Keeling nodded.

'I remember. Stupid, insipid sort of thing. I never could make out why you recommended me to buy it.'

'I can sell it again for more than you paid for it, sir. The price of it has gone up considerably.'

This savoured a little of business.

'No, you needn't do that,' he said. 'It's a handsome book enough. And then there is another Omar Khayyam.'

'Indeed, sir; you've got a quantity of editions of that. But I know it's useless for me to urge you to get hold of the original edition.'

Mr Keeling passed him this latest acquisition.

'Quite useless,' he said. 'What a man wants first editions for, unless they've got some special beauty, I can't understand. I would as soon spend my money in getting postage-stamps because they are rare. But I wanted to talk to you about that poem. What's he after? Is it some philosophy? Or is it a love poem? Or is he just a tippler?'

The conference lasted some time. Keeling was but learning now, through this one channel of books, that attitude of mind which through instinct, whetted and primed by education, came naturally to the younger man, and it was just this that made these talks the very essence of the secret garden. Propert, for all that he was but an employee at a few pounds a week, was gardener there; he knew the names of the flowers, and what was more, he had that comprehension and love of them which belongs to the true gardener and not the specimen grower or florist only. It was that which Keeling sought to acquire, and among the prosperous family friends, who were associated with him in the management of civic affairs, or in business relationships, he found no opportunity of coming in contact with a similar mind. But Propert was freeborn in this republic of art and letters, and Keeling was eager to acquire at any cost the sense of native, unconscious citizenship. He felt he belonged there, but he had to win his way back there. . . . He must have learned the language in some psychically dim epoch of his existence, for exploration among these alleys in his garden had to him the thrill not of discovery, but the more delicate sense of recollection, of revisiting forgotten scenes which were remembered as soon as they disentangled themselves again from the jungle of materialistic interests that absorbed him all the week. Mr Keeling had very likely hardly heard of the theory of reincarnation, and had some modern Pythagoras spoken to him of beans, he would undoubtedly have considered it great nonsense. But he would have confessed to the illusion (the fancy he would have called it) of having known something of all this before when Propert, with his handsome face aglow and his eyes alight, sat and turned over books with him thus, forgetting, as his own absorption increased, to interject his sentences with the respectful 'sir' of their ordinary week-day intercourse. Keeling ceased to be the proprietor and master of the universal stores, he ceased even to be the proprietor of his own books. They and their pictures and their binding and their aroma of the kingdom of intellect and beauty, were common possessions of all who chose to claim them, and belonged to neither of them individually any more than the French language belongs to the teacher who instructs and the pupil who learns.

The hour that Propert usually stayed had to-day lengthened itself out (so short was it) to two before the young man looked at his watch, and jumped up from his chair.

'I'm afraid I've been staying a very long time, sir,' he said. 'I had no idea it was so late.'

Mr Keeling got up also, and walked to the window, where he spoke with his back towards him.

'I should like to know a little more about your family trouble,' he said. 'Any other children beside yourself? I remember you once told me your mother was a widow.'

'Yes, sir, one sister,' said Propert.

'Unmarried? Work for her living?' asked Keeling.

'Yes, sir. I think she'll come and live here

with me,' said he. 'She's got work in London, but I don't want her to live there alone.'

'No; quite proper. What's her work?'

'Clerical work, including shorthand and type-writing.'

'Efficient?'

'Yes, sir. The highest certificates in both. She's a bit of an artist too in drawing and wood-cutting.'

Mr Keeling ceased to address the larch-trees that were the sponsors of his house's name, and turned round.

'And a book-worm like you?' he asked.

Propert laughed.

'I wish I was a book-worm like her,' he said. 'But in London you get so much more opportunity for study of all sorts. She had a British Museum ticket, and studied at the Polytechnic.'

Keeling picked up the Singleton *Morte d'Arthur* and carefully blew a grain of cigarette ash from the opened page.

'Let me know when she comes,' he said. 'I might be able to find her some job, if she still wants work. Perhaps your mother's death has made her independent.'

He paused a moment.

'Naturally I don't want to be impertinent in inquiring into your affairs, Propert,' he said. 'Don't think that. But if I can help, let me know. Going, are you? Good-bye; don't forget to order me Beardsley's *Morte d'Arthur.*'

He walked out with him into the square Gothic hall with its hideous tiles, its castellated chimney-piece, its painted wheelbarrow, its card-bearing crocodile, and observed Propert going towards the green-baize door that led to the kitchen passage.

'Where are you going?' asked Keeling.

'I always come and go this way, sir,' said Propert.

Keeling opened the front door for him.

'This is the proper door to use, when you come to see me,' he said.

He stood a minute or two at the front door, with broken melodies from Omar Khayyam lingering like fragments of half-remembered tunes in his head. 'And Thou, beside me singing in the wilderness,' was one that sang itself again and again to him. But no one had ever sung to him in the wilderness. The chink of money, the flattering rustle of bank-notes had sung to him in the High Street, and he could remember certain ardours of his early manhood, when the thought that Emmeline was waiting for him at home made him hurry back from the establishment which had been the nucleus-cell which had developed into the acres of show-rooms and passages that he now controlled. But Emmeline's presence at home never made him arrive at his work later than nine o'clock next morning. No emotion, caused either by Emmeline or ledger-entries, had ever dominated him: there had always been something beyond, something to which perhaps his books and his Sunday afternoon dimly led. And they could scarcely lead anywhere except to the Wilderness where the 'Thou' yet unencountered, made Paradise with singing. . . . Then with a swift and sudden return to normal consciousness, he became aware that Mrs Goodford's bath-chair was no longer drawn up on the grass below the larches, and that he might, without risk of being worried again, beyond the usual power of Emmeline to worry him, take his cup of tea in the drawing-room before going to evening service.

He found Emmeline alone, just beginning to make tea in the heavily fluted tea-pot with its equipage of harlequin cups and saucers. Alice and John were somewhere in the 'grounds.' Hugh had gone to see his young lady (the expression was Mrs Keeling's), and she herself had suffered a slight eclipse from her usual geniality owing to her mother having stopped the whole afternoon, and having thus interrupted her reading, by which she meant going gently to sleep on the sofa, with her book periodically falling off her lap. The first two times that this happened she almost invariably picked it up, on the third occasion she had really gone to sleep, and the rumble of its avalanche did not disturb her. But the loss of this intellectual refreshment had rendered her rather querulous, and since she was not of very vigorous vitality, her querulousness oozed in a leaky manner from her instead of discharging itself at high pressure. A tea-leaf had stuck, too, in the spout of the tea-pot, which made that handsome piece contribute to the general impression of dribbling at Mrs Keeling's tea-table; it also provided her with another grievance, though not quite so acute as that which took its rise from what had occurred at lunch.

'I'm sure it's years since I've been so upset as I've been to-day, Thomas,' she said, 'for what with you and Mamma worrying each other so at lunch, and Mamma stopping all afternoon and biting my head off, if I said as much as to hope that her rheumatism hadn't troubled her lately, and it's wonderful how little it does trouble her really, for I'm sure that though I don't complain, I suffer twice as much as she does when we get that damp November weather—Dear me, this tea-pot was always a bad pourer: I should have been wiser to get a less handsome one with a straight spout. Well, there's your cup of tea, I'm sure you'll be glad of it. But there are some days when everything combines to vex one, and it will all be in a piece with what has gone before, if Alice forgets and takes some salmon-mayonnaise, and Mr Silverdale goes away thinking that I'm a stingy housekeeper, which has never been said of me yet.'

Keeling failed to find any indication of 'singing in the wilderness' here, nor had he got that particular sense of humour which could find provender for itself in these almost majestic structures of incoherence. At all times his wife's ideas ran softly into each other like the marks left by words on blotting paper; now they exhibited a somewhat greater energy and ran into each other with something of the vigour of vehicles moving in opposing directions.

'I do not know whether you wish to talk to me about your mother, your rheumatism, your teapot, or your housekeeping,' he remarked. 'I will talk about any you please, but one at a time.'

Mrs Keeling gave him his cup of tea, and waited a little before pouring out her own. It was necessary to hold the teapot so long in the air in order to extract a ration of fluid from it.

'Yes, it's very pleasant for you, Thomas,' she said, 'spending the afternoon quietly among your books and leaving me to stand up to Mamma for the way you spoke to her at lunch, when we might have been such a pleasant family party. I don't deny that Mamma gets worried at times, and speaks when she had better have been silent, but——'

Her husband decided that it was her mother she wished to talk about, and interrupted.

'You may tell your mother this,' he said, 'that I won't be called a seller of bad goods by anybody. If another man did that I'd bring a libel action against him to-morrow. Your mother should remember that she's largely dependent on me, and though she may detest me, she must keep a civil tongue in her head about me in my presence. She may say what she pleases of me behind my back, but don't you repeat it to me.'

Mrs Keeling, fractious from her afternoon of absolute insomnia, forced a small tear out of one of her eyes.

'And there's a word to me!' she said. 'Fancy telling me that my mother detests my husband. That's an un-Christian thing to say about anybody.'

'It's an un-Christian feeling, maybe, to have about anybody,' said he, 'but that's your mother's affair and not mine. She may feel about me what she pleases, but I wish her to know she must speak properly to me, or not speak at all. I shouldn't have referred to it again, unless you had begun, but now that you've begun it's best you should know what my opinion on the subject is. Before the children, too: I had better manners than that when I was in the fish-shop myself.'

Mrs Keeling began to fear the worst, and forced a twin tear from her other eye.

'Well, what Mamma will do unless you help her this Christmas, is more than I can tell,' she said. 'Coal is up now to winter prices, and Mamma's cellar is so small that she can't get in enough to last her through. And it's little enough that I can do for her, for with John at home it's like having two young lions to feed, and how to save from the house-money you give me I don't see. I dare say it would be better if Mamma got rid of Blenheim for what it would fetch and went into furnished lodgings.'

'Now who's been talking about my not behaving properly to your mother except yourself?' said Keeling.

'There's other ways of saying a thing than saying it,' said Mrs Keeling cryptically. 'You speak of Mamma detesting you, and not having the manners of a fishmonger, and what's that but another way of saying you're set against her?'

Mr Keeling regarded his wife with a faint twinkle lurking behind his gray eyes.

'Take your tea, Emmeline,' he said, 'and you'll feel better. You haven't had your nap this afternoon, but have been listening to your mother talking all sorts of rabid stuff against me. Don't you deny it now, but just remember I don't care two straws what she says about me behind my back. But I won't stand her impertinence to my face. And as for coal in the winter I can tell you that she still owes me for what she bought at the Stores last January. Perhaps I'll county-court her for the bill. I'm glad you talked about coal, I had almost forgotten about that bill.'

It dawned faintly and vaguely on Mrs Keeling's mind, as on summits remote from where she transacted her ordinary mental processes, that her husband did not quite mean what he said about that county-courting. Possibly there lurked in those truculent remarks some recondite sort of humour.

'Certainly Mamma has no call to be so rude to you, when you do so much for her,' she said.

'Just tell Mamma that,' said he, rising. 'That's what I want her to understand.'

The prospect of Mr Silverdale's presence at dinner that night had filled Alice with secret and gentle flutterings, and accounted for the fact that she wore her amethyst cross and practised several of Mendelssohn's *Songs Without Words* before evening service, in case she was asked to play after dinner. She reaped her due reward for these prudent steps, since Mr Silverdale expressed his admiration for amethysts at dinner, and afterwards came and sat close by the piano, beating time with scarcely perceptible movements of a slim white hand, not in the manner of one assisting her with the rhythm, but as if he himself pulsated with it. He had produced an extraordinarily unfavourable impression on John by constantly calling him by his Christian name, by talking about Tom Brown when he heard he was at Rugby, and by using such fragments of schoolboy slang as he happened to recollect from his boyish days. These in the rapidly changing vernacular of schoolboys were now chiefly out of date, but John saw quite clearly that the design was to be 'boys together,' and despised him accordingly. On Mr Keeling he produced merely the impression of a very ladylike young man of slightly inane disposition, and as Hugh was away, spending the evening at the house of his fiancée, Mr Silverdale was thrown on the hands of the ladies for mutual entertainment. With them he succeeded as signally as he had failed with John, saying that though preaching a sermon might be dry work for his hearers it was hungry work for the performer, eating salmon mayonnaise with great gusto, and remarking across the table to John, 'Jolly good grub, isn't it, John?' a remark that endeared him to Mrs Keeling, though it made John feel slightly sick, and caused him to leave in a pointed manner on his plate the portion of the 'good grub' which he had not yet consumed. Like a wise tactician, therefore, Mr Silverdale abandoned the impregnable, and delivered his assaults where he was more likely to be successful. He had an eager and joyful manner, as of one who found the world an excellent joke.

'Such a scolding as I had before church from

my housekeeper,' he said, 'because I didn't eat the buttered scones she sent me up for tea. I know some one who would have polished them off, eh, John?'

John's eye, which had exactly as much expression in it as a dead codfish's, cowed him for a moment, but he quickly recovered.

'Such a scolding!' he said. 'She said I didn't take sufficient care of myself, and naturally I told her that I had so many others to look after that I must take my turn with the rest. But when I told her that Mrs Keeling was going to take care of me this evening, she thought no more about the scones I hadn't eaten! She knew I should be well looked after.'

Mrs Keeling had had a good nap before dinner, and her geniality had quite returned. She had also seen that Mrs Bellaway was right, and that there was plenty of mayonnaise.

'Well, that does put me in a responsible position,' she said. 'At least I must insist on your having just a morsel more of the mayonnaise before they take it away. It's a very simple dinner I'm giving you to-night: there's but a chicken and a slice of cold meat and a meringue and a savoury to follow.'

Mr Silverdale laughed gleefully.

'Dear me, this is absolute starvation,' he exclaimed. 'I should have eaten my scones.'

Mrs Keeling instantly saw that this was a joke.

'I'll leave my husband to starve you over the port afterwards,' she said.

Again he laughed.

'You and Mr Keeling are spoiling me,' he declared, though it must have required a singularly vivid imagination to trace in Keeling's face any symptom of that indulgent tendency.

Alice, in the depths of her shy, silly heart, found that in spite of his appreciation of the salmon, the chicken, the cold meat, and the meringue, the Galahad aspect of this morning was growing. His housekeeper had told him he did not sufficiently look after himself; it was clear that he was wearing himself out, while the enthusiasm with which presently he spoke of his work deepened the knightly impression. His voice thrilled her; so, too, did the boyish gaiety with which he spoke of serious things.

'I adore my new parish,' he said. 'I was almost afraid when I took the living I should find too little to do. But coming home late last night from a bedside, if I saw one drunken man I must have seen twenty, some roaring drunk, some simply stupidly drunk, dear fellows! I asked two of them to come home with me, and have another drink, and there was I in the middle with two drunken lads, one with a black eye, reeling along Alfred Street. I don't know what my parishioners must have thought of their new pastor. You should have seen my housekeeper's face, when I told her that I had brought two friends home with me.'

Mrs Keeling paused, laying down on her plate the piece of meringue which was actually *en route* for her mouth.

'But you never gave them another drink, Mr Silverdale?' she said.

'Yes, my dear lady, I did. "Ho! Every one that thirsteth!" That was the drink I had for them. Dear lads! They were too tipsy to kneel, but there were tears in the eyes of one of them, before they had been with me five minutes.'

'Was that the one with the black eye?' thought John. If his mouth had not been full he would have said so.

'I saw them home, of course, and next Saturday I'm going to have a regular beano in those slums beyond the church. Don't be shocked, Mrs Keeling, if it's your priest who has a black eye on Sunday morning.'

'And the bedside where you had been before?' asked Alice.

'My dear Miss Alice, I wish you could have been with me. There was such an atmosphere of terror in that room when I went in, that I felt half stifled: the place was thick with the fear of death. I fought against it, it was given me to overcome it, and ten minutes later that disreputable old sinner who lay dying there had such a smile of peace and rapture on his face that I cannot but believe that he saw the angels standing round him.'

'And he got better?' asked Mrs Keeling, with breathless interest, but feeling that this was very daring conversation.

Mr Silverdale laughed as if this was an excellent joke.

'Better?' he asked. 'He got well, and sang his psalms in Heaven this morning. I felt in church as if I could hear his voice.'

Alice remembered the rapt look she had seen there, which her mother almost profanely had taken to be the sign of an insufficient breakfast, and thrilled at knowing the true interpretation of it. The rapt look was there again now, and seemed to her the most adorable expression she had ever seen on a human countenance. Mrs Keeling was more impressed now, and the moisture stood in her kind mild eyes.

'Well, I call that beautiful,' she said, 'and if you'll let me know when the funeral is, I'll send a wreath.'

Mr Silverdale laughed again: John considered he was for ever laughing at nothing at all.

'That would be delightful of you,' he said, 'but pray let us get rid of the dreadful word funeral. Birthday should it not be?'

This was too much for John.

'Oh, I thought birthday was the day you were

born, not the day you were buried,' he said politely.

'John!' said his mother.

Mr Silverdale beamed on him.

'John has had enough shop from his pastor, haven't you, my dear boy?' he said, with the greatest good humour. 'We clergy are terrible people for talking shop, and we don't seem to mind how boring and tiresome we are. You get enough jaw at school, pi'jaw we used to call it, without being preached at when you come home.'

But Alice fixed earnest eyes on him.

'Oh, do tell us a little more,' she said.

Again he laughed.

'My dear Miss Alice, I must come to you and your mother,' he said, 'to learn about my new parishioners. You've got to tell me all about them. I want you to point out to me every disreputable man, woman, and child in the place, and the naughtier they are the better I shall be pleased. We'll rout them out, won't we, and not give them a minute's peace, till they promise to be good.'

Mr Keeling was almost as surfeited with this conversation as was John. It appeared to him that though Mr Silverdale wished to give the impression that he was talking about his flock, he was really talking about himself, and seemed to find it an unusually engrossing topic. This notion was strongly confirmed when he found himself with him afterwards over a cigarette and a glass of port, for Mr Silverdale seemed to have a never-ending fund of anecdotes about besotted wife-beaters and scoffing atheists who were really such dear fellows with any quantity of good in them, as was proved from the remarkable response they invariably made to his ministrations. These stories seemed to be about them, but in each the point was that their floods of tears and subsequent baptism, confirmation, or death-bed, as the case might be, were the result of the moment when they first came across Mr Silverdale, who, as he told those edifying occurrences, had an air of boisterous jollity, cracking nuts in his teeth to impress John, and sipping his port with the air of a connoisseur to impress his host, and interspersing the conversions with knowing allusions to famous vintages. Subconsciously or consciously (probably the latter) he was living up to the idea of being all things to all men, without considering that it was possible to be the wrong thing to the wrong man.

This sitting, though full of sparkle, was but brief, for Keeling was sure that his guest's presence would be more welcome to his wife and daughter than it was to him, and before long he conducted him to the drawing-room where Alice happened to be sitting at the piano, dreamily recalling fragments of Mendelssohn (which she knew very accurately by heart) with both pedals down. She had been watching the door, and so when she saw it opening, she looked towards the window, so that Mr Silverdale was half-way across the room to the piano before she perceived his entrance. Then, very naturally, she got up, and under threat of Mr Silverdale instantly going home if she did not consent to sit down again and continue, resumed her melodies. He came and sat on a low stool close to her, clasped one knee with his slim white hands, and half closed his eyes.

'Now for a breath of Heaven!' he said. 'I am quite wicked about music: I adore it too much. Little bits of anything you can remember, dear Miss Alice; what a delicious touch you have.'

Alice could do better than give him little bits, thanks to her excellent memory and her practice this afternoon, and in addition to several *Songs Without Words*, gave him a couple of pretty solid slow movements out of Beethoven's *Sonatas*. It was not altogether her fault that she went on so long, for once when she attempted to get up, he said quite aloud so that everybody could hear, 'You naughty girl, sit down and play that other piece at once.' But when eventually the concert came to a close, he pressed her hand for quite a considerable time behind the shelter of the piano, and said almost in a whisper, 'Oh, such rest, such refreshment!' Then instantly he became not so much the brisk man of the world as the brisk boy of the world again, and playfully insisted on performing that remarkable duet called 'Chopsticks' with her, and made her promise that if Mr Keeling lost all his money, and she had to work for her living, she would give him lessons on the piano at seven-and-sixpence an hour. There was a little chaffering over this, for as a poor priest he said that he ought not to give more than five shillings an hour, while Mrs Keeling, joining in the pleasantries, urged Alice to charge ten. The only possible term to the argument seemed to be to split the difference and call it seven-and-sixpence, cash prepaid. . . . Mr Keeling was appealed to and thought that fair. But he thought it remarkably foolish also.

Alice's music had lasted so long that already the respectable hour of half-past ten, at which in Bracebridge parties, the crunch of carriage wheels on the gravel was invariably heard, had arrived, but Mr Silverdale had received such rest and refreshment that he sat on the edge of his chair and talked buoyantly and boyishly for another half-hour. The Galahad-aspect had vanished, so, too, had the entranced listener to slow movements, and his conversation was more like that of a rather fast young woman than a man of any kind. He told a Limerick-rhyme with a distinct point to it, having warned them that it was rather naughty, and eventually jumped up with a little scream when the ormolu clock struck eleven, saying that he would get no end of a scolding from his housekeeper for being late.

'And I shall never be asked here again, either,' he said, 'if I inflict myself on you so long. Good-night, Mrs Keeling: I have had a dear evening, a dear evening, though I have wasted so much of it in silly chatter. But if ever I am asked again, I will show you I can be serious as well.'

He shook hands with her and Alice, just whispering to the latter, 'Thank you once more,' and went out with his host. Through the open window of the drawing-room they could hear him whistling 'Oh, happy band of pilgrims,' as he ran lightly along Alfred Road to be scolded by his housekeeper.

CHAPTER III

THOMAS KEELING was seated before the circular desk in his office at the Stores, and since nine that morning, when as usual he had arrived on the stroke of the clock, had been finishing his study of the monthly balance sheets that had come in two days before. For many years now these reports had been very pleasant reading for the proprietor, and for the last eighteen months his accounts had shown a series of record-taking profits. This was no matter of surprise to him, for Bracebridge during the past decade had grown enormously since the new docks at Easton Haven, ten miles away, had converted that town from being a sleepy watering-place into one of the first ports of the kingdom. This had reacted on Bracebridge. Fresh avenues of villas had sprung up mushroom-like for the accommodation of business men, who liked to get away in the evening from crowded streets and the crackle of cobble stones, while simultaneously the opening of the new railway-works at Bracebridge itself had implied the erection of miles upon miles of workmen's dwellings. From a business point of view (to any who had business in the town) these were very satisfactory circumstances, provided that he was sufficiently wide-awake to keep pace with the growing demand, and not, by letting the demand get ahead of his provision for it, cause or permit to spring up rival establishments. Keeling, it is hardly necessary to state, had fallen into no such drowsy error: the growth of Bracebridge, and in particular of those avenues of villas which housed so many excellent customers, had always been kept pace with, or indeed had been a little anticipated by him. He had never waited for a demand to arise, and then arranged about supplying it. With the imagination that is as much at the root of successful shop-keeping as it is (in slightly different form) at the root of successful poesy, he had always foreseen what customers would want. An instance had been the sudden and huge expansion of his furniture department made about the time the first spadefuls of earth were taken out of the hillside for the foundation of the earliest of the miles of villas which held the families of business men from Easton Haven. He had foreseen that profitable incursion, risking much on the strength of his prevision, with the result that now scarcely a new villa was built that was not furnished from the Stores. The expansion of the catering department had been a similar stroke, and the prosperous business man of Bracebridge ate the early asparagus from Keeling's Stores, and drank Keeling's sound wine, as he sat on Keeling's chair of the No. 1 dining-room suite.

To-day as he finished the perusal of these most satisfactory renderings of last month's accounts, Keeling felt that he had arrived at a stage, at a plateau on the high upland of his financial prosperity. It stretched all round him sunny and spacious, and he had no doubt in his own mind as to whether it had not been worth while to devote thirty years of a busy life in order to attain it. The reward of his efforts, namely, the establishment of this large and remunerative business, and the enjoyment of an income of which a fifth part provided him with all that he could want in the way of material comfort and complete ease in living, seemed to him a perfectly satisfactory return for his industry. But as far as he could see, there was no further expansion possible in Bracebridge: he had attained the limits of commercial prosperity there, and if he was to devote his energies, now still in their zenith to a further increase of fortune, he knew that this expansion must take the form of establishing fresh branches of business in other towns. He did not for a moment doubt his ability to succeed elsewhere as he had succeeded here, for he had not in the course of his sober industrious life arrived at any abatement of the forces that drive an enterprise to success. But to-day the doubt assailed him as to whether it was worth while.

He asked himself for what reason he should

continue to rise early and late take rest, and he could not give himself an adequate answer. In material affluence he had all and more than he could possibly need, his family was already amply provided for, and the spur of another ten thousand a year had not, so it appeared now that the time for its application had arrived, a rowel that stimulated him. He had often foreseen the coming of this day, and in imagination had seen himself answer to its call, but now that the day had definitely come he had but a dull ear for its summons. The big manufacturing town of Nalesborough, thirty miles off, was, as he knew, an admirable centre for the establishment of another branch of his business, and he had already secured a two years' option on a suitable site there. There was no reason why he should not instantly exercise this option and get plans prepared at once. True, there was another year of the option still to run, and during that time the site was still potentially his, but he knew well, as he sat and debated with himself, that it was not through such hesitancy as this that his terra-cotta cupolas aspired so high. There was waiting for him, if he chose to put out the energy and capacity that were undoubtedly his, a vast increase of income. But though an increase of income was that which had been the central purpose of his last thirty years, he was still uncertain as to his future course. He was conscious (or some part of him, that perhaps which dwelt in his secret garden, was conscious) that he really did not want any more money, though for years he had so much taken for granted that he did, that the acquisition of it had become a habit as natural to him as breathing.

He folded and docketed the sheets that showed the monthly profits, and most unusually for him at this busy hour of the morning, sat idly at his desk. The business of his stores here whirled along its course automatically, with Hugh who had been so sedulously trained in his father's thorough-going school to look after it, and no longer needed his daily supervision. With the income which came to him from years of prudent investment he wanted no more, and he wondered whether the time was come to turn the business into a company. As vendor he would receive a considerable block of shares and yet leave the company with an excellent return for their money. Hugh would probably become general director, and he himself, sécure in an ample fortune, would have all his time at his own disposal. Next year, it is true, he would be Mayor of Bracebridge, which would leave him but little leisure, for he had no notion of being anything but a hard-worked head of the town's municipal affairs, but after that he could retire from active life altogether, as far as offices and superintendence went. But he by no means looked forward to a life of well-fed, well-housed idleness; the secret garden should spread its groves, he would live permanently in the busy cultivation of it. But it must spread itself considerably: he must be immersed in its atmosphere and lawns and thickets as thoroughly as, hitherto, he had been immersed in the fortunes of the Stores.

Of a sudden vistas not wholly new to him, but at present very vaguely contemplated, rushed into focus. Some three years ago when, at the age of fourteen, John would naturally have taken his place in the Stores, beginning at the bottom even as Hugh had done, Keeling had determined his destiny otherwise, and had sent him to a public school. In taking this step, he had contemplated the vista that now was growing distinct and imminent. John was to enter a sphere of life which had not opened its gate to his father. The public school should be succeeded by the University, the University by some profession in which a perfectly different standard of person from that to which his father belonged made honourable careers. Putting it more bluntly, John was to be a gentleman. Though there was no one less of a snob than Keeling, he knew the difference between what John had already begun to be and himself perfectly well. Already John walked, talked, entered a room, sat down, got up in a manner quite different from that of the rest of his family. Even his mother, the daughter of the

P. & O. captain, even Alice, for all the French, German, and music lessons with which her girlhood had been made so laborious a time, had not —Keeling found it hard to define his thought to himself—a certain unobtrusive certainty of themselves which after three years only of a public school was as much a personal possession of John's as his brown eyes and his white teeth. That quality had grown even as John's stature had grown each time he came back for his holidays, and it was produced apparently by mere association with gentlemen. Little as Keeling thought of Mr Silverdale, he was aware that Mr Silverdale had that quality too. He might be silly and affected and unmanly, but when he and John ten days ago had sat opposite each other on Sunday evening, John sick and disgusted, Silverdale familiar and self-advertising, though he appeared to talk about drunkards, it was easy to see that they both belonged to a different class from the rest of them. Keeling admired and envied the quality, whatever it was, which produced the difference, and, since association with those who had it produced it, he saw no reason to suppose that it was out of his reach.

There were plenty of people in Bracebridge who possessed it, but except at meetings and on official occasions he did not come in contact with them. As ex-fishmonger, as proprietor and managing director of the Stores, he moved in a society quite distinct from those to whom John was learning so quickly to belong. But he could see them tellingly contrasted with each other if he cared to walk along Alfred Street, past the church where he was so regular an attendant on Sunday, to where there stood side by side the two social clubs of Bracebridge, namely the Bracebridge Club to which he himself and other business men belonged, and next door, the County Club from which those of his own social standing were excluded. The Bracebridge Club was far the more flourishing of the two: its bow-windows were always full of sleek and prosperous merchants, having their glass of sherry before lunch, or reading the papers when they arrived in the pleasant hour after offices and shops were shut in the evening. These premises were always crowded at the sociable hours of the business day, and at the last committee meeting the subject of an extension of accommodation had been discussed. There was no such congestion next door, where retired colonels, and occasional canons of the cathedral, and county magnates in Bracebridge for the day spoke softly to each other, or sought the isolation of a screening newspaper in a leather arm-chair. But the quality which Keeling found so hard to define and so easy to recognise, and which to him was perfectly distinct from any snobbish appreciation of position or title, brooded over those portals of the County

Club. In the families of those who frequented it the produce of his own secret garden grew wild, as it were: the culture, the education of which it was the fruit were indigenous to the soil. He did not suppose that Colonel Crawshaw, or Canon Arbuthnot, or Lord Inverbroom discussed *Omar Khayyam* or the *Morte d'Arthur* any more than did Alderman James, or Town-Councillor Phillips, but there was the soil from which culture sprang, just as from it sprang that indefinable air of breeding which already he observed in John. One day he had seen John standing in the window there with Colonel Crawshaw and his son, who was a schoolfellow of John's, and Keeling's heart had swelled with a strange mixture of admiration and envy to see how much John was at ease, sitting on the arm of a big chair, and with a nameless insouciance of respect refusing a cigarette which Colonel Crawshaw had offered him. Lord Inverbroom stood by John; and John was perfectly at ease in these surroundings. That was a tiny instance, but none could have been more typical. Keeling wanted, with the want of a thirsty man, not so much to belong to the County Club, as to feel himself at ease there if he did belong.

He was roused from this quarter of an hour's reverie, most unusual to him in the middle of the morning, by the entrance of one of the porters with a card on a tray.

'His lordship is waiting, sir,' he said, 'and

wants to know if you can see him for ten minutes.'

Keeling took the card which he found to concern the man of whom he had this moment been thinking. Lord Inverbroom was Lord Lieutenant of the County, who lived some six miles outside Bracebridge in a house famed for its library and pictures. Its owner had held office in the last Conservative Cabinet, and was now an indefatigable promoter of county interests. Keeling met him with tolerable frequency on various boards, and there was no one in the world for whom he entertained a profounder respect.

'I'll see him,' he said. 'Show him up.'

Next moment Lord Inverbroom entered. He was small and spare and highly finished in face, and wore extraordinarily shabby clothes, of which no one, least of all himself, was conscious.

'Good-morning, Mr Keeling,' he said, with great cordiality. 'I owe you a thousand apologies for intruding, but I have quite a decent excuse.'

'No excuse necessary, my lord,' said Keeling. 'Please take a chair.'

'Thanks. Now I won't occupy your time more than I can help. I have come to consult you about the County Hospital, of which, as you know, I am chairman. We have a meeting in half an hour from now, the notice of which, by some mistake, never reached me till this morning. That's my excuse for descending on you like this.'

He paused a moment.

'There's a very serious state of affairs,' he said. 'We have a heavy deficit this last year, and unless we can find some means of raising money, we shall have to abandon the building of that new wing, which we began in the spring. I'm glad to say that was not my fault, else I shouldn't have ventured to come to you, for I only became chairman a couple of months ago. Now we are going to have the honour of having you for our Mayor next year, and I wanted to consult you as to whether you thought it possible that the town would lend us a sum of money to enable us to complete this new wing, which, in my opinion, is essential for the proper establishment of the hospital. Would such a scheme have your support? The Committee is meeting, as I said, in half an hour, and, if possible, I should like to be able to tell them that some such project is, or will be, under consideration.'

'What sum do you require?' asked Keeling.

'Eighteen thousand pounds.'

'That means twenty,' said Keeling.

'It probably means twenty,' assented Lord Inverbroom. 'We should pay, I suppose, four or five per cent. on the loan.'

Keeling tapped the table impatiently with his fingers. This was business, and in his opinion rotten business.

'And considering that last year there was a

deficit,' he said, 'where would you get your money to pay the interest?'

'That could be managed. I think I may say I could guarantee that.'

'And how about the repayment of the loan itself?' asked Keeling. 'How will that be guaranteed? The hospital is working at a loss. I don't mind that so much: appeals can be made to wipe off small deficits on working expenses. But an institution that is working at a loss can't get a further loan from a public body without giving some security for its repayment. At least, if I was on that public body, I would resign my place rather than consent to it. What sort of balance sheet would we have to show the taxpayers? No, my lord, that's quite out of the question.'

Secretly he wondered at the obtuseness of this man, who had thought such a scheme within the wildest range of possibilities. For himself he would not have lent a sixpence either of his own or of public money on such an enterprise. Yet he knew that Lord Inverbroom had been a Foreign Secretary of outstanding eminence, diplomatic, large-viewed, one who had earned the well-merited confidence of the public. Without doubt he had great qualities, but they did not appear to embrace the smallest perception on the subject of business.

Lord Inverbroom nodded to him, and rose.

'I quite see your point, Mr Keeling,' he said. 'Now you put it to me so plainly, I only wonder that I did not think of it before. I am afraid we shall have a melancholy meeting.'

As he spoke he became aware that Keeling was not paying the smallest attention to him; he appeared unconscious of him. His finger still tapped his desk, and he was frowning at his ink-bottle. Then he dismissed, as if settled, whatever was occupying his mind.

'How much has been spent on the new wing already?' he asked.

'Approximately eight thousand pounds.'

'And that will be thrown away unless you raise twenty thousand more?'

'Not permanently thrown away, I hope. But it will give us no return in the way of hospital accommodation.'

'And the new wing, on your guarantee, is urgently needed?' asked Keeling.

'I can assure you of that.'

Keeling sat silent for a moment longer. Then he rose too.

'I will present your committee with the entire new wing,' he said. 'It will be called after me, the Keeling wing. I do not wish my gift to be made public as yet. I should like that done as soon as it is complete, at the opening in fact. That should take place during my year of office as Mayor.'

Lord Inverbroom held out his hand.

'I won't keep you any longer, Mr Keeling,' he

said. 'And any words of thanks on my part are superfluous. May I just tell my committee that an anonymous donor has come forward, and that we can proceed with the work?'

'Yes, that will do.'

'I envy you your munificence,' said Lord Inverbroom.

As soon as his visitor was gone, Keeling went straight on with his morning's work. There were a couple of heads of departments to see, and after that, consulting his memoranda, he found he had made an appointment to interview a new private type-writer, in place of one whom he had lately been obliged to dismiss.

Opposite the entry was the word 'Propert,' and he recollected that this was the Miss Propert who had lately come to live with her brother. Presently, in answer to his summons, she came in, and, as his custom was with his employees, he remained seated while she stood.

'I have looked through your testimonials, Miss Propert,' he said, 'and they seem satisfactory. Your work will be to take down my correspondence in the morning, in shorthand, and bring it back typewritten for signature after luncheon. The hours will be from nine till five, with an hour's interval, Saturday half day. Your salary will be twenty-five shillings a week.'

'Thank you very much, sir,' said she.

'You will do the typewriting in that small room off this. You have a machine of your own?'

'Yes, sir. I brought it down this morning.'

'Very well. I engage you from to-day. There is a good deal to do this morning. If you are ready we will begin at once.'

In five minutes Norah Propert had deposited her typewriter in the next room, and was sitting opposite her employer with the breadth of the big table between them. As she had stood in front of him, Keeling noticed that she was tall: now as she sat with her eyes bent on her work, he hardly noticed that she was good-looking, with her light hair, dark eyebrows, and firm full-lipped mouth. What was of far greater importance was that she tore the sheets off her writing-pad very swiftly and noiselessly as each page was filled, and that when she came to some proper name, she spelled it aloud for confirmation. Occasionally when a letter was finished he told her to read it aloud, and there again he noticed not the charming quality of her voice so much as the distinctness with which she read.

For some hour and a half this dictation went on, with interruption when heads of departments brought in reports, or when Keeling had to send for information as to some point in his correspondence. He noticed that on these occasions she sat with her pencil in her hand, so as to be ready to proceed as soon as he began again. Once she corrected him about a date that had occurred previously in a letter, and was right.

'That is all,' he said, at the end. 'I will read them over and sign them, as soon as they are done.'

She had her hands full of the sheets, and he walked with her as far as the door of the very small room where the typewriting was to be done, and opened it for her. It was built out under the tiles, and was excessively hot and stuffy on this warm September morning.

'I shall be here till half-past one, if you want to ask me anything,' he said, and shut the door between her little cabin and his big cool room. This door was heavily padded at the edges, so that the clack of the typewriter hardly reached him.

It was not Keeling's usage to take any step concerning finance or business without considering where that step would take him, though that consideration could often be condensed into a moment's insight. The thought of his sudden munificence with regard to the hospital occupied his mind, when he settled down to work again, as little as did the thought of his new typist whom he had just shut up in the stuffy little chamber adjoining his own. Momentary as had been the time required for his offer, his determination to make it was but the logical next step in the secret ambition which had so long been growing in his mind. Indeed his interview with Lord Inverbroom had been his opportunity no less than the hospital's, and it would have been very unlike him not to take advantage of it. But he was not going to snatch at the fruit which it would help to bring within his reach: he had no wish that the Committee or the town generally should learn the identity of the benefactor until at the opening the name of the new wing should flash on the assembled gathering. That opening must be a day of pomp and magnificence: in course of time he would talk over that with Lord Inverbroom. At present he had plenty of occupations to concern himself with. And noticing the very fluent clacking that came faintly from behind the padded door, he filed the accounts which he had found so satisfactory, and buried himself in business again.

It was barely four o'clock when Miss Propert came in with her sheaf of typewritten correspondence for his inspection and signature. He had thought that this would occupy her for at least an hour longer, and as he read it over he looked for signs of carelessness that should betray haste rather than speed. But none such revealed themselves: all she had done was exceedingly accurate and neat, and showed no trace of hurry. He passed each sheet over to her, when he had read and signed it, for her to place it in its envelope, and looking across the table without raising his eyes he noticed the decision and swiftness of her fingers as she folded the paper with sharp, accurate creases. He liked seeing things handled like that: that was the way to do a job, whether that job was the giving of a wing to the hospital or the insertion of a letter into its envelope. You knew what you meant to do and did it. And though it was not his habit to praise work when it was well done (for he paid for its being well done), but only to find fault with work badly done (since work badly done was not worth the hire of the labourer), he felt moved to give a word of commendation.

'I see you can work quickly as well as carefully,' he said.

'I will do my best to satisfy you, sir,' she answered.

He looked at her, and saw that her face seemed flushed. That, no doubt, was owing to the heat of the room where she had been working. He pushed a ledger and a pile of typewritten sheets towards her.

'I want those entered by hand in the ledger,' he said. 'You can use that table over there in the window. When that is finished you can go.'

For another half-hour the two worked on at their separate tables. The girl never once raised her eyes from her task, but sat with one hand following down the list of names and figures, while with the other she entered them in their due places in the ledger. But her employer more than once looked up at her, and noted, as he had noted before, the decision and quickness of her hands, and, as he had not noted before, the distinction of her profile. She was remarkably like her handsome brother; she was also like the picture of one of the Rhine-maidens in an illustrated edition of the *Rheinegold*. But he gave less thought to that than to the fact that he had evidently secured an efficient secretary.

He came to the end of his day's work before her, and rose to go.

'You can leave the ledger on this table when you have finished,' he said.

She raised her eyes for a half-second.

'Yes, sir,' she said.

'Your brother tells me you are as devoted to books as he,' said Keeling.

This time she did not look up.

'Yes, sir, I am very fond of them,' she said, finishing an entry.

Keeling went out through his book department, where he nodded to Propert, into the bustle of the square, noticing, with a satisfaction that never failed him, as he walked by the various doors of his block of building, how busy was the traffic in and out of the Stores. It was still an hour to sunset: on the left the municipal offices and town-hall rose pretentious and hideous against the blue of the southern sky, while in front to the west the gray Gothic glories of the Cathedral, separated from the square by a line of canonical houses, aspired high above the house-roofs and leaf-laden elm-towers in the Close. The fact struck him that the front of the town-hall, with its wealth of fussy adornment, its meaningless rows of polished marble pilasters, its foolish little pinnacles and finials, was somehow strangely like the drawing-room in his own house, with its decorations selected by the amazingly futile taste of his wife. There was a very similar confusion of detail about the two, a kindred ostentation of unnecessary objects. There was waste in them both, expense that was not represented on the other side of the ledger by a credit balance of efficiency. No one took pleasure in the little pink granite pilasters between the lights of the windows in the town-hall, and certainly they were entirely useless. The money spent on them was thrown away: whereas money spent ought to yield its dividend, producing either something that was useful or something that gave pleasure. If you liked a thing it was worth paying for it, if it was directly useful it was worth paying for it. But where was the return on the money spent on pink pilasters or on the lilies painted on the huge looking-glass above his wife's drawing-room chimney-piece? Those lilies certainly were not useful, since they prevented the mirror exercising its proper function of reflecting what stood in front of it. Or did they yield a dividend in pleasure to Emmeline? He did not believe that they did: he felt sure that she had just bought No. 1 drawing-room suite with extras, as set forth in his catalogue. He knew the catalogues well: with extras No. 1 suite came to £117. It had much in common with the front of the town-hall. So, too, if you came to consider it, had the crocodile with the calling-cards in the abominable hall.

The day, as Miss Propert had already discovered in her little stuffy den, was exceedingly hot and airless, and Keeling, when he had passed through the reverberating square and under the arch leading into the Cathedral Close, found it pleasant to sit down on one of the benches below the elm-trees, which soared loftily among the tombs of the disused graveyard facing the west front of the Cathedral. Owing to Miss Propert's rapidity in typewriting he had left the Stores half an hour earlier than usual, and here, thanks to her, was half an hour of leisure gained, for which he had no imperative employment. The quiet gray graves with head-stones standing out from the smooth mown grass formed his foreground: behind them sprang the flying buttresses of the nave. They were intensely different from the decorations of the town-hall; they had, as he for all his ignorance in architecture could see, an obvious purpose to serve. Like the arm of a strong man akimbo, they gave the sense of strength, like the legs of a strong man they propped that glorious trunk. They were decorated, it is true, and the decoration served no useful purpose, but somehow the carved stone-work appeared a work of love, a fantasy done for the pleasure of its performance, an ecstasy of the hammer and chisel and of him who wielded them. They were like flames on the edge of a smouldering log of wood. He felt sure that the man who had executed them had enjoyed the work, or at the least the man who had planned them had planned them, you might say, 'for fun.' Elsewhere on the battlemented angles of the nave were grotesque gargoyles of devils and bats and nameless winged things with lead spouts in their mouths to carry off the rain-water from the roof. Commercially they might perhaps have been omitted, and a more economical device of piping have served the same purpose, but they had about them a certain joy of execution. There was imagination in them, something that justified them for all their nightmare hideousness. The people who made them laughed in their hearts, they executed some strange dream, and put it up there to glorify God. But the man who perpetrated the little pink granite pilasters on the town-hall, and the man who painted the lilies on the looking-glass above Mrs Keeling's drawing-room chimney-piece had nothing to justify them. The lilies and the pilasters were no manner of good: there was a difference between them and the flying buttresses and the gargoyles. But the latter gave pleasure: they paid their dividends to any one who looked at them. So did the verses in *Omar Khayyam* to those who cared to read them. They were justified, too, in a way that No. 1 drawing-room suite was not justified for the £117 that, with extras, it cost the purchaser.

Dimly, like the moving of an unborn child, the sense of beauty, that profitless thing, without which there is no profit in all the concerns of the world, began to trouble Keeling with a livelier indication of life than any that he had yet experienced from it. In some disconnected way it was connected with John's education and Lord Inverbroom's manner, and the denizens of the windows of the County Club as opposed to those who more numerously gathered in the windows of the Town Club next door. Propert, his salesman in the book department, had a cousinship to these men who made gargoyles and beautiful books, whereas Emmeline was only cousin to the pilasters in the Town Hall and the No. 1 drawing-room suite. Propert's sister, according to her brother's account, had the same type of relationship as himself. But the main point about her was her swiftness in shorthand writing and the accuracy of her transcription on to the typewriting machine. Keeling had never had a secretary who finished a heavy day's work in so short a time. He owed her the extra half-hour's leisure, which had led to this appreciation of the gargoyles and buttresses of the Cathedral. For thirty years he had passed this way almost daily, but until to-day he had never seen them before in the sense that seeing means a digestion of sight.

Behind him, where he sat, ran a thick-set hedge of clipped hornbeams, bordering the asphalt walk that led through the graveyard. It was still in full leaf, and completely screened him from passengers going through the Close. There had been many passengers going along the path there, and he had heard a score of sentences spoken as they passed within a yard of him behind the hornbeam hedge. Sentence after sentence had entered his ears without being really conveyed to his brain. Then suddenly close behind him he heard a voice speaking very distinctly. It said this:—

'It's so horrid to work for a cad, Charles. I haven't done it before. Oh, I know he was awfully kind to you——'

The voice merged into the buzz of autumn noises, and footsteps and other conversation, but it had stood apart and distinct. Keeling knew he recognised the voice, but for the moment could not put a name to its owner; it was a woman's voice, very distinct and pleasant in tone. And in order to satisfy a sudden, unreasonable curiosity, he got up from his seat and, looking out down the path over the hornbeam hedge, saw but a few yards down the path the head of his book department and his sister, the very efficient secretary and typewriter whom he had engaged that morning. Their heads were turned to each other and there was no doubt whatever about their identity.

Well, nothing could possibly matter less to him, so it seemed at that moment, than what his typewriter thought about him. All that mattered was what he thought about his typewriter, whom he considered a very efficient young woman, who got through her work with extraordinary accuracy and speed. He did not care two straws whether she considered him a cad, for what signified the opinion of a girl whose sole connection with you was the nimbleness of her fingers, employed at twenty-five shillings a week? As long as she did her work well, she might take any view she chose about her employer who, for his part, had no views about her except those concerned with the speed and accuracy of her transcriptions. . . . And then, even as he assured himself that he was as indifferent to her opinion as the moon, he found himself hating the fact that she thought him a cad. Why had she thought that, he asked himself. He had been perfectly polite to her with the icy aloofness of the employer; he had even melted a little from that, for he had opened the door for her to go into her typewriting den, because her hands were full of the papers that composed her work. Why a cad then?

He gave orders to his mind to dismiss the matter, and with his long-striding, sauntering walk that carried him so quickly over the ground, continued his way homewards. But despite his determination, he found that his thoughts went hovering back to that unfortunate and unintentional piece of eavesdropping. He wondered whether Charles Propert agreed with his sister (as if that mattered either!) and quite strongly hoped that he did not. Certainly Keeling had been kind enough and generous enough to him. . . . Then, more decidedly still, he pished the whole subject away: there were other things in the world to think about.

For the next week Miss Propert continued to display a galaxy of unvarying excellence in her duties, and Keeling, though he told himself that he had dismissed her overheard criticism from his mind altogether, and perhaps believed that he had done so, acted towards her in sundry little ways, as if he consciously deprecated her opinion and sought to change it. The weather, for instance, continuing very hot, he ordered an electric fan to be placed in the small stuffy den where she did her work, saying nothing about it to her, but setting it going while she was absent for her hour's interval in the middle of the day. On another occasion when he was sitting at his table with his hat on, he took it off as she entered, on a third he cleared a space for her to write at when she came to receive his dictation for the morning. In part, though he would have denied it, his dislike of her verdict on him prompted these infinitesimal courtesies, but in part another incentive dictated them. Vaguely and distantly she was beginning to mean something to him personally, she was acquiring a significance apart from her duties. He began to notice not only the speed and efficiency of her fingers, but the comely shape of her hand: he began to heed not only the distinctness of her voice as she read over her shorthand transcripts to him, but its quality. It reminded him rather of John's voice. . . . And oftener and oftener as he dictated his correspondence he looked up with his gray eyes set deep below their bushy eyebrows at that quiet, handsome face, which hardly ever raised its eyes to his. Somehow her perfect fulfilment of the complete duties of the secretary, devoid of any other human relationship to him whatever, began to pique him. She treated him as if he had no existence apart from his function as her employer. He had never before had so ideal a secretary, so intelligent and accurate a piece of office-furniture, and now, having got it, he was inconsistent enough to harbour a smothered wish that she was a shade more human in her dealings with him. He wished that she would not call him 'sir' so invariably, whenever she spoke to him: he looked out for the smallest indication on her part of being conscious of him in some human manner. But no such indication appeared, and the complete absence of it vexed him, though as often as it vexed him (the vexation was the smallest of annoyances) he strenuously denied to himself that such a feeling existed at all in his mind.

He had made an engagement with her brother that he should come up one Sunday afternoon some fortnight after Miss Propert had entered his employment, to spend a couple of hours among the herbage of the secret garden. The young man had come into his room just before midday closing time on Saturday, with the weekly returns of the lending library that had just been added to the book department, when a sudden idea struck Keeling.

'I shall see you to-morrow afternoon, then,' he said. 'Perhaps you will bring your sister with you, as you tell me she is a book-lover too.'

She was at the moment in the little typewriting den adjoining, the door of which was open. Through it he could just see her hands arranging the papers on her table; the rest of her was invisible. But as he spoke in a voice loud enough to be heard by her, he observed that her hands paused in the deft speed of their tidying and remained quite motionless for a second or two. And he knew as well as if some flawless telegraphic communication had been set up between her brain and his that she was debating in her mind whether she should come or not. 'She thought him a cad, but no doubt she wanted to see his books;' that was the message that came to him from her.

Keeling nodded towards the room where the hands had become busy again. He knew she had heard, overheard if you will, and since she did not choose to give her answer herself, he did not choose to convey the invitation to her again. Some faint stirrings of human relationship began at that moment to enter into living existence, for each set up their little screen of pride. Neither would have done that had there not been something, ever so small, to screen.

'Will you ask her?' he said to her brother. 'She is in there.'

He waited, hat and stick in hand, while a couple of sentences passed between them. Then Charles came out.

'She is very much obliged to you, sir,' he said. 'She will be very much pleased to come.'

'Damned condescending of her,' thought Keeling to himself. What right had a secretary at twenty-five shillings a week to send him messages through her brother? But if a message was to be sent, he was glad it was that one.

Keeling received the two next afternoon in his secret garden, and had taken the trouble to bring in a couple of more comfortable chairs. For the first time he looked at his secretary without the sundering spectacles of the employer, and on the instant became aware that she, on her side, had, so to speak, taken off the blinkers of the employed. She was here as his guest, asked by him personally because he wished to welcome her and show her his books, and her eyes, instead of being glued to her work, met his with a frank cordiality. He was not accustomed to shake hands with her brother on his Sunday visits here, but the girl advanced to him with her hand out, presupposing his welcome. Whatever hesitancy she might have had in accepting his invitation, she had, by the fact of her accepting it, put her indecision completely away, and for the first time she smiled at him.

'It was so good of you to let me come and see your books, Mr Keeling,' she said. 'My brother has often told me what delightful Sunday afternoons he has passed with you here.'

He did not fail to notice that he was 'sir' no longer, but 'Mr Keeling,' nor did he fail to grasp the significance. He was 'sir' in his office, he was Mr Keeling in his house. Somehow that pleased him: it was like a *mot juste* in a comedy.

'Your brother has often been very useful to me in my collecting,' he said, with a hint of 'employer' still lingering in his attitude towards him.

She sat down in one of the big chairs that Keeling had brought in. That was the purpose for which he had fetched them, but for the moment he put on his employer-spectacles again to observe the unusual sight of his secretary sitting unbidden while he stood. Then the girl's complete and unconscious certainty that she knew how to behave herself, whisked them from in front of his eyes again, and he saw only his guest sitting there, to whom were due his powers of entertaining and interesting her.

'Charles tells me you go in for beautiful books rather than rare ones,' she said. 'Charles, have you told Mr Keeling about the official Italian book on Leonardo?'

'No; I was going to mention it to you to-day, sir,' he said.

'Leonardo?' asked Keeling.

'Yes, Leonardo da Vinci . . .'

Immediately she saw that he had never heard of him, and without pause conveyed incidental information.

'It will reproduce all pictures certainly by him,' she said, 'and a quantity of his sketches, with his drawings of flying machines, the Venice ones, you know. It will be published to subscribers only.'

Keeling nodded to Charles.

'Will you see to that for me?' he asked.

'Yes, sir. It's published at £25, isn't it, Norah?'

'Yes, or is it £30? Ah, there's the Singleton Press *Morte d'Arthur*. May I look at that? It is one I have never seen. Ah, what a page! What type!'

For the next hour the three burrowed into or nibbled at Keeling's volumes, now losing themselves completely in the interest which was in common between them, now for a moment conscious of their mutual relations as employer and employed. But those intervals grew rarer, and in Keeling's mind were replaced by the new consciousness of his secretary with her mask off. She, on her part, found no difficulty in separating her employer from Mr Keeling with this really wonderful collection of beautiful modern books, and indeed there was little in common between them. The hobby was like a thawing sun of February that uncongealed the ice of the office, and, as long as it shone on them, the melting seemed not less than a complete break up of the frost.

'Lord Inverbroom lives near, does he not?' she asked. 'That's a wonderful library. Is the public allowed to see it? I suppose not. I would not trust Charles within arm's length of a Caxton if I had one.'

'Kind of you,' remarked Charles. 'My

sister designed and cut a book-plate for him, sir.'

Keeling saw her out of the corner of his eye just shake her head at her brother, and she instantly changed the subject. The reason seemed clear enough in the midst of these walls of books that had no such decoration. But she need not have shown such delicacy, he thought to himself, for he had no notion of ordering a plate from her. And very soon she rose.

'We must be off, Charles,' she said, 'if we are to have our walk. Thank you so much, Mr Keeling, for showing me your treasures.'

He was sorry she was going, but made no attempt to detain her, and presently she was walking back along the still sunny road with her brother.

'I'm sorry I called him a cad,' she said. 'He's only a cad in his office perhaps. My dear, did you see the crocodile holding a tray for cards? What an awful house.'

'Nice books,' said Charles.

'Very. He's worthy of them too: he really likes them. Perhaps they'll civilise him. Do you know, I feel rather a brute for having gone there.'

'Why?'

'Because I don't like him. But he's kind; and that makes it worse. What does he think about apart from his books? Just money, I suppose. I won't go there again anyhow.'

'Until he gets the Leonardo book.'

She sighed.

'I shall have to then, if he asks me,' she said. 'Or couldn't you manage to steal it?'

Charles made no definite promise on this point, and they walked on for a little in silence.

'I'm not even quite certain if I do dislike him,' she said.

'Have you been thinking about that all this time?' he asked.

'I suppose I must have been. Let's think about something else.'

CHAPTER IV

ALICE KEELING was sitting close to the window of her mother's room making the most of the fading light of a gray afternoon at the end of October, and busily fashioning leaves of gold thread to be the sumptuous foliage of no less sumptuous purple pomegranates, among which sat curious ecclesiastical fowls, resembling parrots. The gold thread had to be tacked into its place with stitches of gold silk, and this strip of gorgeous embroidery would form when completed part of the decoration of an altar-cloth for the church which till but a few weeks ago, had not even had an altar at all, but only a table. Many other changes had occurred in that hitherto uncompromising edifice. The tables of commandments had vanished utterly; a faint smell of incense hung permanently about the church, copiously renewed every Sunday, candles blazed, vestments flashed, and a confessional, undoubtedly Roman in origin, blocked up a considerable part of the vestry. But chief of all the changes was that of the personality of the vicar, and second to that the state of mind of the parish in general to which, taking it collectively, the word Christian could not properly be applied. But taking the parish in sections, it would not be in the least improper to apply the word ecstatic to that section of it to which Alice Keeling belonged, and the embroidery on which she, like many other young ladies, was employed was not less a work of love than a work of piety. As the blear autumnal light faded, and her mother dozed quietly in her chair, having let her book fall from her lap for the third time, Alice, short-sightedly peering at the almost completed leaf, would have suffered her eyes to drop out of her head rather than relinquish her work. She was sewing little fibres and shreds of her heart into that pomegranate leaf, and it gave her the most exquisite satisfaction to do so.

It would have been easy, so the simple and obviously-minded person would think, for her to have turned on the electric light, and have saved her eyes. But there were subtler and more compelling reasons which stood in the way of doing that. The first was that the light would almost certainly awaken her mother, who, by beginning to talk again, as she always did when a nap had refreshed her, would put an end to Alice's private reflections which flourished best in dusk and in silence. A second reason was that it was more than likely that Mr Silverdale would presently drop in for tea, and it was decidedly more interesting to be found sitting at work, with her profile outlined against the smouldering glow of sunset, than to be sitting under the less becoming glare of an electric lamp. For the same reason she did not put on the spectacles which she would otherwise have worn.

The leaf was all but finished when her mother began to talk with such suddenness that Alice wondered for the moment whether she was but talking in her sleep. But the gist of her remarks was slightly too consecutive to admit of that supposition.

'Though it looks very odd,' she said, beginning to give utterance to her reflections in the middle of a sentence, 'that your father and Hugh should go to Cathedral, while you and I go to St Thomas's. But the Cathedral is very draughty, that's what I always say, and with my autumn cold due, if not overdue, it would be flying in the face of Providence to encourage it by sitting in draughts. As for incense and confession and——'

Her voice suddenly ceased again, as if a tap had been turned off by some external agency, and Alice wisely made no reply of any kind, feeling sure that in a minute or two her mother would begin to give vent to that faint snoring which betokened that she had gone to sleep again. That did not interrupt the flow of her ecstatic musings, whereas her mother's general attitude to all the novel institutions which were so precious to her gave her a tendency to strong shudderings. Only half an hour ago Mrs Keeling had said that she was sure she saw nothing wrong in confession and would not mind going herself if she could think of anything worth telling Mr Silverdale about. . . . Alice had drawn in her breath sharply when her mother said that, as if with a pang of spiritual toothache.

There came a slight sound from the drawing-room next door which would have been inaudible to any but expectant ears, and Alice bent over her work with more intense industry. Then the door opened very softly, and Mr Silverdale looked in. He was dressed in a black cassock and had a long wooden shepherd's crook in his hand. He saw Alice seated in the window, he saw Mrs Keeling with her mouth slightly open and her eyes completely shut in a corner of the sofa, and rose to his happiest level.

'Hush !' he said, very gently, and tiptoed across the room to where Alice sat. He took her hand in his, pressing it, and spoke in the golden whisper which she was getting to know so well in the vestry.

'My dear girl,' he said, 'how good and industrious you are.'

'I shall get it done well before Christmas,' whispered Alice.

'How pleased the herald angels will be !' he answered.

Alice gave a great jerk of emotion which most unfortunately upset her embroidery-frame, which fell off the table with a crash that might have awaked the dead, and certainly awoke the living.

'And vestments,' said Mrs Keeling again going on precisely at the point where sleep had overtaken her, 'I can't see that there's any harm in them, though your father——'

There was a moment's dead silence as she became drowsily aware that there was somebody else in the room. Mr Silverdale's gay laugh, as he gave a final pressure to Alice's hand, told her who it was.

'Dear lady,' he said. 'Go on with your Protestant exhortations. I have been exhorting all afternoon, and I am so tired of my own exhortations. We will listen, and try to agree with you, won't we, Miss Alice?'

Mrs Keeling got up in some confusion.

'Bless me, to imagine your having come in while I was so busy thinking about what I had been reading that I never heard the door open,' she said, hastily picking up the book which had fallen face downwards on the floor. 'Well, I'm sure it's time for tea. How the evenings draw in! But there are unpleasanter things than a muffin and a chat by the fire when all's said and done.'

Alice seemed inclined to prefer her pomegranates to muffins, and had to be personally conducted from her work, and told she was naughty by Mr Silverdale, who sat on the hearthrug with woollen stockings and very muddy boots protruding from below his cassock, for he had had a game of football with his boys' club before his afternoon preaching. He had only just had time to put on his cassock and snatch up his shepherd's crook when the game was over, and ran to church, getting there in the nick of time. But he had kicked two goals at his football, and talked to twice that number of penitent souls afterwards in the vestry, so, as he delightedly exclaimed, he had had excellent sport. And he poked the fire with his shepherd's crook.

'And you didn't go home and change after your football?' asked Alice. 'You are too bad! You promised me you would!'

He held up apologetic hands, and spoke in baby voice.

'I vewy sowwy,' he said. 'I be dood to-morrow!'

'I'm not sure I shall forgive you,' said Alice radiantly.

'Please! If I have another cup of tea to keep the cold out?'

'Well, just this once,' said Alice, pouring him out another cup.

He fixed his fine eyes on the fire, and became so like the figure of Jonah in the stained-glass window that Alice almost felt herself in Nineveh.

'I'm getting spoiled here,' he said, 'all you dear ladies of Bracebridge positively spoil me with your altar-cloths and your extra cups of tea. I'm getting too comfortable. And here's Miss Alice with a cigarette at my elbow. But I don't know whether it's allowed. Have one with me, Miss Alice, and then your mother will have to scold us both, and I know she's too fond of you to scold you.'

This was slightly too daring an experiment for Alice, but she resolved to have a try in her bedroom that night.

'Indeed, it's allowed,' said Mrs Keeling, 'but as for Alice smoking, well, that is a good joke. And as for your being too comfortable I call that another joke.'

'I call it a very bad one,' said Alice delightedly. 'Mr Silverdale is very naughty. You mustn't encourage him, Mamma, to think he is funny when he is only naughty!'

She went to the window and brought back her strip of pomegranates.

'You're naughty too,' he said. 'This is playtime. And now there's something else I want to talk about. You ladies are the queens of your homes: don't you think you could persuade Mr Keeling not to think me the thin edge of the Pope, so to speak?'

'Delicious!' said Alice, beginning to be naughty with her pomegranates.

Mrs Keeling shook her head.

'It's no use,' she said. 'You can have incense or Mr Keeling, but not both. And such a draughty pew as he's got in the Cathedral!'

'It isn't only his attendance there that I mean,'

said Mr Silverdale. 'But you know his Stores are in my parish, and he employs some four hundred work-people there. I went to see him at his office this morning, and asked him if I couldn't have a daily service for them.'

'He didn't refuse?' said Alice.

'He said they might all do what they liked out of their work hours, but he couldn't have them encroached on. I was tempted to give him a good rap with my shepherd's crook, but there was a lady present. So I appealed to her for her assistance in persuading him.'

'Indeed, and who was that?' asked Mrs Keeling.

'He introduced me: it was his secretary. Such a handsome girl. I think she tried to snub me, but we poor parsons are unsnubbable. She told me that she quite agreed with Mr Keeling.'

'His typewriter dared to say that!' hissed Alice. 'Oh——'

'Then he began dictating to her something about linoleums. But I've not done with him yet. The dear man! I'll plague his life out for him if you'll only help me.'

A pink lustre clock of horrible aspect suddenly chimed six, and he jumped up.

'Evensong at half-past!' he said. 'Blow evensong! There!'

He picked up his crook.

'I've got to get hold of all you dear people,' he said, grasping Alice's long lean fingers in one hand,

and Mrs Keeling's plump ones in the other and, kissing them both. 'What an hour of refreshment I have had. Blessings! Blessings!'

He ran lightly across the room, kissed his hand at the door, and they heard him running across the drawing room.

'Blow evensong!' said Alice ecstatically. 'Wasn't that delicious of him. And the Pope, too; the thin end of the Pope. But how could father be so rude as to begin dictating about linoleum?'

'Your father doesn't like working hours interfered with, my dear,' said Mrs Keeling. 'But we'll do what we can. Anyhow, Mr Silverdale will have to change before he goes to church.'

'Oh, I hope so,' said Alice, extending her long neck over her embroidery.

'Not that it will do any good talking to your father,' continued Mrs Keeling placidly, 'for I'm sure in all these thirty years I never saw him so vexed as when you and I said we should keep on going to St Thomas's after the incense and the dressing-up began. But I had made up my mind too.'

Alice flushed a little.

'I wish you would not call it dressings-up, Mamma,' she said. 'You know perfectly well that they are vestments. They all signify something: they have a spiritual meaning.'

'Very likely, my dear,' said Mrs Keeling

amiably, 'and I'm sure that's a beautiful bit of figured silk which he has his coat made of.'

Alice drew in her breath sharply.

'Cope, Mamma,' she said.

'Yes, dear, I said coat,' rejoined her mother, who was not aware that she was a little deaf.

Alice did not pursue the subject, and since there was now no chance of Mr Silverdale's coming in again, she put on her spectacles, which enabled her to see the lines of the pomegranate foliage with far greater distinctness. Never before had she had so vivid an interest in life as during these last two months; indeed the greater part of the female section of the congregation at St Thomas's had experienced a similar quickening of their emotions, and a 'livelier iris' burnished up the doves of the villas in Alfred Road. The iris in question, of course, was the effect of the personality of Cuthbert Silverdale, and if he was not, as he averred, being spoiled, the blame did not lie with his parishioners. They had discovered, as he no doubt meant them to do, that a soldier-saint had come among them, a missioner, a crusader, and they vied with each other in adoring and decorative obedience, making banners and embroideries for his church (for he allowed neither slippers nor neckties for himself) and in flocking to his discourses, and working under his guidance in the parish. There had been frantic discussions and quarrels over rites and doctrines; households had been divided among themselves, and, as at The Cedars, sections of families had left St Thomas's altogether and attached themselves to places of simpler ceremonial. The Bishop had been appealed to on the subject of lights, with the effect that the halo of a martyr had encircled Mr Silverdale's head, without any of the inconveniences that generally attach to martyrdom, since the Bishop had not felt himself called upon to take any steps in the matter. Even a protesting round-robin, rather sparsely attested, had been sent him, in counterblast to which Alice Keeling with other enthusiastic young ladies had forwarded within a couple of days a far more voluminously signed document, quoting the prayer-book of Edward VI. in support of their pastor, according to their pastor's interpretation of it at his Wednesday lectures on the history of the English Church.

Cuthbert Silverdale was not unaware of the emotion which he had roused in so many female breasts, and it is impossible to acquit him of a sort of clerical complacency in the knowledge that so many young ladies gazed and gazed on him with a mixture of religious and personal devotion. Though a firm believer in the celibacy of the clergy, he did not feel himself debarred from sentimental relations with both married and unmarried members of his flock, indeed the very fact that nothing could conceivably come of these little mawkishnesses made them appear perfectly licit. He held their hands, and took their arms, and sat at their knees, and called them 'dear girls two or three at a time, finding safety perhaps in numbers, and not wishing to encourage false hopes. He was an incorrigible if an innocent flirt; a licensed lap-dog practising familiarities which, if indulged in by the ordinary layman, would assuredly have led to kickings. In some curious manner he quite succeeded in deceiving himself as to the propriety of those affectionate demonstrations, and considered himself a sort of brother to all those young ladies, who worked for him with the industry (and more than the excitement) of devoted sisters. To do him justice he was just as familiar with the male members of his congregation, and patted his boys on the back, and linked his arm in theirs, but it would be idle to contend that he got as much satisfaction out of those male embraces.

There was no question, however, about the devotion and strenuousness of his life. His congregation, in spite of the secession of such plain men as Mr Keeling, crammed his church to the doors and spilt into the street, and he kindled a religious fervour in the parish, which all the terrors of hell as set forth by his predecessor had been unable to fan into a blaze. In a thoroughly cheap but in a masterly and intelligible manner he preached the gospel, and in his life practised it, by incessant personal exertions, of which others as well as himself were very conscious. It was more his surface than his essential self which was so deplorable a mass of affectation and amorousness, and the horror he inspired in minds of a certain calibre by his skippings and his shepherd's crook and his little caresses was really too pitiless a condemnation. Indeed, the gravest of his errors was not so much in what he did, as his omission to consider what effect his affectionate dabs and touches and pawings might have on their recipients. He would, in fact, have been both amazed and shocked if he could have been an unseen witness of Alice Keeling's proceedings when she found herself in the privacy of her own bedroom that night.

She had gone up to bed early, feeling that nameless stir of the spirit which can only find expansion in solitude. She wanted to let herself go, to be herself, and the presence of her family forced her to wear the carapace of convention. But having pleaded fatigue at ten o'clock, though her eyes sparkled behind her spectacles, she escaped from the cramping influence of the drawing room, and locked herself into her own bedroom with her thoughts and her glowing altar-cloth.

She spread it over the side of her bed, and in front of it proceeded to her evening devotions. In the pre-Silverdale days these were the briefest and most tepid orisons, now they were invested with sincerity and heart-felt worship. First she thought over her misdoings for the day, a series of the most harmless omissions and commissions, which she set honestly before herself. She had not got up with the punctuality she had vowed: she had not kept her mind free from irritation when she went to see her grandmother: she had been guilty of gluttony with regard to jam pancakes; she had said she was tired just now when she never had felt fresher in her life. Then followed her prayers; like the rest of her vicar's numerous Bible-class she read a chapter from the Gospels, and she finished up with the appointed meditation from the devotional book which Mr Silverdale had given her.

Up to this point there would have been nothing to surprise or amaze him; he might not even have blushed to see how, when her meditations were done, she pored over the title page where he had written her name with good wishes from her friend C. S. She kissed that page before putting the book away in a box, which contained two or three notes from him, which she read through before locking them up again. They were perfectly harmless little notes, only no man should ever have written them. One had been received only this morning, and she had not read it more than a dozen times yet. It ran—

'Won't I just come in this afternoon after my football and my preachment, and get some opodeldoc for my bruises and some muffins for my little Mary, and some refreshment for my silly tired brain. God bless you!

'Your friend,

'Cuthbert S.'

That required much study. He had never signed himself like that before. She wondered if she could ever venture to call him Mr Cuthbert, and said 'Mr Cuthbert' out aloud several times in order to get used to the unfamiliar syllables. 'Preachment' too: that was a word he often used; once when he came to see them he entered the room chanting,—

'I admit the soft impeachment
That I've been making preachment.'

Alice thought that quite lovely, even when she subsequently found out that the identical effusion had already been chanted on his arrival at the house of Mrs Fyson the day before. Julia Fyson, her most intimate friend and co-adorer of the vicar, had told her.

She locked up those treasures, and going to the window drew aside the curtain and looked out. The autumnal fall of the leaf from the trees in the garden had brought into view houses in the town hidden before; among these was St Thomas's Vicarage, that stood slightly apart from the others and was easily recognisable. With the aid of an opera glass she could distinguish the windows, and saw that a light was burning behind the blinds of his study. He had come in, then, and for a full minute she contemplated the luminous oblong. Later, she had sometimes seen that a window exactly above that was lit. She liked seeing that, for it meant that he was going to bed, and would soon be asleep, for he had mentioned that he went to sleep the moment he got into bed. Once she had watched till that light went out also.

She let the curtain fall into place again, and sat by the fire for a little feeling alive to the very tips of her fingers. To-morrow would be a busy day; she had her lesson for her Sunday-school to get ready (she and Julia Fyson were going to prepare that together); there was a hockey-match for girls in the afternoon, at which Mr Silverdale—she said 'Mr Cuthbert' aloud again—had promised to be referee, she was going to read the paper to her grandmother (this was now a daily task directly traceable to the vicar), and her altar-cloth would fill up any spare time.

But as the fire began to die down, the invigorating prospect of next day lost its quality, and there began to stir in her mind a vague disquiet. Hitherto it had really been enough for her that Mr Silverdale existed; to put him on a pedestal and adore in company with other reverential worshippers had satisfied her, and the inspiration had resulted in many useful activities. But to-night she began to wish that there had not been so many other worshippers, towards whom he exhibited the same benignant and affectionate aspect. There was Julia Fyson, for instance: he would walk between them with an arm for each, and a pressure of the hand for Julia as well as herself. In moments of expansion she and Julia had confided to each other their adoration and its rewards; they had sung their hymns of praise together, and had bewailed to each other the rare moments when he seemed to be cold and distant with them, each administering comfort to the other, and being secretly rather pleased. But now Alice felt that any story of his coldness to Julia would give her more than a little pleasure. She would like him to be always cold to Julia. She wanted him herself. And at that moment the truth struck her: she was in love with him. Till then, she had not known it: till then, perhaps, there had been nothing definite and personal to know. But now, as the fire died down, she was aware of nothing else, and her heart starved and cried out. She had admired and adored before; those were self-supporting emotions. But this cried out for its due sustenance.

She got up and went to her looking-glass, turning on the electric light above it. Certainly Julia was much prettier than she, with her mutinous little pink and white face and her violet eyes. But she was such a little thing, she hardly came above Alice's shoulder, and Alice, who knew her so well, had often thought, in spite of her apparent earnestness nowadays, that she was flighty and undependable. With the self-consciousness that was the unfortunate fruit of her newly found habits of self-examination and confession, she told herself that Julia had not a quarter of her own grit and character. Only the other day, when he was walking between them, he had said, 'I always think of my friends by nicknames.' Then he had undeniably squeezed Julia's arm and said, 'You are "Sprite," just "Sprite."' Julia had liked this, and with the anticipation of a less attractive nickname for Alice, had said, 'And what is she?' Then had come a memorable reply, for he had answered, 'We must call her Alice in Wonderland: she lives in a fairyland of her own.' And he had squeezed Alice's arm too.

It was comforting to remember that, and Alice saw wonder and wistful pensiveness steal into the reflection of her face. There was the girl who would upset all his convictions about a celibate clergy; indeed, he had said that he did not think it morally wrong for them to marry. It was a case of the thin end of the wedge again, not this time of the Pope, but of Benedick, the married man.

Alice went once more to the window, and lifted the curtain. There was an oblong of light in the window above his study. She kissed her hand to it, and once more said aloud, 'Good-night,

Mr Cuthbert.' . . . But it would have been juster if she had wished him a nightmare.

Had Alice been in a condition to observe any windows and the lights in them, except those of the dark study and the illuminated bedroom at the Vicarage, she would have seen that, late as it was, there was a patch of gravel on the garden-wall outside her father's library window which smouldered amid the darkness of the night and showed there was another wakeful inhabitant in the house. He had gone to his room very shortly after Alice's disappearance from the drawing room, leaving his wife talking about table linen to Hugh. He, like Alice, wanted, though more dimly than she, the expansion of solitude. But when he got into that retreat, he found he was not quite alone in it. He had intended to look through the Leonardo publication which had just arrived, and for which he thought he thirsted. But it still lay unturned on the table. He had but unpacked and identified it, and in ten minutes had forgotten about it altogether. Another presence haunted the room and disquieted him.

It was nearly a month since the Sunday afternoon when he had held conference with the two Properts here. He had gone back to his office on the following Monday morning, feeling that he had shown a human side to Norah. She had done the same to him: she had talked to 'Mr

Keeling'; not to 'sir'; there was some kind of communication between them other than orders from an employer to an employed, and obedience, swift and deft from the employed to the employer. When he arrived at the office, punctual to nine o'clock, with a large post awaiting his perusal, he had found she had not yet come, and had prepared a little friendly speech to her on the lines of Mr Keeling. She arrived not five minutes afterwards, and he had consciously enjoyed the sound of her steps running along the passage from the lift. But when she entered she had no trace of the previous afternoon.

'I am late, sir,' she said. 'I am exceedingly sorry.'

At that, despite himself, the Sunday afternoon mood dried up also. She was in the office again, was she? Well, so was he. If she had only looked at him, had called him Mr Keeling, he would have been Mr Keeling. As it was, he became 'sir' with a vengeance.

'I hope it won't happen again,' he said. 'I cannot allow unpunctuality. Open the rest of the letters, and give me them.'

She had frozen into the perfect secretary. With incredible speed she had the sheaf of letters before him, and with her writing pad in her hand awaited his dictation. Twice during the next hour she, with downcast eyes, corrected some error of his, once producing an impeccable file to show him that a week before he had demanded a reduction on certain wholesale terms, once to set him right in a date regarding previous correspondence. She had been five minutes late that morning, but she had saved him fifty in future correspondence. She seemed to know her files by heart: it was idle to challenge her for proof when she made a correction.

Then she had gone back with her shorthand notes to her room, and all morning the noise of her nimble fingers disturbed him through the felt-lined door. He was in two minds about that: sometimes he thought he would send her into Hugh's room, where another typewriter worked. Hugh was accustomed to the clack of the machine, and two would be no worse than one. Then again he thought that the muffling of the noise alone disturbed him, that if she sat at the table in the window, and did her work there, he would not notice it. It was the concealed clacking of the keys that worried him. Perhaps it would even help him to attend to his own business to see how zealously she attended to hers. Those deft long fingers! They were the incarnation of the efficiency which to him was the salt of life.

Five days had passed thus, and on the next Saturday he had asked her brother and her, this time giving the invitation to her, to visit his library again. She had refused with thanks and a 'sir,' but Charles had come. Keeling had determined not to allude to his sister's refusal, but had suddenly found himself doing so, and Charles, with respect, believed that she was having a friend to tea. And again, despite himself, he had said on Charles's departure, 'I hope I shall see you both again some Sunday soon.'

Well, he was not going to ask twice after one refusal of his favours, but, as the next week went by, he found the 'sir' and the dropped eyes altogether intolerable. These absolutely impersonal relationships were mysteriously worrying. She had shown herself a compatriot of the secret garden, and now she had retreated into the shell of the secretary again. This week the weather turned suddenly cold, and since there was no fireplace in her room, he invited her to sit at the table by the window in his, which was close to the central-heating hot-water pipes. A certain employer-sense of pride had come to his aid, and now he hardly ever glanced at her. But one day the whole card-house of this pride fell softly on the table, just as he took his hat and stick after the day's work.

'I wonder if you would do a book-plate for me, Miss Propert,' he said. 'I should like to have a book-plate for my library.'

She paused in her work but did not look at him.

'Yes, sir, I will gladly do you one,' she said. 'Shall I draw a design and see if you approve of it?'

'No, I know nothing of these things. But I

should like a book-plate. Similar to the sort of thing you did for Lord Inverbroom.'

He hesitated a moment.

'As regards size,' he said, 'perhaps you will come up and have a look at my books again, and get a guide from them.'

She smiled, or he thought she smiled, and that together with her reply enraged him.

'That won't be necessary,' she said. 'Book-plates will suit any volume except duodecimos. I don't think you have any. If so, I could cut the margin down, sir. But I should like to submit my design to you before I cut the block.'

'That also will not be necessary,' he said. 'Something in the style of Lord Inverbroom's. Good-afternoon, Miss Propert.'

'Good afternoon, sir,' said she.

It was extraordinary to him how this girl got on his mind. He thought he disliked her, but in some obscure way he could not help being interested in her. There was somebody there, somebody from whom there came a call to him. He wanted to know how she regarded him, what effect he had on her. And there were no data: she sat behind her impenetrable mask, and did her work in a manner more perfect than any secretary who had ever served him. She declined to come to his house with her brother, she had retreated again inside that beautiful shell. He noticed infinitesimal things about her: sometimes she wore a hat, sometimes she left it in her room. One day she had a bandage round a finger of her left hand, and he wondered if she had cut herself. But her reserve and reticence permitted him no further approach to her: only he waited with something like impatience for the day when she would bring the block of his book-plate or an impression of it. There would surely be an opportunity for the personal relation to come in there.

He had begun to know that moment which few men of fifty, and those the luckiest of all, are unaware of. He wanted a companion, somebody who satisfied his human, not his corporal needs. While we are young, the youthful vital force feeds itself by its own excursions, satisfies itself with the fact of its travel and explorations. It is enough to go on, to lead the gipsy life and make the supper hot under the hedge-side, and sleep sound in the knowledge that next day there will be more travel and fresh horizons, and a dawn that shines on new valleys and hillsides. But when the plateau of life is reached, those are the fortunate ones who have their home already made. For thirty years he had had his own fireside and his wife, and his growing children. But never had he found his home: some spirit of the secret garden had inspired him, and now he felt mateless and all his money was dust and ashes in his mouth. Two things he wanted, one to be different in breed from that which he was, the other to find a companion. The shadow of a companion lurked in his room, where were the piles of his books. Somewhere in that direction lay the lodestone.

Another week passed, and still he waited for some word from his secretary about the book-plate. He was not going to be eager about it, for he would not confess to himself the anxiety with which he awaited an opportunity that his twenty-five shillings a week secretary had denied him. But day by day he scrutinised her face, and wondered if she was going to say that the book-plate was finished.

The event occurred at the most inopportune moment. He had concluded a bargain, a day or two before, for the purchase of the entire vintage of a French vine-grower in the Bordeaux district, and had just opened a letter to say that owing to the absence of a certain payment in advance, the stock had been disposed of to another purchaser, and he had lost one of the best bargains he had ever made. But he felt sure that he had drawn the cheque in question: he remembered drawing it in his private cheque-book, just before leaving one afternoon, when the cashier had already gone home. He opened the drawer where he kept his cheque-book and examined it. There it was: it was true he had drawn the cheque, but he had forgotten to tear it out and despatch it, meaning no doubt to do so in the morning.

Never in all his years of successful business had he made so stupid an omission, an omission for which he would at once have dismissed any of his staff, telling him that a man who was capable of doing that was of no use to Keeling. And it was himself who had deserved dismissal. He could remember it all now: he had locked the cheque up again as it was necessary to send a certain order form with it, and that was inaccessible now that his secretary had gone. He would do it in the morning, but when morning came he had thought of nothing but the request he was going to make that Norah should do him a book-plate. That, that trivial trumpery affair, utterly drove out of his head this important business transaction. He was furious with himself for his carelessness: it was not only that he had lost a considerable sum of money, it was the loss of self-respect that worried him. He could hardly believe that he had shown himself so rotten a business man: he might as well have sold stale fish, according to the amiable hint of his mother-in-law as have done this. And at that unfortunate moment when he was savage with himself and all the world Norah Propert appeared. Instantly he looked at his watch to see if she was again late. But it had not yet struck nine, it was he himself who was before his time.

She carried a small parcel with her, of which she untied the string.

'I have brought the block of your book-plate, sir,' she said, 'with a couple of impressions of it.'

He held out his hand for it without a word. She had produced a charming design, punning on his name. A ship lay on its side with its keel showing: in the foreground was a faun squatting on the sand reading: behind was a black sky with stars and a large moon. He knew it to be a charming piece of work, but his annoyance at himself clouded everything.

'Yes, I see,' he said. 'What do you charge for it?'

'Ten pounds,' she said. 'That will include a thousand copies.'

He looked at the block in silence for a moment. There did not seem to be much work on it: he could get a woodcut that size for half of the price. It was but three inches by two.

'Ten pounds!' he said. 'I shouldn't dream of giving more than seven for it. Even that would be a fancy price.'

He put the block down, laid the two impressions on the top of it, and turned over the leaves of his cheque-book in order to pay for the thing at once. But she picked up her work, and without a word began wrapping it up in the paper she had just taken off it. Already he knew he had made a blunder, and the blunder was the act of a cad. It had been his business to ask the price beforehand, if he wanted to know it, not to quarrel with it afterwards. But the cad in him had full possession just then.

'What are you doing?' he said, and glancing up he found that for once she was looking at him with contemptuous anger, held perfectly in control.

'I am going to take my work away again, sir, as you do not care to pay the price I ask for it,' she said.

'Nonsense. Seven pounds is a very good price. I know the cost of woodcuts.'

He had written the cheque and passed it over to her. She took no notice whatever of it, tied the string round her parcel and put it on the table in the window. Then, still without a word, she took up her pencil and her writing-pad, and sat down to receive his dictation.

In his heart he knew he was beaten. She had given him even a sharper lesson than he had given himself in the matter of the cheque he had forgotten to post. And that was but business: the error was expensive, but it was merely a matter of money as far as its effects went. He very much doubted whether money would settle this. He still thought that ten pounds was an excessive charge, but that did not detract from the fact that he had behaved meanly. His pride still choked him, but he knew that sooner or later he would be obliged to capitulate. He would have to apologise, and hope that his apology would be accepted.

The morning's work went on precisely as usual, and not by the tremor of an eyelash did she betray whatever she might be feeling. Just that one look had she given him of sovereign disdain, and the remembrance of it stiffened him against her, and he battled against the surrender that he knew must come. If she was going to be proud, he could match her in that, and again he told himself that seven pounds was a very good price. He was not going to be imposed on. . . .

All the morning the see-saw went on within him, and when she rose to go for her hour's interval he noticed that she took the parcel containing the wood-block with her. And very ill-inspired he made an attempt at surrender.

'Come, Miss Propert,' he said. 'Let's have an end of this. I should have asked the price before I commissioned you to do the work. Let me give you a cheque for ten pounds.'

She smiled: there was no doubt about that.

'I'm afraid that's quite impossible, sir,' she said, 'now that you have told me that you don't consider my work worth that. Good-morning, sir.'

Up flamed his temper again at this. What on earth did the girl want more? He had offered her the price she asked; he had said he was wrong in not inquiring about it before. She might go hang, she and her niceties and her contempt.

She had come back in the afternoon without her parcel, and his imagination pictured her telling her brother all that had happened. He felt he must have cut a sorry figure. 'That's the end of his books and his book-plates for me,' would be the sort of way Norah would sum it all up. Probably they did not discuss it much: there really was very little need for comment on what he had done. The simple facts were sufficient: perhaps she had smiled again as she smiled when she rejected his first overtures.

All afternoon they worked within a few yards of each other, all afternoon his accusing conscience battered at his pride; and as she rose to go when the day's work was over, he capitulated. He stood up also, grim and stern to the view, but beset with a shy pathetic anxiety that she would accept his regrets.

'I want to ask your pardon, Miss Propert,' he said, 'for my conduct to you this morning. I am sure you did not charge me more than your work was worth. I like your design very much. I shall be truly grateful to you if you will let me have that plate. I am sorry. That's all . . . I am sorry.'

It cost him a good deal to say that, but at every word his burden lightened, though his anxiety to know how she would deal with him increased.

She raised her eyes to his, quite in the secret garden manner, and she smiled not as she had smiled when she left him this morning.

'Thank you so much, Mr Keeling,' she said.

'I shall be delighted to let you have the block if you feel like that about it. I will bring it back with me to-morrow, shall I?'

To-night as he thought over this, when the hour was quiet, and upstairs Alice kept vigil, Norah's presence seemed to haunt the room. She had only been here once, but he could remember with such distinctness the trivial details of that afternoon, that his imagination gave him her again, now standing by the book-shelves, now seated in one of the chairs he had brought in that day, and kept here since. They would be needed again, he hoped, next Sunday, for with the arrival of the Leonardo book he had an adequate excuse for asking her again, and, he hoped, an adequate cause for her acceptance. There it lay on the table still unopened, and in the clinking of the ashes in the grate, and the night-wind that stirred in the bushes outside, he heard with the inward ear the sound of her voice, just a word or two spoken through the wind.

CHAPTER V

ONE night early in December Norah Propert was busily engaged in the sitting-room of her brother's house just off the market-place at Bracebridge. She had left him over a book and a cigarette in the dining-room, and as soon as she had finished her supper had gone across the passage to her work again. The room was very simply decorated: to Mrs Keeling's plush-and-mirror eye it would have seemed to be hardly decorated at all. There were a few framed photographs or cheap reproductions of famous pictures on the walls, a book-case held some three hundred volumes, the floor had a fawn-coloured drugget on it, and there was not a square inch of plush anywhere.

The table at which she worked was covered with small cardboard slips, bearing in her neat minute handwriting the titles and the authors of the books in Mr Keeling's library. Each appeared twice, once under its author, once under its title, and these she was sorting out into an alphabetical file from which she would compile her catalogue. She had been at work on it for about a fortnight, and the faint hopes she had originally entertained of getting it finished by the end of the year had now completely vanished. He had been buying books in very large numbers; already wing-bookcases had begun to invade the floor space of his room, and he intended in the spring to build out farther into the garden. But Norah was not at all sure that she regretted the vanishing of those hopes: the work interested her, and she had the true book-lover's pride in making all the equipment connected with books as perfect as it could be. Three times a week she went with her brother after supper for a couple of hours' work in Mr Keeling's library: the other evenings she brought into order at home the collection of slips she had made there.

Those evenings spent at Mr Keeling's house had a great attraction for her. She enjoyed the work itself, and as she made her slips she had refreshing glances at the books. It was a leisurely performance, not like her swift work in the office. Charles helped her in it, making author-slips or illustration-slips as she made title-slips. There was a fire on the hearth, a tray of sandwiches for them before they left, and more often than not Mr Keeling came and sat with them for half an hour, unpacking fresh volumes if any had come in, and looking through the book-catalogues that were sent him. And Norah was honest enough with herself to confess that it was not the work alone that interested her. Friendship, no less than friendship sudden and to her quite unexpected, had been the flower of the original enmity between her and the man, who was never 'sir' to her even in the office now. It dated from the moment when he had made his unreserved apology to her over the matter of the book-plates. She knew what it must cost to a man of his type to say what he had said to his typewriter, and she had to revise all her previous estimates of him, and add him up honestly again. She found the total a very different one from that which she had supposed was correct. True, a woman does not like or dislike a man directly because of his qualities, but his qualities are the soil from which her like or dislike springs. They are part at any rate of his personality, in which she finds charm or repulsiveness. The upshot was, to take it at its smallest measure, that instead of disliking her work for him, she had grown to like it, because it was for him that she did it.

She was deep in her work now when her brother joined her. Charles was suffering from a cold of paralysing severity, and she looked up with a certain anxiety as a fit of coughing took him, for he was liable to bad bronchitis.

'Charles, you ought to go to bed,' she said, 'and stop there to-morrow.'

'I dare say, but I shan't,' said Charles hoarsely.

'Why? It is very unwise of you. I'll tell Mr Keeling as soon as I get there in the morning. I'm sure he'll think you were right.'

'Oh, I shall be better,' said he. 'Considering

that he saw me through an illness last year, the least I can do is to hold on as long as I can.'

'So that he may have the pleasure of seeing you through another one this year,' remarked Norah.

'Don't be so optimistic. I may die instead.'

'You can if you like,' she said, 'but it would worry me very much.'

Charles subsided into his book again for a little, but presently put it down.

'What about your work at Keeling's to-morrow night?' he said, 'if I'm not fit to come out? You can't very well go up there alone, can you?'

Norah paused before she answered.

'Why on earth not?' she said. 'I sit with him alone all day in his office. Besides, I know he has a dinner-party to-morrow. I shan't see him.'

'And how do you know that?' he asked.

'Because a note came to the office from his wife, which I opened, not knowing her writing, which had something to do with it. He began dictating a reply for me to type-write, but I suggested he had better write a note himself.'

'What awful impertinence!'

'He didn't think so. He's rather touching. He said, "Then you don't despair of making a gentleman of me in time." '

'I remember you told me once he was a cad. I shall go to bed, I think.'

'You had much better. And do let me tell

him you have stopped there to-morrow morning,' she said.

'I doubt it. Good-night. I dare say I shall be all right to-morrow.'

Charles was no better next day, but merely obstinate, and went up to his work, as usual, with his sister. Keeling appeared shortly after, and, as usual, began the dictation. Now and then he gave sharp glances at Norah, and before long stopped in the middle of a letter.

'What's the matter, Miss Propert?' he said. 'Better tell me and not waste time, unless it's private.'

He had no difficulty in making her look at him now. She looked up with a half smile.

'How did you guess there was anything the matter?' she asked.

'How do I guess it is warm or cold? I feel it. Tell me.'

'I'm rather anxious about Charles,' she said. 'He has got an appalling cough.'

'Have you sent for the doctor?'

'No. He insisted on coming up to his work.'

Keeling got up.

'I'll soon settle that,' he said, going out.

He came back in a very short space of time.

'You'll find him in bed when you get home,' he said.

'Oh, thank you so much. I am so grateful.'

'You needn't be. I told him he wanted to

make me pay a big doctor's bill for him instead of his paying a little one. He deserved that for being so idiotic as to come out. Read the letter, please, which we stopped in the middle of.'

All day the work went forward as usual: there was a heavy budget to answer, and it was not till nearly six that Norah had her letters ready for his signature. He made no payment to her for such over-time work, for the balance was more often on the other side, and she got away before her time. As he passed her back the last of the batch, he said,—

'You are coming to the library this evening, are you not?'

'I had meant to, if it is convenient to you.'

'Perfectly. Perhaps you would leave a line on the table to say how your brother is. I don't suppose I shall see you to-night.'

Mrs Keeling's party that night, which sat down very punctually at half-past seven, and would disperse at half-past ten, was of the only-a-few-friends nature. Julia Fyson, Alice's bosom friend, whom she had begun to dislike very cordially, was there, with her father and mother, the former, small and depressed, the latter, large and full-blooded and of a thoroughly poisonous nature. The four Keelings were there, and the extremely ladylike young woman whom Hugh had lately led to the altar. She was a shade too lady-like, if anything, and never forgot to separate her little finger from the others when she was holding a cup or glass. They were ten in all, Mr Silverdale and Dr Inglis completing the number. As was usual at the table of that generous housekeeper Mrs Keeling, there were vast quantities of nitrogenous food provided in many courses, and it was not till nine that the dining-room door was opened, on the run, by Mr Silverdale to let the ladies leave the room. He made a suitable remark to each as she passed him, and Julia Fyson and Alice, with waists and arms interlaced, stopped to talk to him as they went out. Precisely at that moment, while they were all in the Gothic hall together, the boy covered with buttons opened the front door and admitted Norah Propert. The door into the dining-room was still being held wide by Silverdale, as the interlaced young ladies answered his humorous laments over the setting of the sun now that the ladies were leaving, and through it Keeling standing at the head of the table saw Norah there. She had had but one moment for thought as the front-door was opened to her, but the light from the hall streamed full on to the step and she judged it better to come in than, having been already seen, retreat again. Without looking up she walked across to the library door while still Mrs Fyson stared, and let herself in. She heard the dining-room door opposite close again while she fumbled for the switch of the electric light; she heard indistinguishable murmurs from the hall. Only one caught her ear intelligibly when Mrs Keeling said, 'Oh, Mr Keeling's typewriter. She is cataloguing his books.'

It had begun to snow thickly outside, and she stood for a minute or two before the fire, shaking from her cloak the frozen petals, which fizzed on the coals. Certainly she had felt a disconcertment at the moment of her entry and passage through the hall, had found fault with the ill luck that had caused her to meet the gorged galaxy from the dining-room on the one and only night when her brother had not been with her. But the encounter did not long trouble her, and like warmth coming over frozen limbs, the fact of being here alone gave her a thrill of pleasure that surprised her. She was in his secret garden all by herself, without Charles to intrude his presence, without even Keeling himself. She did not want him here now; she was surrounded with him, and presently she plunged like some ecstatic diver into the work she had come to do for him. Soon the buzz of men's conversation drifted past the door, prominent among which was Silverdale's expressive and high-pitched voice, and without intention she found herself listening for Keeling's. Then the murmur was cut off by the sound of a shutting door, and she went on with her work on the catalogue cards. Faint tinkles of a piano were heard as Alice performed several little pieces, faint screams as Julia Fyson sang. Keeling was there, no doubt, and still she did not want him in his bodily presence. He was more completely with her in this room empty but for herself.

She had settled in her own mind to get away before the party broke up, but she grew absorbed in her work, and it came with something of a surprise and shock to her when again she heard the gabble of mixed voices outside, saying what a pleasant evening they had had, and realised that she must wait till those compliments were finished. She had not yet written the note which Keeling had asked her to leave on the table, regarding her brother's health, and this she did now as she waited, giving a promising account of him. Soon the front-door closed for the last time, leaving silence in the hall, and she heard a well-known foot cross it in the direction of the drawing-room, pause and then come back. Keeling entered.

'Good-evening, Miss Propert,' he said. 'I want you, if you will, to leave your work now, and come into the drawing-room to talk to my wife and daughter for a few minutes, while I ring for a cab for you. It is snowing hard.'

'Oh, I would rather not do that,' said Norah. 'I have got great big overshoes: there they are filling up the corner of the room; I shan't mind the snow. And, Mr Keeling, go back to the drawing-room, and say I've gone.'

It was clear to each of them that the same

situation, that of Norah having been seen entering the house alone after dinner, and going to his private room, was in the mind of each of them. Norah, for her part, had a secret blush for the fact that she considered the incident at all, but her reply had revealed that she did, for she remembered that her brother had alluded to the question of her coming up here alone. But Keeling saw no absurdity in, so to speak, regularising the situation, and his solution commended itself to him more than hers.

'I should prefer that you came and were introduced to Mrs Keeling,' he said. 'I think that is better.'

Norah got up, smiling at him. Her internal blush had filtered through to her face.

'If you think it best, I will,' she said. 'Whatever we do, don't let us waste time here.'

'Come then,' he said.

He showed her the way to the drawing-room, where his wife and Alice were standing by the fire.

'I have brought in Miss Propert,' he said, 'while I am getting a cab for her to take her home. It is snowing heavily. And this is my daughter, Miss Propert.'

Mrs Keeling made a great effort with herself to behave as befitted a mayoress and the daughter of a P. and O. captain. She thought it outrageous of her husband to have brought the girl in here without consulting her, not being clever enough to see the obvious wisdom, both from his standpoint and that of the girl, of his doing so. But she had the fairness to admit in her own mind that it was not the girl's fault: Mr Keeling had told her to come into the drawing-room, and naturally she came. Therefore she behaved to her as befitted the Mayoress talking to a typewriter, and was very grand and condescending.

'I am sure you are very useful to Mr Keeling,' she said, 'in helping to arrange his books, and it must be a great treat to you to have access to so large a library, if you are fond of reading.'

The pretentious solemnity of this was not lost on Norah's sense of humour. She was rather annoyed at the whole affair, but it was absurd not to see the lighter side of it, and answer accordingly.

'Yes, I am very lucky,' she said. 'I was lucky in London too, where I had access to the library at the British Museum.'

This seemed a very proper speech to Mrs Keeling. It was delivered in clear, pleasant tones, with the appearance of respect, and she could not make out why Alice gave one of her queer, crooked smiles, or why she said,—

'I suppose that is bigger than my father's, Miss Propert.'

Norah looked up at her, laughing.

'At a guess I should say it was,' she said.

Decidedly there was something here that Mrs Keeling did not wholly comprehend, and when she did not comprehend she called it being kept in the dark. She comprehended, however, that Norah was exceedingly good-looking, and that there was a certain air about her, which she supposed came from reading books. Simultaneously she remembered Mrs Fyson asking her who it was who had come in and passed into Mr Keeling's library; and on being informed that lady had said, 'How very odd,' and at once changed the subject. Instantly she began to consider if it was very odd. But for the present she determined that nothing should mar the perfect behaviour of the Mayoress.

'Pray sit down, Miss Propert,' she said. 'I fancy your brother is one of Mr Keeling's clerks too.'

'Yes; he usually comes with me in the evening,' said Norah, 'but he is in bed with a very bad cold.'

'Indeed. Oh, indeed!' said Mrs Keeling.

Conversation came to a dead halt here, and again Mrs Keeling, with growing resentment, took in Norah from head to foot. The seconds were beaten out sonorously by the pink clock on the chimney-piece, and at last Norah, now growing thoroughly uncomfortable in this hostile atmosphere, rose.

'I think Mr Keeling had much better not bother about a cab for me,' she said. 'I can perfectly well walk home.'

Mrs Keeling became a shade statelier, without abatement of her extremely proper behaviour.

'Mr Keeling will do as he thinks wisest about that,' she said.

It seemed, however, not to be in Mr Keeling's power to do what he thought wisest, for after a minute or two of ringing silence, he appeared with the news that there were no cabs to be got. It was snowing heavily and they were all out.

Norah held out her hand to Mrs Keeling. 'I won't keep you up any longer,' she said. 'I shall walk home at once.'

'It's impossible,' said he, 'there's nearly a foot of snow now.'

'All the more reason for getting home before there are two,' said she.

'I'll see you home then,' he said. 'You can't go alone.'

'Indeed you shall do nothing of the sort,' said she. 'It is quite unnecessary. I absolutely forbid it.'

For a moment it was a mere tussle of will between them, and Norah's reasons were the stronger. She looked at him a moment, and knew she had won, and without more words went back to the library and put on her over-boots, and gathered up the book-slips she had made that evening. He followed her as far as the hall, and waited for her.

'Don't look at my feet,' she said gaily. 'They

are officially invisible like the legs of the Queen of Spain.'

The grim mouth smiled, and the stern eyes grew kindly. She knew that transformation so well now.

'You are very obstinate,' he said. 'Why don't you let me walk home with you?'

'I am right,' she said. 'And I think your plan was wrong.'

'They weren't rude to you?' he asked, growing grim again.

'Ah, you shouldn't have asked that,' she said. 'They were exceedingly polite.'

He let her out into the snow, and felt that fire went with her; then returned to the drawing-room where he found unquestionable ice. Little sour wreaths of mist were already afloat in Mrs Keeling's mind, which, though not yet condensed into actual thought, were chilling down to it in that narrow receptacle. Alice took her embroidery, and went upstairs, but his wife sat rather upright by the fire, looking at the evening paper which she held upside down. She meant to behave with perfect propriety again, but wished him to begin, so as to launch her propriety on a fair and even keel.

For his part he had known so many of those evenings, when the dinner-party went away precisely at half-past ten, and he was left to hear long comments by his wife on the soup and the beef and the grouse and the pudding and the savoury, and what Dr Inglis said, and what Mrs Fyson thought. He hoped, when he first came back, after seeing Norah fade into the snow-storm, that he was to be regaled with such reminiscences, but hoped rather against hope. No reminiscences came to his aid, and he began to be aware, from the ice-bound conditions, that he must expect something far less jovial and trivial. But he had no accusing conscience, and if she chose to read her evening paper upside down in silence, he could at least read the morning paper the right way up. Then, as he would not give her a lead, make some remark, that is to say, to which she could take exception, she had to begin.

'I must say I am surprised at your not seeing Miss Propert home,' she said. 'After bringing her into my drawing-room and forcing me to be civil to her, you might have had the civility yourself to see her to her house.'

He was aware that she was intending to exercise the dead-weight somewhere. It was not many weeks ago that she had brought it into play regarding Mr Silverdale and his Romish practices, when she had refused to leave his church for the simpler rites of the Cathedral. He had yielded there, because he did not really care whether she and Alice chose to attend a milliner-church or not. They might if they liked: it did not seriously matter. But the dead-weight, if she was intending to exercise it over the question of Norah, mattered very much.

'Would it have pleased you better if I had seen her home?' he asked.

'I can't say whether I should have been pleased or not,' she said. 'It didn't happen. But I'm sure I don't know why you sent your typewriter in here to talk to me. I don't know what you think I should find to say to her. With Alice here too.'

She had said too much, and knew it the moment she had said it. But the mists had congealed, and she felt obliged, as she would have expressed it, say, to Mrs Fyson, to speak her mind. She did not really speak her mind; she spoke what some perfectly groundless jealousy dictated to her.

He dropped the paper, and stood up by the fireplace.

'You said, "With Alice here too,"' he said. 'Oblige me by telling me what you mean.'

She saw that in a reasonable frame of mind she would not have meant anything. But she was cross and surfeited, and the cold in the head which had spared her so long was seriously threatening. She wanted, out of sheer perverseness, to defend an indefensible position.

'Well, I'm sure Alice must have thought it very odd your bringing your typewriter into my drawing-room,' she said.

'No, you didn't mean that!' said Keeling.

Mrs Keeling got up.

'If you only want to contradict me,' she said, 'you can do it by yourself, Thomas. I'm not going to answer you. That rude girl came in here——'

'Rude? You said, "rude." How was she rude?'

He knew he was being unwise in bandying stupid words with his wife. But she continued to make accusations, and his want of breeding, to use a general term, did not allow him to pass them over in the silence that he knew they deserved.

'How was she rude?' he repeated.

'She said something about the British Museum Library that I did not understand,' she said.

'And because you couldn't understand, you think she was rude? Was that it?'

'Well, if you had heard her say it——' she began.

'You know I did not. But I am quite certain that Miss Propert was not rude. And now about Alice's being here, when I brought her in. What of that? I wish you to tell me if you meant anything. If you did not, I wish you to say so.'

He knew quite well that he was adopting a bullying tone. But he had no inclination to be bullied himself. One or other of them had to be vanquished over this, and he was quite determined that he would not hold the white flag. There was something to be fought for, something which he could not give up.

'You must allow it was very odd that your secretary should appear in the middle of my dinner-party,' she said, 'and simply stroll across to your room. I had been talking of your room half dinner-time with Mr Fyson, saying that none of us was allowed there. And then, in came this girl——'

He cut her short.

'What has that to do with Alice?' he repeated.

'I was going to say that, only you always interrupt me,' she said. 'Then when our guests are gone, you bring her in here, just as if she was Julia Fyson, into my drawing-room. And Alice —well, Alice would think it very odd too, just as Mrs Fyson did. Of course it was not that which Mrs Fyson thought odd: I know you will try to catch me up, and ask me how Mrs Fyson knew, but that is always your way, Thomas. I know quite well that Mrs Fyson had gone away before you brought her in here.'

'I don't want to catch you up,' he said. 'I only want to know why Alice should not be here when I bring Miss Propert in to wait for a cab. You can't give me any reason because there is no reason. Let's get that clear, and then I want to talk about something else.'

Suddenly the whole of the vague internal movements of her mind flashed into his vision, as intelligible as some perfectly simple business proposition. She had a certain justification too: it was awkward that Norah had run into the exit of the ladies, that his wife had been saying that none of them ever entered the library. He knew the mind of Bracebridge pretty well, the slightly malicious construction that women like Mrs Fyson would find themselves compelled to put on it all. He knew also the mind of his wife, and the effect which it clearly had had on her. Her sense of propriety, of dignity had been assaulted: it was a queer thing to have happened. Then there was Norah's presence in her drawing-room. He had insisted on that, for, at the moment, it seemed the most straightforward thing to do. But he was beginning to think it had been a mistake. Something about the girl, her beauty (and never had that struck him so forcibly as when he saw her standing by Alice), her air of breeding, of education, of simplicity in front of those draped easels and painted looking-glasses had stirred some long latent potentiality for jealousy in his wife. It was that suggestion which suddenly enraged him.

'Don't be such a damned fool, Emmeline,' he said angrily, answering his own thoughts. He had divined hers quite correctly, and the justice that lay behind this rude speech struck her full. Her only course was to take refuge in her own propriety. *She* knew how to behave.

'Well, Mr Keeling,' she said, 'you can't expect

me to say anything more about it, if all you want to do is to swear at me. Perhaps you would like to swear at me again. Pray do.'

'No, that's all,' he said. 'I've told you not to be a damned fool, and I meant it. The wisest thing you can do is to take my advice.'

She moistened her lips very genteelly with the tip of her tongue.

'Then if you have finished with that,' she said, 'shall we pass on to the other matter you said you wanted to talk to me about.'

'By all means. Your Mr Silverdale is stuffing Alice's head with ridiculous notions. He's doing the same to that other girl. Of course she's no business of yours or mine, but Alice is. She'll soon be fancying herself in love with him, if she doesn't already.'

'And do you want my opinion on the subject?' asked the Mayoress.

'Of course. I am consulting you.'

'Then I think you are quite mistaken. They are great friends, and Mr Silverdale has the most wonderful and spiritual influence over her. She is quite changed. She is always doing something now for somebody else; she reads to Mamma, she takes a Sunday school, she is busy and happy and active.'

Mr Keeling considered this.

'My idea is that she's doing it all for Mr Silverdale. She could have read to your mother before

Dr Inglis went to the Cathedral. Silverdale is the somebody she's doing things for.'

'It is due to his influence certainly. I know you dislike him, but then that is your opinion, and it does not agree with other people's. His parishioners generally adore him.'

'Especially the young ladies, and of these especially the silly ones. He can have an influence with my poor Alice without holding her hand and whispering to her. He's a flirt, and I don't like flirts, especially those who wrap up their nonsense in religion. Can't you do something to stop it? He's always coming here, isn't he? I don't like all that pawing and touching, and saying it is spiritual influence.'

Mrs Keeling felt shocked at this positively carnal view of Mr Silverdale's tendernesses. At the same time she thought they had a promising aspect besides the spiritual one.

'Well, I hope you'll not say or do anything to put him off,' she said, the practical side of the question claiming her. 'I'm sure it's high time Alice was married, and never yet has she taken to a young man as she's taken to Mr Silverdale.'

Poor Keeling's head whirled: a moment ago his wife had said that the two were great friends only on the spiritual plane, now she was saying precisely what she had begun by contradicting. He was satisfied, however, that he had her true opinion at last. It did not appear to him to be worth anything, but there it was. He got up.

'If I thought Silverdale had the slightest intention of marrying Alice,' he said, 'I shouldn't mind how much he pawed her. But I don't believe he has. I've a good mind to ask him.'

'Indeed, I hope you will do nothing so indelicate,' said she.

A humorous twinkle came into his eye.

'I wish you would flirt with him yourself, Emmeline,' he said, 'and take him away from Alice. Perhaps you do: some of these clergy flirt with every decent-looking woman within reach, and you're twice as handsome as Alice.'

This also was dreadfully indelicate, but it is not to be wondered at that Mrs Keeling cast a glance into the looking glass, where her reflection looked out like a Naiad amid the water-lilies, even while she reproved her husband for the broadness of his suggestion.

'I never heard of such talk,' said she. 'Pray don't let us have any more of it. For shame!'

But she went up to her bed in a far better temper than she would otherwise have done, and quite abandoned any idea of lying awake to punish him for his previous brutality.

He went back to his library when his wife left him, where an intangible something of Norah's presence lingered. There was the chair she had sat in, there was her note to him about her brother on the table, and the blotting paper on which she had blotted the entries she had made on the catalogue cards. He took up the top sheet and held it to the light, so as to be able to read the titles of the books. There were the authors' names in big firm capitals, the book-titles in smaller writing but legible. She had done a lot to-night, for he remembered having put clean blotting paper for her, and the sheet was covered with impressions. Here she had been sitting at work, while he talked and listened to those people in the drawing-room who meant nothing to him. . . .

He laid the sheet down with an impatient exclamation at himself, and thought over the incident of Norah's meeting the party of ladies in the hall. Mrs Fyson had thought it odd, had she? So much the more mistaken was Mrs Fyson. There was nothing odd about it at all. His wife had been disposed to take Mrs Fyson's view, and he had given her his opinion on that point pretty sharply. Nothing had ever passed between Norah and himself that might not with perfect propriety have taken place in the middle of the market-square with Mrs Fyson and all the ladies of Bracebridge straining their eyes and ears to detect anything which could have given one of them a single thing to think about. But the complete truth of that was not the whole truth. A situation which was in process of formation underlay that truth, and just now that situation had expressed itself in eloquent silence when he took up the blotting-paper and read what Norah had written on the cards. He had not given a thought to the titles of the books and their authors, though probably his eyes had observed them: his mind had been wholly occupied with the knowledge that it was she who had written them.

It was that which his wife had expressed in her manner and her words: it was that for which he had chosen to swear at her. He had given her a good knock for hinting at it, and had followed up that knock by the stupid sort of joke about the superiority of her charms to those of Alice, which she was sure to appreciate. She had done so; she had said, 'For shame!' and gone simpering to bed. Perhaps that would take her mind off the other affair. He sincerely hoped it would, but he distrusted her stupidity. A cleverer woman would have probably accepted the more superficial truth that there had never passed between him and Norah a single intimate word, but a stupid one might easily let a dull unfounded suspicion take root in her mind. It was difficult to deal with stupid people: you never knew where their stupidity might break out next. Emmeline had a certain power of sticking, and Mrs Fyson had a brilliant imagination. Together they might evolve some odious by-product, one that would fumble and shove its way into the underlying truth.

He got up with a shrug of the shoulders. There was no use in making conjectures about it all. Perhaps if he gave Emmeline a pearl-pendant for her birthday, which fortunately occurred next week, he could distract her mind. But it was impossible to tell about Emmeline: her stupidity was an incalculable item.

He went to the front door in order to make sure he had put the chain on, and then taking it off, opened the door and looked out into the night. The snow was still falling fast, and the prints of wheels and footsteps outside were already obliterated. Mr Silverdale had walked home, light-heartedly predicting a 'jolly good snowballing match' with his boys next day, and Keeling found himself detesting Mr Silverdale with acute intensity. Norah had walked home also. . . . In a moment he was back in the hall, putting on a mackintosh. He would have liked to put on boots as well but for that he would have had to go up to his dressing-room next door to his wife's bedroom. Then gently closing the door behind him, he went out into the night. He must just walk as far as her house to make sure she was not still tramping her way through the snow, and traverse the streets she had traversed. It was absolutely necessary to satisfy himself about that, and he did not care how unreasonable it was—rational considerations had no application; an emotional dictate made him go. There was but a mile of gas-lit thoroughfare between his house and hers, but he, striving to smother the emotion he would not admit, told himself that he must be satisfied she was not still out in this frozen inclement night. He gave that as a sop to his rational self; but he knew he threw it as to some caged wolf, to keep it from growling.

There was a moon somewhere above the snow-clouds that already were beginning to grow thin from the burden they had discharged, and the smug villas on each side of the road were clearly visible. She had to go up the length of Alfred Road, then turn down the street that led by St Thomas's Vicarage, and emerge into West Street, where she lived with her brother. Already, a fortnight ago he had ascertained the number of their house, not asking for it directly, but causing her to volunteer the information, and since then he had half a dozen times gone through the street, on his way to and from the Stores in order to take a glance at it as he passed. He had wanted to know what the house looked like; he had wanted to construct the circumstances of her life, to know the aspect of her environment, to see the front-door out of which she came to her duties as his secretary. That all concerned her, and for that reason it concerned him. He knew the house well by now: he knew from chance remarks that he had angled for that her bedroom looked into the street, that Charles's looked on to an old disused graveyard behind. There was the dining-room and the sitting-room in front, and a paling behind which Michaelmas daisies flourished in a thin row. She cared for flowers, but not for flowers in a six-inch bed. They rather provoked her: they were playing at being flowers. She liked them when they grew in wild woodland spaces, and were not confined between a house-wall and a row of tiled path.

The empty streets, dumb with snow, flitted silently by him, and as they passed, he seemed to himself to be standing still while some circular movement of the earth carried him past the silly Vicarage and into West Street. It brought him up to the house: it showed him a red blind on the first floor lit from within. That was what he had come to see, and he waited a moment on the white pavement opposite watching it. She had got home, that was all right then, yet still he looked at the blind.

He turned and retraced his steps. Now that the object of his expedition was secured he was conscious of all the discomforts and absurdity of what he had been doing. The snow was deep, his evening shoes were wet through, his mackintosh heavy with clinging flakes, and his rational self made its voice heard, telling him what a fool's errand was in progress. He heard, but his emotional self heeded nothing of that: it would not argue, it would not answer, it was well satisfied with what he had done, telling him, now that he was going homewards again, that he would find there the blotting paper on which she had pressed the wet ink of her catalogue slips, reminding him that at nine next morning he would see her again. It would attend to no interruptions, its thoughts sufficed for itself. But he knew that his reason, his prudence were ringing him up, as it were, on the telephone. The bell tinkled with repeated calls for him to listen to what they had to say. But he refused to take the receiver down; he would not give his ear to their coherent message, and let them go on summoning him unheeded. He knew all they had to say, and did not want to hear it again. They took an altogether exaggerated view of his affairs, when they told him that the situation might easily develop into a dangerous one. He, with his emotional self to back him up, knew better than they, and had assured them that his self-control had the situation well in hand. They need not go on summoning him, he was not going to attend. In the leafless elms above there sang in this wintry and snow-bound night the shy strong bird of romance: never in his life had he heard such rapture of melody.

Despite his fifty years, and the hard dry business atmosphere of his life, there was something amazingly boyish in the inward agitation in which Keeling, arriving ten minutes before his time at his office next morning, awaited Norah's coming. His midnight excursion, dictated by some imperative necessity from within had, even if it was not a new stage in his emotional history, revealed a chapter already written but not yet read by him. He expected too, quite irrationally, that some corresponding illumination must have come to the girl, that she, like himself, must have progressed along a similar stage. He pictured himself telling her how he had left his house in order to have the satisfaction of seeing her lit window; he had a humorous word to say about the state of his dress shoes (in place of which he must not forget to order a pair from the boot and shoe department this morning). He could see her smile with eyes and mouth in answer to his youthful confession, as she always smiled when, as often happened now, some small mutual understanding flitted to and fro between them, and could easily imagine the tone of her reply, 'Oh, but how dreadfully foolish of you, Mr Keeling. You want to be laid up too, like Charles.' She would not say more than that, but there would be that glimmer of comprehension, of acceptance, that showed she had some share in the adventure, that she allowed it, looked on it with the kind eye of a friend.

There was never a swifter disillusionment than when she came in, and he stood up, as he had now learned to do, at her entrance. He had heard her step along the passage, and the bird of romance, hidden perhaps behind the sofa or in the case of files, gave out a great jubilant throatful of song. But next moment it was as if some hand, Mrs Fyson's perhaps, had wrung its neck and stopped its singing. She had a perfectly friendly smile for him, but the smile was not one shade more friendly than usual, her eyes did not hold lit within them a spark of closer intimacy than had habitually been there for the last fortnight. Whatever had happened to him last night, he saw that nothing whatever had happened to her. No sixth sense had conveyed to her the smallest hint of his midnight walk: she had been through no nocturnal experiences that the most sanguine could construe into correspondence with that, and on the moment he could no more have told her about his midnight walk, or have been humorous on the subject of disintegrated shoes than he could have taken her into his arms and kissed her. And by the standard of how incredibly remote she seemed, he could judge of the distance of his spirit's leap towards her, when he stood outside her window last night. The very absence of any change in her was the light by which he saw the change in himself.

She had his letters opened for him with her usual speed, but as she worked he could see by the soft creased line between her eyebrows, even as he had seen it yesterday morning, when she was anxious about her brother, that something troubled her. To-day, however, he did not question her: she might tell him if she felt disposed, and guessing that it was connected with the events of last night, his instinct told him that it was for her to speak or be silent. Then, when she had opened the letters, she placed them by him, and without a word, took up her writing-block and pencil for the shorthand dictation. But still her brow did not clear, the smudge of shadow lay perpendicularly between her eye-brows, as fixed as if it was some soft pencil mark on the skin.

To-day the work was not heavy, and nearly an hour before the interval for lunch he had finished the dictation of his answers. She knew his business engagements as well as himself, and reminding him that a land-agent was coming to see him at twelve on some private matter, took her papers into the little inner room. Then she came back for her typewriter, which stood on the table in the window where she usually worked, paused and came over to his table.

'May I speak to you a moment?' she asked.

'Certainly, Miss Propert. What is it?'

She fingered the edge of the table, and with her instinct for tidiness, put straight a couple of papers that lay there.

'It's about last night,' she said. 'I told Charles what had happened, and he doesn't want me to come up to your house again like that in the evening. He knows as well as I do——'

She broke off, and the trouble cleared from her face, as she looked up at him smiling.

'Charles wanted to write to you,' she said, 'but I said I would really prefer to explain. People are such fools, you know, aren't they?'

There was mingled chagrin and pleasure for him in this speech. He admired the frank friendliness with which she spoke: but he would have liked to have seen in her some consciousness of the underlying truth which last night he had hugged to himself. But in her frankness there seemed to be a complete unconsciousness of any of his own sentiments, no twitter, however remote, of the bird of romance that had sung to him from the snowy trees.

He assented to the fact that people were fools. 'But is that the end of my library catalogue?' he asked.

'No; I must finish it. I thought perhaps I could go there for an hour in the middle of the morning, when you were down here. I could still get your letters done in time for the evening post. If I went there every day for an hour I could get through as much as I did on alternate evenings.'

He knew this to be a sound and sensible plan, but he did not in the least wish to assent to it. In the first place, it would look as if he acknowledged some basis of reason in his wife's attitude the evening before; in the second place, he would no longer have those half-hours after dinner in his library with Norah and her brother. He knew that they had become the pearl of the day to him.

'But since people are such fools,' he said, 'does it matter?'

'Yes. I think it does. I don't want to make unpleasantness.'

'For me?' he asked. 'You make none.'

She flushed a little.

'Yes. Personally I don't care two straws. But Charles does rather.'

Keeling stood up.

'I'm ashamed of myself,' he said. 'Your brother is perfectly right. Go down, then, as you suggest in the morning.'

'We'll settle it like that then,' she said. 'But I am so sorry. I liked those evenings.'

'I didn't object to them myself,' said he. As she turned, their eyes met again, and Norah knew she had done right. But that knowledge gave her no atom of satisfaction.

The land-agent was announced, and Norah left the two together. Of late years Keeling had been buying both building-sites and houses in Bracebridge, and Simpson, his agent, had been instructed to inform him of any desirable site that was coming into the market. But at the moment he felt singularly little interested in any purchase that Simpson might recommend.

'Good-morning, Simpson,' he said. 'What have you come about?'

In the next room the typing machine had begun its clacking that came staccato and subdued through the baize-lined door. That seemed to him more momentous than anything his agent could tell him about.

'Well, sir, there's a building site just beyond your little place,' began Mr Simpson. 'It's coming up next month for sale, but if you make an offer now, I think you might get it cheap.'

Keeling forced his mind away from the sound that came from next door, and looked at the map that the agent had spread out. But the purchase did not appeal to him.

'Too far out,' he said. 'And I think the villa-building is being a bit overdone. Anything else?' he said.

'Yes, sir, if you'll pay the price, there's an important site which the owner wants to sell the freehold of. It's the site of the County Club. The price asked seems rather high, but then I consider the Club are getting their premises absurdly cheap. You might fairly ask a much higher rental.'

Suddenly Keeling felt himself interested in this, and the clacking of the typewriter came to his ears no longer.

'What lease has the Club got?' he asked.

'I have ascertained that there is a break in it next Midsummer on both sides, notice to be given at Lady Day. The present owner had determined to put up their rent then, and the Committee, I believe, thought that quite reasonable. But he wants cash, and has instructed me to look out for a purchaser.'

Keeling had that faculty, which had stood him in such good stead all his life, of being able to make up his mind quickly when all the data were put before him. He did not hesitate now, and ten minutes after, when the details of the ownership and present lease were in his possession, he had authorised his agent to purchase for him.

'I gather that the owner wishes the transaction to be private,' he said. 'And I wish the same.'

'Certainly. I think you have made a wise purchase, sir,' said Simpson. 'I am told that the landlord is ex-officio a member of the Club. Good-morning, sir. I will have the deed made out with your lawyer without delay.'

Keeling nodded. The last speech had given him something to think about.

CHAPTER VI

Mrs Keeling had much enjoyed the sense of added pomp and dignity which her husband's mayoralty gave her. She liked seeing placards in the streets that a concert in aid of some charity was given under the patronage of the Lady Mayoress, and would rustle into the arm-chair reserved for her in the middle of the front-row with the feeling that she had got this concert up, and was responsible not only for the assistance it gave to the charity in question, but for the excellence of the performance. She assumed a grander and more condescending air at her parties, and distinctly began to unbend to the inhabitants of Alfred Road instead of associating with them as equals. She knew her position as Lady Mayoress; it almost seemed to her that it was she who had raised her husband to the civic dignity, and when one morning she found among her letters an invitation from Lady Inverbroom for herself and him to dine and sleep one day early in December, at their place a few miles outside Bracebridge, she was easily able to see through the insincerity of Lady Inverbroom's adding that it would give her husband such pleasure to show Mr Keeling his library. It was an amiable insincerity, but

Emmeline was secretly sure that the Lady Mayoress was the desired guest. She tried without success to control the trembling of her voice when she telephoned to Keeling—who had just left for the Stores (those vulgar stores)—the gratifying request He was quite pleased to accept it, but she could detect no trembling in his voice. But men controlled their feelings better than women. . . .

She took the parlour-maid as her maid, though her husband altogether refused to pass off the boy covered with buttons as his valet, and enjoyed a moment's supreme triumph when she was able to reply to Lady Inverbroom, who hoped, when she showed her her room that she would ask the housemaid for anything she required, that she had brought her own maid. Then Lady Inverbroom (to hide her natural confusion) had poked the fire for her and pointed out the position of the bathroom, which communicated with her bedroom. Certainly that was most convenient, and dinner would be at half-past eight.

Mrs Keeling felt a little strange: the magnificence of this great house rather overawed her, and she had to remind herself several times, as she dressed, that she was Lady Mayoress. There were quantities of tall liveried footmen standing about when she went down, but she remembered to put her nose in the air to about the angle at which Lady Inverbroom's nose was naturally levelled, and walked by them with an unseeing eye, as if they were pieces of familiar furniture. She had soup on a silver plate, and was quite successful in avoiding what she would have called 'a scroopy noise' made with her spoon as she fed herself off that unusual material. Then when Lord Inverbroom alluded casually to the great Reynolds over the chimney piece, she flattered herself that she made a very apposite remark when, after duly admiring it, she said, 'And who is the heir to all this beautiful property?' for she was well aware that her hosts were childless. There were no guests in the house, except themselves, and though it would have been nice to let slip the names of illustrious people when alluding to this visit afterwards in Bracebridge, she felt glad at the time that there was no one else, for she was on the verge of feeling shy, which would never have done for a Lady Mayoress.

A few small incidents during dinner rather surprised her; once Lady Inverbroom, in helping herself to some hot sauce let a drop of it fall on the fingers of the footman who handed it to her. Instantly she turned round in her chair and said in a voice of real concern (just as if the man had not been a piece of furniture), 'I beg your pardon; I hope I didn't burn you!' After dinner again, when cigarettes came round, she was rather astonished at being offered one, and holding her head very high, turned abruptly away. No doubt it was a mistake, but there would have been words at the Cedars next morning, if the parlour-maid had offered a cigarette to any lady. Indeed she was rather astonished that Lord Inverbroom lit his without first asking her if she minded the perfume.

But what surprised her even more than her hostess's politeness to a footman, or the handing of a cigarette to herself, was her husband's obvious unconcern with the magnificence of his surroundings. He seemed perfectly at his ease, and though there was nothing in his manner which suggested a sort of haughty polish which she felt was suitable in these exalted places, he behaved as simply as if he was at home. In fact his simplicity almost made his wife blush once, when, on the occasion of a large puff of smoke coming down the chimney he said to Lord Inverbroom, 'I can show you a new cowl which will quite stop that.' But Lord Inverbroom did not seem the least uncomfortable at this sudden peeping out of the mercantile cloven hoof, and merely replied that a cowl that would prevent that chimney from smoking would be worth its weight in gold. That was very tactful, and Mrs Keeling was vexed that her husband would not leave the subject: instead he laughed and said that the cowl in question did not cost much more than its weight in iron. Then luckily the talk drifted away on to books, and though Mrs Keeling knew that by all the rules of polite behaviour her husband should have been engaging his hostess in light conversation while she talked to her host, Keeling and Lord Inverbroom quite lost themselves in discussing some Italian book with pictures that had lately appeared. Lord Inverbroom said he could not afford it, which must be a joke. . . .

In consequence of the two men talking together she was left to Lady Inverbroom, but as she had taken the trouble to read the small paragraphs in a Society journal that day, she could give her little tit-bits of information about the movements of the King and the Royal Family, while with half an ear she continued to listen to her husband, so as to interrupt in case he tended to unsuitable topics again. But she was so dumbfoundered when, à propos of book-plates (which sounded safe enough), she heard Lord Inverbroom say that he had a charming one lately made for him by a Miss Propert, that the apposite talk she was engaged in died on her lips.

'She has just made one for me,' said her husband. 'Perhaps you didn't know that she lives in Bracebridge with her brother. She is my secretary and typewriter.'

'Indeed? I wonder if you would let her come over here one day. I should like to show her my books with her book-plate in them. Saturday, perhaps, if that is a half-holiday. Would she come to lunch, do you think, and spend the afternoon?'

Mrs Keeling was quite horrified; she longed

for her husband to tell him that Miss Propert was quite a humble sort of person. Then luckily it occurred to her that no doubt the idea was that she should have her lunch in the housekeeper's room. This relieved her mind, and she continued to tell Lady Inverbroom the last news from Windsor. Shortly afterwards, with a little pressing on the part of her hostess, she was induced to precede her out of the dining-room, leaving the men alone.

The new wing of the hospital was a subject about which Lord Inverbroom wanted to talk to his guest, and for a little while that engaged them. This open weather had allowed the building to go on apace, and by the end of March the wing should be advanced enough to permit of the opening ceremony. The Board of hospital directors would see to that, and Lord Inverbroom sketched out his idea for the day. The ceremony of the opening he proposed should be in the morning, and for it he hoped to secure the presence of a very distinguished personage. Lunch would follow, and if Mr Keeling approved, he would at the luncheon announce the name of the munificent giver. Then he paused a moment.

'Mr Keeling,' he said, 'I think there is no doubt that the Prime Minister would wish to submit your name to the King as the recipient of some honour in public recognition of your munificence. Would you allow me in confidence to tell him who our benefactor is? And would you in case he sees the matter as I do, be disposed to accept a baronetcy? I may say that I do not think there is the slightest doubt that he will agree with me. Perhaps first you would like to mention it to Mrs Keeling.'

Keeling had no doubts on this subject at all, and felt sure his wife would have none. He was not in the least a snob, and to wish to be a baronet implied nothing of the kind.

'I should be very much gratified and honoured,' he said.

'Very well. Perhaps you would mention it to your wife and let me know. The town and county generally owe you the deepest debt of gratitude.'

Now there was another subject on which Keeling had made up his mind to speak to Lord Inverbroom, and this intelligence encouraged him to do so. By purchasing the freehold of the County Club, he had acquired the right of membership, but with that streak of pride which was characteristic of him, he did not want to get elected to the Club as a right. He had, since he had made the purchase, thought this over, and wished to stand for election, could he secure a proposer and seconder, like any other candidate. That being so, he did not intend to tell Lord Inverbroom that he would, ex officio, become a member of the Club at the next quarter-day, when he entered into possession of his property, but had determined to ask him if he, as president, would propose him in the ordinary course. The next election, he had already ascertained, took place early in April, when his blushing honours as benefactor to the hospital and baronet would be fresh upon him. There could be no more suitable opportunity for his request than the present.

'I wonder if you would do me a great favour,' he said bluntly.

'I feel sure it would be a pleasure to me to do you any favour that is in my power,' said the other.

'Would you then be kind enough to propose me for election to the County Club next April?' said Keeling.

There was a pause, the very slightest, quite imperceptible to Keeling, though John would probably have noticed it. But instantly Lord Inverbroom made up his mind that it was quite impossible to refuse this thing which he wished had not been asked. He had not the smallest personal objection to having Keeling as a member, but in that infinitesimal pause he divined, he was afraid unerringly, the feeling of the club generally. Ridiculous it might be, as many class-distinctions are, but he knew that it existed, and in general he shared it. He succeeded, however, in keeping cordiality in his voice, in consenting to do what he felt unable to refuse.

'I shall be delighted to,' he said. 'Have you

got a seconder? Ah, I think that is not necessary when the President proposes a candidate. I will certainly put down your name when I go into Bracebridge next.'

Again there was a slight pause, and he rose, trying to avoid the appearance of breaking off a distasteful subject.

'Well, Mr Keeling,' he said. 'I mean to keep you up a long time in my library to-night, so shall we go into the drawing-room at once, till the ladies go up to bed? Dear me, that awful chimney! It would be very good of you if you would let me have the cowl you told me of.'

Late as it was when Keeling went upstairs, he found a jubilant and wakeful wife waiting for him, with a positive cargo of questions and impressions which she had to unload at once. Her elation took a condescending and critical form, and she neither wanted nor paused for answers.

'Well, I'm sure it's been a very pleasant if a very quiet evening,' she said. 'There's nothing nicer than to dine, as you may say, tête-à-tête like that and have a little agreeable conversation afterwards, not but what I should have been sorry to have as tough a pheasant as that served at my table, for I declare I could hardly get my teeth into it though it did come on a silver plate, and nothing but a nut and an apple for dessert, though you can get choice grapes so cheap now. But there! what does that matter when you dine with friends? Such a pleasant talk as I had too with Lady Inverbroom, who, I'm sure, is a very sensible and agreeable sort of woman. Nothing very gifted, I dare say, but a great deal of common sense. Common sense now! I often wish it was commoner. But the time passed so quickly while you and Lord Inverbroom were talking together in the dining-room that I was quite surprised when you came in. The soup, too, did you not find it insipid? But I expect Lady Inverbroom does not have the sort of cook that I have always been accustomed to. No jewels either, just that little diamond brooch, which made me feel that I was too fine with the beautiful pearl pendant you gave me for my birthday. Don't you agree with me, Thomas?'

'You have talked about fifty things, my dear. I don't know which you want me to agree with you about,' said he.

'Well, we will let it pass. Was it not odd that Lord Inverbroom had a book-plate by your Miss Propert? Quite a coincidence! But you made me feel quite hot when you talked about supplying him with a chimney-cowl, just as if he was a customer. Not that it really matters, and I thought you got on wonderfully well, though no doubt you felt a little strange at first. And what did you and Lord Inverbroom talk about when we left you? Books, I suppose.'

Keeling sat down by the fire.

'If you want to know I will tell you,' he said.

'Of course I want to know. What should I ask for unless I wanted to know? Parkinson tells me they had quite a common supper in the room, nothing out of the way, just some of the fish that was left over and cold beef. I must ask Lady Inverbroom to drop in to lunch some day when she is in Bracebridge, and let her see how a pheasant should be served.'

'I am going to tell you what we talked about, if you will be quiet for a moment. You do not yet know that I have given them the new wing to the hospital——'

'What? You gave the new wing. Well, to think of your having kept me in the dark all this time! I do call that very generous, but generous you always are, as I've often told Mamma, about your money. I suppose that will cost a great deal of money.'

'Yes, a great deal. Kindly allow me to get on. You are not to tell anybody about it till the day it is opened, when it will be announced. Lord Inverbroom thinks I shall be given a baronetcy. He suggested that I should tell you and see what you thought about it.'

Mrs Keeling sat straight up in bed.

'Well, I never!' she said. 'Indeed Mamma was right when she said some people got on in the world. Sir Thomas Keeling, Bart., and Lady Keeling. It sounds very well, does it not? I do call that money well laid out, however much it was—Sir Thomas and Lady Keeling! I hope Parkinson will pick it up quickly, and not stumble over it. "My lady" instead of "Ma'am." She will have to practise.'

It was easy to see out of the depths of these futilities that Mrs Keeling was pleased, and her husband retired to his dressing-room and shut the door on her raptures.

It was largely the remembrance of this visit, and the future accession of dignity which it had foreshadowed that inspired Mrs Keeling, as she drove home in her victoria after morning-service at St Thomas's, a few Sundays later, with so comfortable a sense of her general felicity. The thought of being addressed on her envelopes as Lady Keeling, and by Parkinson as 'My lady,' caused her to take a livelier interest in the future than she usually did, for the comfortable present was generally enough for her. And with regard to the present her horizon was singularly unclouded, apart from the fact that Alice was suffering from influenza, an infliction which her mother bore very calmly. Her mind was not nimble, and it took her all the time that the slowly-lolloping horse occupied in traversing the road from the church to The Cedars in surveying those horizons, and running over, as she had just been bidden to do by Mr Silverdale in his sermon, her numerous causes for thankfulness. She hardly knew where to begin, but the pearl-pendant, which her husband had given her on her birthday, and now oscillated with the movement of the carriage on the platinum chain round her ample neck, formed a satisfactory starting-point. It really was very handsome, and since she did not hold with the mean-spirited notion that presents were only tokens of affection, and that the kind thought that prompted a gift was of greater value than its cash-equivalent, she found great pleasure in the size and lustre of the pearl. Indeed she rather considered the value of the gift to be the criterion of the kindness of thought that had prompted it, and by that standard her husband's thought had been very kind indeed. She had never known a kinder since, now many years ago, he had given her the half-hoop of diamonds that sparkled on her finger. And this gift had been all 'of a piece' with his general conduct. She knew for a fact that he was going to behave with his usual generosity at Christmas to her mother, and he had promised herself and Alice a fortnight's holiday at Brighton in February. Perhaps he would come with them, but it was more likely that business would detain him. She found she did not care whether he came or not. It was her duty to be contented, whatever happened, when everything was so pleasant.

This imaginative flight into the future fatigued

her, or at any rate demanded an effort on the part of her brain, and very naturally she went back to the blessings that she found it easier to call to mind since they already existed. Quite high among these, a little lower perhaps than the pleasure of being Lady Mayoress, but higher than the fact that Alice was distinctly better this morning, was the sensible way in which her husband had behaved about those odd evening visits of Miss Propert when she worked at his library catalogue. Faint was the remembrance of that unpleasant moment when she had suddenly appeared among all the guests at the close of dinner, and was subsequently introduced into the drawing-room. But after that those visits had ceased altogether, and instead Miss Propert came in the middle of the morning when her husband was at his office. That was perfectly in accordance with the rules of correct behaviour, and when she chanced to meet Norah going into the library or leaving it at the conclusion of her work, she always had a civil and condescending word for her. She had no doubt whatever that the girl was a very decent young woman in her station of life, which was as much as could be said about anybody.

At this point she sat rather more upright in her carriage in order to be able to show how distant and stately was her recognition of Mrs Fyson, who was walking (not driving) in her direction. She gave her quite a little bow without the hint of a smile, for that was just how she felt to Mrs Fyson, and the more clearly Mrs Fyson grasped that fact the better. She could barely see Mrs Fyson, that was the truth of it, and it was not wholly the sunlit mist of Inverbroom magnificence that obscured her. It is true that since the Inverbroom visit (followed up by a Lady Inverbroom lunch at The Cedars, when she had shown her how a pheasant should be served) Mrs Keeling had adopted to Alfred Road generally the attitude of a slowly-ascending balloon, hovering, bathed in sun, over the darkling and low-lying earth below it, and this would very usefully tend to prepare Alfred Road for the greater elevation to which she would suddenly shoot up, as by some release of ballast, when in the spring a certain announcement of honours should be promulgated. But it was not only that Alfred Road was growing dim and shadowy beneath her that prompted this stateliness to Mrs Fyson. That misguided lady (not a true lady) had been going about Bracebridge assuring her friends that Mr Silverdale had been so very attentive to her daughter Julia, that she was daily expecting that Mr Silverdale would seek an interview with Mr Fyson, and Julia a blushing one with her. Now, as Mrs Keeling was daily expecting a similar set of interviews to take place at The Cedars, it was clear that unless Mr Silverdale contemplated bigamist proposals (which would certainly be a very great change from his celibate convictions) Mrs Fyson must be considered a mischievous and jealous tatler. Several days ago Alice had appeared suddenly in her mother's boudoir, murdering sleep like Macbeth, to inform her that she was never going to speak to Julia again, nor wished to hear her name mentioned. She gave no reason, nor did Mrs Keeling need one, for this severance of relations beyond saying that certain remarks of Mrs Fyson were the immediate cause. She then immediately went to bed with influenza, which her mother attributed to rage and shock.

This, though the last of Mrs Fyson's misdeeds, was not the first, and Mrs Keeling almost forgot the duty of thankfulness for blessings when she remembered that dreadful occasion. Shortly after Norah's final appearance in the evening, Mrs Fyson had called, and under the pretext of a digestion-visit after her dinner had hissed out a series of impertinent questions as to how 'it had all ended.' Fool though she might be, Mrs Keeling was not of that peculiarly hopeless sort that confides domestic difficulties to the ears of gossips, and had with some appearance of astonishment merely said that she and Miss Propert had had a very pleasant chat while Mr Keeling was telephoning for a cab to take Miss Propert home. On which Mrs Fyson had looked exactly like a ferret and said, 'Did he bring her into your drawing-room? That was *very* clever!'

The remembrance of this odious suggestion was the only thing that seemed to cloud the serenity of Mrs Keeling's horizon: indeed it scarcely did that, and corresponded rather to a very slight fall in the barometer, though no signs of untoward weather were anywhere visible. She did not often think of it, but she knew that it had not (like so many more important things) entirely vanished from her mind, and when she did think of it, it produced this slight declension from weather otherwise set fair. But immediately afterwards her thistle-down reflections would flutter away to the pearl-pendant, the Inverbroom visit, and the baronetage.

She had arrived at the front door of The Cedars, and as it was rather too cold to wait for the boy covered with buttons to remove her rug, she managed to do that for herself. Just as she stepped into the Gothic porch, the front-door opened and Norah came out. This was something of a surprise: it had not previously occurred to her that the catalogue-work went on on Sundays. But it was no business of hers whether her husband's secretary chose to behave in an unsabbatical if not heathenish manner. That was quite her own concern, and a small elephantine reproach was all that the occasion demanded.

'Why, Miss Propert,' she said. 'Fancy working on Sunday morning when all good people are at church!'

Norah looked not only surprised but startled, but she instantly recovered herself.

'I know; it is wicked of me,' she said. 'But I so much wanted to get on with my work. You are back early, aren't you?'

This was true: the sermon on the duty of thankfulness had been short though joyous, and there was no Litany. Mrs Keeling had already congratulated herself on that, for she would have time to rest well before lunch and perhaps see Alice when she had rested. But when after a few more gracious remarks, she found herself in the hall, she did not immediately go to her boudoir to rest. Perhaps some little noise from the library, only half-consciously heard, caused her to pause, and then, Mrs Fyson's unforgotten remark occurring to her, she went to that door and opened it. Her husband, whom she supposed to be at the cathedral, was standing in front of the fire.

'Back from Cathedral already, Thomas?' she said.

'Yes, my dear, and you from church. I sat in the nave, if you want to know, and came out before the sermon.'

He paused a moment.

'Probably you met Miss Propert at the door,' he said. 'She has been working at the catalogue, I find. How is Alice this morning? Have you seen her?'

The pearl-pendant gently wagged at Mrs Keeling's

throat: Mrs Fyson's comment gently stirred in her head. She would have said this was clever too, this introduction of Miss Propert's name without waiting for his wife to mention it. Clever or not, it served its immediate purpose, for she gave him news of Alice.

'The sooner you take her off to the seaside the better,' he said. 'Change of air will do her good. I should go this week, if I were you.'

It seemed to Mrs Keeling that this was not being clever but stupid. She felt that it was a designed diversion to distract her thoughts. She was being 'pearl-pendanted' again without the pearl, and was not going to be put off like that.

'Oh, I have too many engagements to think of that,' she said, 'and you would not be able to come with me!'

'There is little chance of that whenever you go,' said he.

An awful, an ill-inspired notion came into poor Mrs Keeling's head. She determined on light good-humoured banter. Her intentions were excellent, her performance deplorable.

'Too busy over the catalogue, eh?' she asked. 'Coming away before the sermon too. Naughty, as Mr Silverdale would say. Oh, I understand, my dear.'

The effect of this light humour was not at all what she had anticipated. He turned swiftly round to her, with a face appallingly grim.

'Never mind what Mr Silverdale would say,' he said. 'Tell me what it is that you understand. Now, quick, what is it you understand?'

She retreated a step with a fallen face.

'What's the matter?' she said. 'Dear me, what is the matter? It was only my joke.'

Instantly he saw his mistake. He had had the opportunity to treat the subject in the same playful spirit. But he had been unable to: it was all too serious to him. The grim Puritan streak in him, which had not prevented his falling in love with Norah, made it impossible for him to jest or suffer a jest about it. He was not a flirt, and did not care to have that tawdry cloak thrown on to his shoulders. But he had made a mistake: he ought to have accepted that ridiculous decoration with a grin as ridiculous. Now he tried to recapture the belated inanity.

'Ah, you're just chaffing me,' he said, 'and there's no harm in that. But I didn't care for what Mr Silverdale would say. He's naughty too, if he's not going to ask poor Alice to marry him, when she's recovered from her influenza. Or have you done as I asked you, and cut your daughter out yourself? That's a joke too: one bad joke deserves another, Emmeline.'

Suddenly it struck him that the situation was parallel to, but more significant than that which had occurred in her drawing-room when Norah had come into it for a few minutes one snowy evening. Then, as now, his wife had hinted at an underlying truth, which he was aware of: then, as now, he had scolded her for the ridiculous suggestion her words implied. But to-day the same situation was intensified, it presented itself to him in colours many tones more vivid, even as the underlying truth had become of far greater concern to him. And, unless he was mistaken, it had become much more real to his wife. Her first vague, stupid (but truly-founded) suspicion had acquired solidity in her mind. He doubted whether he could, so to speak, bomb it to bits by the throwing to her of a pearl-pendant.

She looked at him a moment with eyes behind which there smouldered a real though a veiled hostility, and he found himself wishing that she would put it into words, and repeat definitely and seriously the accusation at which her dismal little jest about the work of the catalogue keeping him here in Bracebridge, had hinted. Then he could have denied it more explicitly, and with a violence that might have impressed her. But his roughness, his fierce challenging of her stupid chaff had effectively frightened her off any such repetition, and she gave him no opportunity of denial or defence. Only, as she left him, with the intention of seeing Alice before lunch, he noted this intensified situation. It had become more explosive, more dangerous, and now instead of taking it boldly out into the open, and encouraging it to explode, with, probably, no very destructive results, he had caused his wife to lock it up in the confined space of her own mind, hiding it away from his anger or his ridicule. But it was doubtful whether she had detached the smouldering fuse of her own suspicions. They were at present of no very swiftly inflammable stuff : there was but a vague sense that her husband was more interested in Norah than he should be, and had he answered her chaff with something equally light, she might easily have put out that smouldering fuse. But he had not done that : he had flared and scolded, and his attempt to respond in the same spirit was hopelessly belated. She began to wonder whether Mrs Fyson was not right. . . . True, Mrs Fyson had said very little, but that little appeared now to be singularly suggestive.

The various sale departments at the Stores were thronged all day from morning to night during this week before Christmas with crowds of purchasers, but the correspondence on business matters, such as engaged Norah, fell off as the holidays approached, and next morning, when she arrived, she found not more than a dozen letters for her to open. Charles, however, was being worked off his feet in the book-department, where were a hundred types of suitable Christmas gifts (the more expensive being bound in stuffed morocco, so that the sides of them resembled flattish cushions) and Norah intended, as soon as she had finished her shorthand transcription, to proceed at once with the typewriting, and then ask leave of Keeling to go and help her brother. He arrived but a few minutes after her, and in half an hour her shorthand dictation was finished.

'I was going to typewrite these at once,' she said, 'if you'll allow me, and then go and help Charles in the book department.'

Keeling pushed back his chair as he often did when he was disposed for a few minutes' talk, putting a gap between himself and his business table. He gave her a smile and a long look.

'Have you seen the books?' he said. 'I'm almost ashamed to get a profit out of such muck. Beastly paper, beastly printing, and squash bindings. The more expensive they are, the more loathsome.'

She laughed.

'They are pretty bad,' she said. 'But there's a big sale for them. May I go and help Charles?'

'And not do any work in my library this morning?' he asked.

'Unless you wish me to.'

He paused.

'I do rather,' he said. 'I want that work to go on as usual. Monday is your regular day to go there.'

Now yesterday, when Norah met Mrs Keeling in the porch, the latter had been so very normal and condescending that she had scarcely given another thought to the encounter. Mrs Keeling had often met her coming or going to her work, and had always a word for her even as she had had yesterday. But instantly now, when Keeling expressed a wish that she should go there this morning, she connected it in her mind with that meeting.

'I will go if you like,' she said.

'I shall be obliged if you will. I have a certain reason for wishing it. It's a rubbishy reason enough, and I needn't bother you with it.'

She looked up at him, and it was clear to each when their eyes met, that the same species of thought was in the mind of both: both at any rate were thinking of what had occurred yesterday. But immediately she looked away again, silently pondering something, and he, watching her, saw that soft frown like a vertical pencil-mark appear between her eyebrows. Then it cleared again, and she looked at him with a smile that conveyed her comprehension of the 'rubbishy reason,' and a sudden flush that came over her face confirmed that to him. Naturally it was as awkward, even as impossible for her to speak of it, as it was for him; she could but consent to go or refuse to.

'I expect I see your point,' she said. 'I will go.'

For the first time it occurred to him that she had a voice in the matter, that it was only fair to her to suggest that she should give up these visits to his house altogether. He would not be there when she went, but she understood now (indeed she had understood long ago, when she made her entry into the dinner-party) that Mrs Keeling had, so to speak, her eye on them. It was due to Norah that she should be allowed to say whether she wanted that eye taken off her.

'Don't go unless you wish,' he said suddenly. 'Give up the catalogue altogether if you like.'

The moment he suggested that, her whole nature, her consciousnesss of the entire innocence of her visits there, was up in arms against the proposal. Not to go there would imply that there was a reason for not going there, and there was none. Whatever had passed between Mrs Keeling and her husband yesterday was no business of hers; she intended to finish her work. This conclusion was comprised in the decision with which she answered him.

'Why should I give up the catalogue?' she said. 'I have no intention of doing so unless you tell me to. My business is to finish it.'

Keeling hesitated: he wanted to say something to her which showed, however remotely, the gleam of his feelings, something which should let that spark of unspoken comprehension flash backwards and forwards again.

'Yes, it's just a matter of business, isn't it?' he said.

She met his eyes with complete frankness: there was nothing to show whether she had caught the suggestion that lurked in his speech or not.

'Then shall I go down to your house now, and get on with my business?' she said.

He was half disappointed, half pleased. But, wisely, he gave up the idea of conveying to her that there was anything more than 'business' for him in her working among his books. If she understood that her handling them, her passing hours in his room, her preparing his catalogue was something so utterly different from what it would have been if any one else was doing it for him, she would have found the hint of that in what he had said. If she did not—well, it was exactly there that the disappointment came in. He pulled his chair a little nearer to the table again, where his work lay.

'There is one other thing,' he said. 'You get four days' holiday at Christmas, you and your brother. Are you going to spend them here?'

'I suppose so.'

'Then take my advice and make your brother go to the seaside with you instead. You've been rather overworked lately and he has too. A change would do you both good.'

'Oh, I don't think we shall go away,' she said.

He fidgeted with his papers a moment. When money concerned business, he could discuss and bargain with the nonchalance of a man who had passed his life in making it. But when money began to trespass on the privacies of life, there was no one in the world more shy of mentioning it.

'Miss Propert,' he said, 'don't think me impertinent, but if there's any question of expense about your going away, please let me advance you the money I shall be paying you for my catalogue. You've done a good deal of work on it already: it is quite a reasonable proposal.'

The moment he said that Norah knew that she did not want to be paid at all for her work on the catalogue. When she undertook to do it, he had just mentioned the question of payment, saying that she would let him know her charges some time, but since then the thought of what she was going to charge had not entered her head. And now, when she thought of those pleasant hours in his library, she disliked the thought of payment.

'I don't want to be paid at all,' she said. 'It was most of it work done in office hours, when otherwise I should have been in the office here. I have done a certain amount in the evening, but I enjoyed it: I found it much more amusing than playing Patience.'

'No, I can't allow that for a moment,' he said.

'What if you have to?' she asked, smiling.

'I shall not have the catalogue completed. And I shall insist on paying for what you have done. I shall get an estimate of your work made and a price fixed.'

He did not smile back at her: he looked at the table and drummed it with his fingers, as she had often seen him do when he was discussing some business point on which he did not intend to yield.

'Are you serious?' she asked.

'I was never more so.'

'But I have really enjoyed doing it. I—I have done it for the sake of books. I like doing things for books.'

Keeling stopped his drumming fingers, and looked up with his grim face relaxing.

'Don't remind me of that affair over my bookplate,' he said. 'You are putting me into an odious position. It isn't generous of you.'

'What am I to do then?' she asked.

He took his cheque-book out of his drawer and wrote.

'Take that on account, please,' he said. 'If you want to be business-like, give me a receipt. And I advise you to spend some of it on a little holiday.'

She looked at the cheque.

'I can't take that as part payment,' she said. 'It is fully as much as the completed catalogue will cover.'

'You are very obstinate,' he said. 'I will get an independent estimate of what is a fair price for the completed catalogue when you have finished it, and adjust my payment by that. Will that satisfy you?'

'Quite. But it seems to me I am far from obstinate. I have given way.'

'Of course. I credit you with so much sense.'

Suddenly Norah found she did not mind yielding to him. She was rather surprised at that, for she knew there was some truth in Charles's criticism that she preferred her own way to anybody else's. It was an amiable way, but she liked having it. But now when Keeling so much took it for granted that she was going to do as he suggested, she found she had no objection to it. She wondered why. . . .

'Thank you very much,' she said. 'I will try to persuade Charles to take your advice too, and come away for a few days. And now I'll go down to your house. Oh, your receipt. Shall I write it and file it?'

He had already pulled a sheaf of papers towards him, and was turning them over.

'Please,' he said.

It was a crisp morning, with touches of frost lingering in shadowed places where the warmth of the primrose-coloured winter sunshine had not reached them, and Norah preferred walking to taking the bus that would have set her down at the corner where Alfred Street became Alfred Road. She was keenly sensitive to the suggestion of brisk sunshine or the depression of heavy weather, but the kindly vigour of this winter morning did not wholly account for the exhilaration and glee of her blood. There was more than that in it: the drench of a December gale would hardly have affected her to-day. As she went, she let herself examine for the first time the conditions that for the last six weeks had caused her every morning to awake with the sense of pleasure and eager anticipation of the ensuing day. Hitherto she had diverted her mind from causes, and been contented with effects. Her office-work (that work which had begun so distastefully) pleased and interested her, her catalogue work enthralled her, and now she turned round the corner, so to speak, of herself, and asked herself why this sunshine was spread over all she did.

She made no reservation on the subject: she told herself that it was because these things were done with Keeling or for him. With equal frankness, now that she had brought herself face to face with the question, she affirmed that she was not in love with him, and as far as she could know herself at all she knew that to be true. But it was equally true that she had never met any one who so satisfied her. Never for a moment had the least hint of sentimentality entered into their day-long intercourse. He could be, and sometimes was, gruff and grim, and she accepted his grimnesses and gruffnesses because they were his. At other times he showed a comprehending consideration for her, and she welcomed his comprehension and his considerateness, for exactly the same reason. She knew she would not have cared the toss of a brass farthing if Mr Silverdale had comprehended her, or a railway porter had been considerate of her. All her life she had been independent and industrious, and that had sufficed for her. She had not wanted anything from anybody except employment and a decent recompense. Her emotional life had vented itself on those beloved creatures called books, and on that divine veiled figure called Art that stood behind them, and prompted, as from behind some theatre-wing, her deft imaginative work in designing and executing the wood blocks for bookplates. In every one there is a secret fountain which pours itself out broadcast, or quietly leaks and so saves itself from bursting. Books and the dreams she wove into her blocks had given her that leakage, and here had her fountain thrown up its feather of sparkling waters.

She had not been without certain expression of herself in more human terms. She had for years borne patiently with a querulous mother, but her patience and care for her had been the expression of decent and filial behaviour rather than of herself. When that task was over she had gone with comradeship to her brother, with whom she had a greater affinity of tastes. But now, as she walked westwards in the snap of wintry air and the joy of wintry sun, she realised how completely sisterhood and the kinship of a bookish mind accounted for her devotion to him. They were the best of friends, they lived together in the most amicable equality, in a comfortable atmosphere of courtesy and affection. She gave and she took, they lived and worked together equally, and that sense of 'fairness,' of reasonable contract between brother and sister was the root of their harmonious companionship.

And now, so she instinctively recognised, that sort of satisfaction in human intercourse had become to her childish and elementary. It was good (nothing could be better) as far as it went, but this morning she felt as some musician might feel, if he was asked to content himself with a series of full plain common chords on the piano. Nothing could be better (as far as it went) than that uncomplicated common chord: nor (as far as it went) could anything be better than living with so amiable and understanding a brother. Only now she wanted to give, instead of to give and take: she wanted to lose the sense of fairness, to serve and not to be served.

She had the satisfaction—and that made her step the more briskly and gave the sunshine this mysterious power of exhilaration—of knowing that she was serving and supplying. She loved the knowledge that never had Keeling's type-writing been done for him so flawlessly, that never had the details of his business, such as came within her ken, been so unerringly recorded. He might ask for the reference to the minutest point in a month-old letter, and she could always reinforce his deficient memory of it, and turn up the letter itself for confirmation of her knowledge. When days of overwhelming work had occurred, and he had suggested getting in a second type-writer to assist her, she had always, with a mixture of pride in her own efficiency, and of jealousy of a helping hand, proved herself capable of tackling any task that might be set her. Probably she could not have done it for any one else, but she could do it for him. It was easier, so she told herself, to do his work herself, than to instruct anybody else what to do. She allowed herself just that shade of self-deception, knowing all the time that there were plenty of 'routine' letters that any one else could have done as well as she. But she did not want anybody else to do them.

She was passing through the disused graveyard of the Cathedral where the clipped hedge of hornbeam bounded the asphalt path. The browned leaves still clung to the trees, and she suddenly remembered how she had passed down this path with Charles, and had said how distasteful it was to work for a cad. Her own words seemed to hang on the air, even as the leaves still clung to the hedge, and she tried in vain to remember the mood in which those words were green as the hornbeam leaves had then been, instead of being brown and lifeless. Lifeless they were, there was no vitality in them. They but clung to her memory, as the brown leaves to the hedge. She was scarcely ashamed of them : she only wondered at them, just as, in parenthesis of her thought, she wondered at the clothed twigs, when all the other trees had shed their foliage. They were not evergreen : they were just dead.

She came out, by this short cut across the Cathedral close, where the motor-bus would have taken her, and saw the row of separated houses stretch westward in Alfred Road. A quarter of a mile away was The Cedars, with the delightful big library, and the abominable residuum of the house. Very likely she would see Mrs Keeling, or Miss Keeling. . . .

It was not only in matters of office work, of swift shorthand, of impeccable typewriting that she was of use to him. She guessed that he found in her a companionship that Mrs Keeling with her pearl-pendant and her propriety could not supply. Norah knew all about the pearl-pendant : Mrs Keeling had told her, as it wagged at her throat, that her husband had given it her on her birthday, and was it not handsome? It was tremendously handsome : there was no doubt whatever about that. But the pearl-pendant mattered to Norah exactly as much as did the cheque which she had just been given. It mattered less, indeed: it did not express anything.

She faced the conclusion that her vague exhilaration of thought had brought her to. She did not only serve him in his office: she served him here in The Cedars. Neither Mrs Keeling nor his daughter could make his book-catalogue for him. Irrespective of their inability, he would not have allowed them to attempt it. But she could do it: he gave her access to his library and a free hand to do as she liked there.

She turned in at the gate and went up the drive to the Gothic porch. He gave her more than that: he gave her his need of her. He had expressed that when he had said her catalogue work was a pure matter of business. What he meant and what she understood was that it was not.

The boy covered with buttons opened the door to her. She hoped that Mrs Keeling would not be richly crossing the Gothic hall. She wanted only to get quietly into the library and go on with letter M. Letter M implied a quantity of cardboard slips.

She wanted to be left alone in the library, working for him. It did not matter whether he paid her for her work or not. She only wanted to go on working for him.

CHAPTER VII

ALICE KEELING had arrived at that stage of convalescence after her influenza when there is dawn on the wreck, and it seems faintly possible that the world will again eventually prove to contain more than temperature thermometers and beef-tea. She was going to leave Bracebridge with her mother next day for the projected fortnight at Brighton, and had tottered up and down the gravel path round the garden this morning for half an hour to accustom herself to air and locomotion again. While she was out, she had heard the telephone bell ring inside the house, a sound that always suggested to her nowadays an entrancing possibility, and this was confirmed when Parkinson came out to tell her that Mr Silverdale would like to speak to her. At that she ceased to totter: her feet positively twinkled on their way to the little round black ear of the machine. And the entrancing possibility was confirmed. Might Mr Silverdale drop in for the cup that cheered that afternoon? And was she better? And would she promise not to be naughty and get ill again? Indeed, she was vastly better on the moment, and said down the telephone in a voice still slightly hoarse, 'I'm not naughty: me dood,' in the baby-dialect much affected by her and Mr Silverdale.

Alice was not of a prevaricating or deceptive nature, but having suddenly remembered that her mother was opening a bazaar that afternoon, and would not be back for tea, she gaily hastened to forget that again, for the chance of having tea alone with Mr Silverdale must not be jeopardised by such infinitesimal proprieties. She hastened also to forget to tell her mother that he had proposed himself, and only remembered to change her dress after lunch for something more becoming. She choose with a view to brightening herself up a daring red gown, which made her, by contrast, look rather whiter than the influenza had really left her. But she did not mind that: it was obviously out of the question to look in rosy and blooming health, and the best alternative was to appear interestingly pale. She remembered also to order hot buns for tea, though the idea of eating one in her present state was provocative of a shuddering qualm, and having seen her mother safely off the premises, sat waiting in Mrs Keeling's boudoir ready to ring for tea as soon as her visitor appeared. Punctually came the sound of the front-door bell, and according to his custom, he came running across the drawing-room, tapped at the boudoir door, and peeped in, his head alone appearing.

'May me come in?' he said. 'And how are us?'

He took her hand and playfully pretended to feel her pulse.

'Now this is doctor's orders,' he said. 'You are to sit cosily by the fire, and talk to any poor parson who comes to see you. The dose is to be taken at exactly half-past four!'

He sat down on the hearth-rug in front of her chair, and looked round the room.

'This is the pleasantest club I know,' he said. 'And where's the president?'

Alice guessed what he meant in a moment.

'I don't think mother is in yet, 'she said. 'We won't wait tea for her. Buns? There they are. And it's two lumps of sugar, isn't it? And how are you?'

'Better,' he said, 'better already. Poor parson has been lonely without his dear kind Helper. But now he's got her again.'

Alice gave a little quiver of delight, and the cup she handed him rocked on its saucer.

'But poor parson's going to be lonely again, isn't he?' he went on. 'Didn't ickle bird tell him that Helper was going to spread wings and fly away to Brighton for a fortnight? He mustn't be selfish, mustn't poor parson, but only be glad to think of Helper sitting in the sun, and drinking in life and health again.'

Alice wished that Julia Fyson could hear him say that. (Julia Fyson probably would have if she had had the influenza too, but that benumbing possibility did not enter Alice's head.) He had called her Helper before, but the oftener he called her that the better.

'And now Helper is going to ask questions,' she said, formally adopting the name. 'She wants to know if poor parson has been good, and not been overworking himself.'

He turned to her with an air of childlike frankness.

'He's been pretty good,' he said. 'Not bad enough to be scolded. But if Helper will get nasty nasty influenza, why parson must do some of her work.'

Alice could not keep up this pretty jesting tone any longer: it was much too serious and wonderful a thing to jest about that she should really be his Helper.

'Oh, Mr Silverdale,' she said, 'have I really been of any use to you?'

He began to be firmly conscious of a wish that Mrs Keeling would appear. Alice's pale eyes were fixed on him with an almost alarming expression of earnestness. He took refuge in the pretty jesting again.

'Once upon a time,' he said, 'there was a young lady of such a modest disposition that though she had a Sunday School and a boys' class, and made a beautiful, beautiful, altar-cloth—Oh, Helper,' he broke off, 'we had your altar-cloth in use for the first time last Sunday, and you not there to see how smart it looked.'

That was another of the ways in which he made religious matters real to many of his congregation. He used the phraseology, even the slang, of ordinary life about them, speaking of 'such a ripping prayer' or 'such a jolly celebration.'

'Oh, I hope it fitted well,' said Alice, diverted for the moment by the mention of this piece of ecclesiastical finery.

'It was a perfect fit. I wish my coats fitted as well. I looked round to see if I couldn't catch the eye of my Helper, and there wasn't a Helper there at all. I wondered if you were ill. I could think of nothing else that would have kept you away, and just said a wee bitty prayer for Helper. And then after church I heard that she had horrid old flue. And now may I make chimney smoke? Smoke not smell nasty to poor Flu-flu?'

This was a joke of well-established standing, and asked permission to light a cigarette. Leave was given him, and he insisted that she should strike the match and hold it to the end of his cigarette.

'Poor parson has no business to indulge himself,' he said, and blew the inhaled smoke up the chimney in a gay puff.

He had steered the conversation away from the tidings that gleamed from Alice's earnest eyes, he had taken it past that dangerous corner of religion, from which she might bolt back again to earnestness, and had brought it to its congenial base of legitimate clerical flirtation, which allowed him to talk baby-talk with adoring parishioners, and squeeze hands and dab on the presumption that all this meant no more to anybody else than to him. This was pure assumption: it meant much more to poor Alice. . . .

For one brief moment a certain clear-sightedness penetrated her infatuation, a certain business-like unidealising vision, inherited probably from her father, came to her aid, giving her a warning both peremptory and final. For that one moment she saw this adored priest as he was, more or less, to whom this baby-talk and this squeezing of hands and this lighting of matches were not symbols of anything that lay behind them, but only expressive of an amorous anæmia. Had he been in earnest with a hundredth part of her intention, he would have caught at it, made plain his want, and even if marriage was not within the scope of his desire, reached a hand to the love she brought him, and claimed the comradeship of it, even if he could do no more. But, in this moment of clear vision, she saw and she knew that he did not even do that. He but sat on the hearth-rug and wagged his tail and barked for biscuits. . . . Then the clouds of her own foolishness, derived perhaps from her mother's side, and strangely swollen by her individual temperament obscured that brief ray of common sense, and she yielded herself up to the entrancement of having Mr Silverdale sitting on the floor at her feet and lighting his cigarette from her match.

A sudden idiotic courage possessed her; she proposed to put things to the touch. The flickering firelight and her sense of convalescence inspired her. He had called her 'Helper,' he had said a thousand things behind which meaning might lurk. It was her business, like that of every sensible girl who wants to be married, to show him that his shy priest-like advances met a slightly less shy welcome. A wave of calculating fatuousness combed over her.

'Poor parson doesn't indulge himself as much as he ought,' she said. 'He won't think a wee bitty about his own happiness, and so he makes others think of it for him.'

Alice looked not at him as she said these remarkable words but at the pink clock on the chimney-piece. She had the recklessness of physical weakness in her, she did not care what happened, if only one thing happened. If he would not take that lure, she was quite prepared to try him with another.

He half took it: he rose at it, but, so to speak, rose short. He continued to use baby-language, in order to indicate the distance that separated him from the earnest eyes that so pointedly looked at the pink clock.

'Poor parson knows kind friends are thinking

for him,' he said. 'He knows it too well perhaps: he is so selfish that he leaves his happiness in the hands of others, and doesn't bother about it himself.'

Suddenly it struck this unfortunate clergyman that his words might conceivedly bear a disastrous interpretation to his adorer. Anything was better than to let such an interpretation become coherent: he felt that Alice had been encouraged to be on the point of proposing to him. Without a moment's delay (since every moment was precious so long as Alice did not take possession of it) he switched off violently on to religious topics. Just now they had seemed dangerous to him, at this awful moment they presented the appearance of an Ark of Refuge.

'Parson has got too much to think about,' he hastily continued, 'to allow him to think of his own happiness. Isn't it true, dear Miss Alice, that we only get our own happiness when we are thinking not about ourselves? I thought about myself for half an hour this morning, and I did get so dreadfully bored. I thought how pleased I should be if—and how delighted I should be if—and then, thank God, I found myself yawning. It was all so stupid!'

'I don't believe you could be stupid,' said Alice with her infernal calmness, that again terrified him.

'Stupid? I am always stupid,' he said. 'I

want to *do* something for everybody committed to my charge. I want to give myself to the drunkards and the drabs and the unbelievers. But I am like a foolish cook: I do not know how to serve myself up so as to become palatable.'

He could not help drawing a long breath of cigarette smoke mixed with relief. He thought that the corner had been quite safely steered round. There they were back again in parish work, and what could be nicer? He disregarded Alice's gasp of appreciation at his modesty, and proceeded with an increased sense of comfort.

'Give, give!' he said. 'Give and ask nothing. What you get doesn't matter. Does it?'

He was feeling so comfortable now that he scarcely wished for Mrs Keeling's entry. Alice's earnest eyes, so he told himself (thereby revealing his ignorance of psychology) were dim with the perception of this fine interrogation. He was being wonderful, as he had so often been before, and the perception of that would surely fill her soul with the altruistic glee that possessed himself. He began, in the sense of personal security which this gave him, to get a little incautious. He did not wait for her acceptance of the prodigious doctrine that nothing you get matters to the problematical getter, but construed his own sense of security into her acquiescence.

'So let us give,' he said, just as if he was perorating in the pulpit, 'let us give till we have spent all our energies. That will take a long time, won't it: for the act of giving seems but to increase your capability of it. Dear Miss Alice, I have a thousand plans that are yet unrealised, a thousand schemes for this little parish of ours. We must have more schools for religious education, more classes, more lives unselfishly lived. I want all the help I can get. I want to transfuse St Thomas's with the certainty that the doubting disciple lacked. But I can't do it alone. Those who see must lend me their eyes—I am a mere stupid man. I——'

And then the fatuous voice suddenly ceased. To his extreme terror Alice with her earnest eyes leaned forwards towards him. She was husky through influenza, but the purport of what she said was horribly clear.

'Oh, Mr Silverdale,' she said, 'do you really mean that? That you can't work alone as a mere man? Do you——'

Alice drew a long breath that wheezed in her poor throat and covered her eyes with her hands, for she was dazzled with the vision that was surely turning real. To her, to his Helper, he had said that he was no use as a mere man. Surely the purport of that was clear.

'Do you mean me?' she said.

Mr Silverdale got up off the hearthrug where he had been sitting nursing his knees with miraculous celerity. She behind her hidden eyes heard him and knew, she felt she knew, that in another moment would come the touch of his hands on hers as he took them, and bade her look at him. Perhaps he would say, 'Look at me, my darling'; perhaps his delicious joking ways would even at this sublimest of moments still assert themselves and he would say 'Peep-o!' But whatever he did would be delicious, would be perfect. But no touch came on her hands, and there was a long, an awful moment of dead silence, while behind poor Alice's hands the dazzle died out of her vision. Before it was broken, she perceived that beyond a shadow of doubt he did not 'mean her,' and both were tongue-tied, he in the shame of having provoked a passion he had no use for, she in the shame of having revealed the passion he had not invited. She had come to the wrong house: she was an unbidden guest who must be directed outside the front-door again.

She got up, the sense of being wronged for the moment drowning her shame. It was his fault; he had made her think that he wanted her. She had long been termed his Helper, and now he had made himself clear by terming himself the mere man. At least she had thought he made himself clear. But the silence made him clearer.

'I see you don't mean me,' she said quietly.

There was nothing for it but to confirm the justness of this perception.

'My dear Miss Alice,' he said, 'I am infinitely distressed.'

From the mere habit of pawing, he laid his hand on hers.

'Infinitely distressed,' he repeated. 'I had no idea that you ever looked upon me——'

He could not complete that outrageous falsity with Alice's eyes fixed on him. She waited, she longed to withdraw her hand from under his: it itched to pluck itself away and yet some counter-compelling influence from herself kept it there, delighting in his touch. The resentment at the encouragement she had received, which had provoked this ghastly fiasco, faded from her, her shame at having precipitated it faded also, and her mind, even in this cataclysm, but sunned itself in his presence. But that lasted only for a moment, her shame toppled it off its pre-eminence again, and again her sense of the wanton flirting of which she had been the victim banished her shame. Never in all the years of her placid existence had her mother felt the poignancy of any one of those emotions which made tumult together in Alice's heart. And as if that was not enough, another added its discordant shrillness to the Babel within her. She pulled her hand away.

'Tell me one thing,' she said. 'Is there some one else? Is it Julia Fyson? Oh, Mr Silverdale, do tell me it is not Julia Fyson!'

Mr Silverdale suffered at that moment a profound disappointment. He had been telling himself that his hand was exercising a calming and controlling influence over this poor lady, and that presently she would say something very sensible and proper, though he could not quite tell what this would be. Instead, it was as if a wild cat had suddenly leaped out at him.

'Certainly it is not Miss Julia Fyson,' he exclaimed, in great dismay. For the moment his chronic fatuous complacency in the possession of his habitual adorers quite faded from his mind. They were intended to adore him tenderly, reverentially, fervently, but not to make proposals of marriage to him. He really did not care if he never put his arm round Julia Fyson's waist again.

'I assure you it is not Miss Fyson,' he reiterated, wiping his moist forehead. 'I wonder at your suggesting it. Besides, you surely know my views about the celibacy of the clergy.'

The humorousness, as it would have struck a bystander, of this amazing anticlimax escaped Alice. She knew it was an anticlimax, for she was not giving two thoughts to his principles, but was only involved in his practices. Anger suddenly flamed in her, giving her an odd grotesque dignity.

'I dare say I have heard you express them,' she said, 'but I have also heard you express intimacy and affection towards me. You always encouraged me, you held my hand, you whispered to me, and once, after my confession, you——'

'No, no,' said Mr Silverdale hurriedly.

'But you did: you kissed me on the forehead and called me a little child,' said Alice, with indignation that waxed as she recalled those tokens.

Mr Silverdale clasped his hands together.

'I am infinitely distressed,' he began. But Alice, with her temper rising to heights uncontemplated, interrupted him.

'You said that twice before,' she said. 'And I don't believe you care a bit.'

'Hush!' said Mr Silverdale, holding up his hand as he did at the benediction.

'I won't hush. You did all those things, and what was a girl to make of them except what I made of them? I put the natural construction on them. And you know it.'

The hand of benediction did not seem to be acting well, and Mr Silverdale took it down. He used it instead to cover his eyes. He was quite genuinely sorry for Alice, but at the back of his mind he could not help considering what a wonderful person he must be to inspire this passion without ever having meant to. There was a fascination about him. . . .

'I am deeply grieved,' he said, 'but as you will not listen to anything I say, there is no use in my saying any more. Good-bye, Miss Alice.'

He put back his head in a proud, misunderstood attitude, and instantly at the thought of his leaving her like this, Alice's anger began to ooze out of her. She pictured what the room would be like when the boudoir door had closed behind him, its intolerable emptiness. But she had still enough resentment left not to stop him.

'Good-bye,' she said.

'Aren't you going to shake hands?' he asked.

The dying flame flickered up again.

'We've got nothing to shake hands about,' she said.

He bowed his head with a marvellous proud meekness, and left her.

Alice sat down again by the fire, and picked up a piece of buttered bun with a semicircular bite out of it which had fallen on the carpet. He must have been in the middle of that mastication when the fiasco began. . . . Yet, he could not have been, for he had begun to smoke. Perhaps he took another bun after he had finished his cigarette. . . . She considered this with a detached curiosity; it seemed to occupy all her mind. Then the boy covered with buttons came in to remove the tea-tray, and she noticed he had a piece of sticking plaster in the middle of his forehead. That was interesting too and curious. . . . And then she had a firm, an absolute conviction that Mr Silverdale had not gone away, that he was waiting in the hall, unable to tear himself from her, and yet forbidden by his pride to come back. He had only left the room a couple of minutes; and surely she would find him seated in one of the Gothic chairs in the hall, with his hand over his face. She must go to him; their eyes would meet, and somehow or other the awful misunderstanding and estrangement in which they had parted would melt away. He would say, 'Life is too strong for me; farewell the celibacy of the clergy,' or something like that: or he would hold her hand for a long, a very long time, and perhaps whisper, 'Then blessings on the fallings out,' or 'Whatever happens, nothing must interrupt our friendship.' Perhaps the farewell to the celibacy of the clergy was an exaggerated optimism, but she would be so content, so happy with much less than that (provided always that he did not say his farewell to celibacy with Julia Fyson). She would be enraptured to continue on the old terms, now that she understood what he meant and what he did not mean. And perhaps she had spoiled it all, so that he would never again hold her hand or whisper to her, or kiss her with that sort of tender and fraternal affection as once in the vestry when she had made her guileless confession to him. It was a brother-kiss, a priest-kiss, coming almost from realms above, and now she had thrown that in his teeth. She had altogether failed to understand him, him and his friendship, and his comradeship (and his pawings). In the fading of her anger she longed for all that which she had thought meant so much, but which she prized now for its own sake. Surely she would find him still lingering in the hall, sorrowful and unhappy and misunderstood, but not reproachful, for he was too sublime for that. He had said he was infinitely grieved several times, and he would be great enough to forgive her. Perhaps he would be too deeply hurt to make any of those appropriate little speeches she had devised for him, and if so, the reconciliation for which already she yearned, the re-establishment of their relations on the old maudlin lines, must come from her initiative. Already with that curious passion some women have for being beaten and ill-treated, she longed to humble herself, to entreat his forgiveness.

She did not wait to put on a shawl, but walked quickly across the drawing-room, where she had so often heard his nimble tripping approach, and across the inner hall and out into that Gothic apartment where she would surely find him. Before she got there she had only one desire left, to abase herself and be raised up again. She was short-sighted, and as she came into the outer hall, her heart for a moment leaped within her, for she thought she saw him standing in the dusky corner by the library door. Then, with a sickening reaction, she saw the phantom resolve itself into a coat and hat of her father's hanging up there, and she saw that the hall was empty, and Mr Silverdale gone. Still she would not give up; he might be standing just outside, unable quite to leave her like this, and opening the front door, she looked out on to the star-sown dusk. But certainly there was no one there.

She went back to her mother's room and deliberately proceeded to torture herself. She had been to blame throughout, and not a spark of anger or resentment came to comfort her. All these past months he had brought joy and purpose into her aimless life, and she had but bitten the hand that fed her, and even worse than that, had scolded its owner for his bounty. It was with a sense of incredulity that she recalled some of her awful phrases, her rude, snappish interruptions, and yet in the midst of her self humiliation she knew that she felt thrills of excitement, both at what had happened and what was taking shape in her brain as to what was going to happen. She had just that pleasure in her agonies of self-reproach, as does the penitent who scourges himself. She liked it to hurt, she gloried in the castigation that was surely doing her good.

Tingling from her self-inflicted penance, she went to her mother's writing table, for she had to complete her humiliation by writing to him without delay, and expressing fully and unreservedly all that had made this last half-hour so replete with the luxury of self-reproach. But the expression of it was not so easy as the perception of it had been, and she made half a dozen beginnings without satisfying herself. One began, 'Oh, Mr Silverdale, how could I?' but then she despaired of how to proceed. Another began, 'I have honestly gone over every moment of this afternoon, and I find there is not a single point in which I am not entirely to blame,' but that was too business-like and lacked emotion. But when she was almost in despair at these futile efforts, a brilliant idea came into her head. She would write in baby-language, which would surely touch his heart when he remembered how many serious things he and she had discussed together in this pretty jesting fashion.

'Me vewy sorry,' she wrote. 'Me all messy with sorrowness. O poor parson, your Helper is vewy miserable. May things be as before? Will 'oo forget and forgive, and let everything be nicey-nicey again? Fvom your wicked little Helper who hates herself.'

She could not improve on that either for silliness or pathetic sincerity, and unable to contemplate the delay which the post would entail, she gave it to the boy covered with buttons to carry it at once by hand to the Vicarage and wait for an answer. That would take half an hour: there were thirty delicious minutes of suspense, for though she did not doubt the purport of his answer, it was thrilling to have to wait for it.

The thrillingness was slightly shorn of its vibrations by the return of her mother, who had a great deal to say about the felicitous manner in which she had opened the bazaar. She had brought back with her a small plush monkey climbing a string, and a realistic representation of a spider's web, with a woolly spider sitting in the middle of it. The rim of the web was fitted with hooks, so that you could hang it up anywhere. She selected the base of the pink clock as the most suitable site.

'Is it not clever and quaint?' she said. 'I must really tell Jane that it is not a real one, or she will be dusting it away. And the monkey too, that is even quainter. You can bend its arms and legs into all sorts of attitudes. I made a little speech, dear, and there was Lady Inverbroom on one side of me, and Mrs Crawshaw on the other. It was quite a gathering of county people. Lady Inverbroom asked after you; no, I think I told her you had the influenza first, and then she asked after you. Yes, that was the way of it. She had a mantle on which I don't think can have cost more than four guineas, but then I'm sure it's not her fault if she has to economise. For my part, if I had all those pictures with that great house to keep up, I should get my husband to sell one or two, and treat myself to a bit of finery and a better dinner in the evening.'

'Perhaps they are entailed,' said Alice, thinking that by now her note would have arrived at the Vicarage.

'Very likely, my dear,' said her mother, 'though it's poor work entailing your pictures if you haven't got anybody to leave them to. Indeed, I don't see how they could be entailed unless you had somebody nearer than a second cousin to entail them for. I shouldn't think the law would allow that for so distant a relation, though I'm sure I don't know. Bless me, you've put on your new red dress. Whatever have you done that for? Just to sit quietly before the fire at home?'

Alice had the sense not to conceal a perfectly ordinary and innocent event, which if concealed and subsequently detected would make the concealment of it significant.

'Oh, Mr Silverdale came to tea,' she said. 'He telephoned.'

'All alone with you?' said Mrs Keeling archly. 'Well I'm sure! What did you talk about? or is it stupid of me to ask that?'

Alice felt her colour rising till she imagined her face as red as her gown. She decided to treat the question humorously.

'Very stupid, Mamma dear,' she said. 'I couldn't dream of telling you all we said to each other.'

At this moment the boy covered with buttons entered.

'Mr Silverdale's not at home, miss,' he said.

'But he will be given your note when he comes in, and send an answer.'

Now Mrs Keeling had a very high opinion of her powers of tact and intuition. Here was a situation that promised to drive the final nail into the cheap and flimsy coffin of Mrs Fyson's hopes. Mr Silverdale had come to tea all alone with Alice, and here was Alice writing him a note that required an answer not half an hour afterwards. Her intuition instantly told her that Mr Silverdale had made a proposal of marriage to Alice, and that Alice had written to him saying that he must allow her a little time to think it over. (Why Alice should not have said that, or why Alice should not have instantly accepted him, her intuition did not tell her.) But it was certain that no other grouping of surmises would fit the facts. Then her intuition having done its work, though bursting with curiosity she summoned her tact to her aid, and began to talk about the spider's web again. She was determined not to pry into her daughter's heart, but wait for her daughter to open the door of it herself. Alice (and this only served to confirm Mrs Keeling's conjectures) responded instantly to this tactful treatment, and began to talk so excitedly about the spider's web, and the plush monkey, and their journey to Brighton next day, that Mrs Keeling almost began to be afraid that she was feverish again. But presently this volubility died down. and she sat, so Mrs Keeling rightly conjectured, listening for something. Once she was certain that she heard steps in the next room, and went to see if her father had come in : once she was almost sure that the telephone bell had rung, and wondered who it could be disturbing them at their chat over the fire. Then, without doubt, the telephone bell did ring, and on this occasion she pretended she had not heard it, but hurriedly left the room on the pretext of taking her tonic. She left the door open, and Mrs Keeling could distinctly hear her asking her tonic apparently who it was, though well aware that it was strychnine. . . . Then after a pause she heard her thanking her tonic ever ever so much, and she came back looking as if it had done her a gread deal of good already.

Odd as it may appear, there were limits to Mrs Keeling's tact, or to state the matter in other terms, none to her curiosity. For a little while she resisted the incoming tide ; but when Alice had informed her brightly for the third time that their train started at 11.29 next morning, she felt so strongly that a mother was her daughter's proper confidante, that her tact retreated rapidly towards vanishing point.

'I saw Mrs Fyson this afternoon,' she said, beginning gently.

'And did she see you?' asked Alice, with a sort of idiotic eagerness. All the time there was ringing in her head, like a peal of baritone bells through the quackings of the telephone, the lovely words, 'My dear little Helper! Bless you, my dear little Helper.'

'I imagine so, as I was opening the bazaar,' said Mrs Keeling, with some dignity.

'Of course, yes,' said Alice, with enthusiasm. 'How stupid of me not to have thought of that. That lovely spider! Do remember to tell Jane not to dust it away. I haven't seen Mrs Fyson for a long time, nor Julia. I must write a note to Julia wishing her good-bye before I go to Brighton. Dear Julia.'

She got up and overturned a tray of pens in her eagerness to write to Julia. This, of course, gave fresh provender to her mother's intuition. She could put two and two together as well as most people, and hardly ever failed to make the result 'five.' It was quite obvious that Mr Silverdale had proposed to Alice, and that in consequence Mrs Fyson's ill-founded expectations for Julia had fallen as flat as a card-house. No wonder Alice could afford to forgive her friend.

'Well, I'm glad to hear you speak like that, dear,' she said, 'because the last time you mentioned Julia's name was to tell me that you didn't want to hear it mentioned again. Mrs Fyson, too, I dare say she is a very well-meaning woman, though she does go about saying that all sorts of things are happening without any grounds except that she wants them to.'

Alice made a large blot on her paper in agitation at hearing this allusion, and took another sheet of paper.

'And I am sure Julia has an excellent heart,' she said enthusastically, recalling Mr Silverdale's definite assurance that 'it' was not Julia. At the time she had been so full of more personal emotion that she had scarcely cared; now the balm of that was divinely soothing.

'Quite an excellent heart,' she said. 'Julia has always been my friend, except just lately. And now it is all right again. Don't you think that quarrels sometimes lead to even warmer attachments, Mamma?'

Mrs Keeling tried to recollect something about quarrels she had been party to. There was the case of the two little tiffs she had had lately with her husband, once when he had distinctly sworn at her, once when he had asked her so roughly what she meant with regard to her little joke about Norah and the catalogue. One of those, so it suddenly seemed to her now, had led to a pearl-pendant, which seemed to illustrate Alice's theory of quarrels leading to warmer attachments. She had not connected the two before. She wondered whether Mrs Fyson would say that that was very clever too. . . . She determined to think it over when she had leisure. At present she was too curious about Alice to attend to it. But she would think it over at Brighton.

'Don't you think they lead to warmer attachments, Mamma?' repeated Alice, finding she got no answer.

Mrs Keeling was very cunning. She would apply this to Alice's quarrel with Julia and just see what Alice would say next.

'Well, dear,' she said. 'You couldn't well be more warmly attached to Julia than you were. I'm sure you used to be quite inseparable.'

Alice gave a little hoarse laugh.

'Oh, *that*,' she said. 'Dear Julia; I hope we shall be great friends again, when I come back from Brighton. I shall be very glad to, I am sure.'

Clearly the quarrels which led to warmer attachments had nothing to do with Alice's late fury about Fysons, and her mother, throwing tact and delicacy about a daughter's heart to the winds, tried another method of battering her way into it. She could not conceive why Alice did not tell her that Mr Silverdale had proposed to her.

'I've been thinking, dear,' she said, 'that it would be but kind to ask Mr Silverdale down to Brighton while we are there. He looks as if a holiday would do him good. I would take a nice room for him in the hotel, and of course he would use our sitting room. Of course, I should make it quite clear to him that he was my guest, just as if he was staying with us here. Such walks and talks as you and he could have! What do you think of that for a plan?'

Alice was so stiff with horror at 'that for a plan' that she could barely articulate. Of course Mr Silverdale would refuse to come, the horror was but due to the mere notion that he should be asked.

'Oh, I don't think that would do at all, Mamma!' she said. 'It would be a very odd thing to propose.'

'I don't see why. You and he are such friends. I shall write to him and suggest it, or you might; perhaps that would be best: he can but say he cannot manage it, though for my part I should be very much surprised if he did not accept.'

Alice got up from the table where she had just written an affectionate little note to Julia, and came up to her mother's chair, quivering with apprehension.

'You really must do nothing of the sort,' she said. 'There are reasons against it: I can't tell you them.'

Mrs Keeling's powers of intuition could make nothing of this. Starting with the firm conviction that Mr Silverdale had proposed to her daughter, there seemed no place where it would fit in.

'You are very mysterious, dear,' she said. 'You seem to forget that I am your mother. And if you tell me that I must speak to nobody about it yet, you may be sure I shall not do so without your leave. I was always famous for my ability to keep a secret. Why, not so long ago your father told me something which I am sure will make Mrs Fyson turn quite green with odious jealousy when she hears it, and I have not breathed a word to anybody. Not a word. So don't be so mysterious, dear; I remember going to tell Mamma the moment your father spoke to me, and it was in the garden behind Mamma's house; I could show you the very place, if you don't believe me.'

'But Mr Silverdale hasn't spoken to me like that,' said poor Alice.

'Well then, there's a reason the more for asking him to Brighton,' said Mrs Keeling, now quite out of sight of her tact, 'I know very well what all his attentions to you mean. I've never seen a man so devoted, for I'm sure your father never made such a fuss over me as that. You've got to meet a man half-way, dear; it's only right to show him that you are not indifferent to him (or do I mean that he's not indifferent to you? some words are so puzzling). He wants a wife, I can see that, and you may trust me that it's you he wants. I shall invite him to Brighton, and if you only behave sensibly, he'll ask you before we're even thinking of coming back.'

'But I don't want him to ask me,' said Alice, *splendide mendax*.

Mrs Keeling looked positively roguish.

'Oh, you just wait till he does, and that won't be a very long wait,' she said. 'You think you'll be shy and nervous, but you won't when your turn comes. I'll be bound you like him well enough really.'

This was about as pleasant to Alice as the prodding of an exposed nerve. But she held on unshaken to the main point.

'If you ask him to Brighton,' she said, 'I shall instantly write to tell him that I am not going. That's my last word. And if you knew what has happened, you would agree with me. He won't come, but I can't have him asked.'

Alice, in spite of her influenza and the shattering events of this afternoon, had something adamantine about her. She paused a moment.

'Please promise me at once not to suggest this to him,' she added.

Mrs Keeling rose from her chair. The dressing-bell had already sounded, and she had not had a moment's rest since before lunch.

'Well, I'm sure it's little reward one gets for being a mother in these days,' she said, 'or a wife either, for what with your father's typewriter lording it in the library, and you telling me what's right and what isn't in my own room, there's little left for me to be mistress of. I wear myself to the bone in doing my duty to you and him, and all I get is to be sworn at and scolded, and when I lie awake at night making plans for your future, you tell me that I might just as well have gone to sleep, for you won't permit them. Pray may I go and dress, or have you any other orders for me?'

'No, I just want your promise that you won't ask Mr Silverdale to Brighton,' said Alice, unmoved by this withering sarcasm.

'Well, what's the use of repeating that like a parrot?' observed Mrs Keeling. 'Haven't I promised?'

'I didn't hear you,' said Alice.

'Well, then, you may have your own way, and be crowed over by Mrs Fyson, since you prefer that to being taken care of by me.'

Alice's smart red dress was good enough for a purely domestic dinner, and she sat down again by the fire when her mother had bewailed herself out of the room. She had got her way there, and that was a relief; she was Mr Silverdale's Helper again, and that was a glow that had penetrated her very bones. When she wrote the little baby-note to him, she felt that if only she was granted such a welcome back as had been conveyed to her down the telephone, she would swoon with happiness. But already that which she thirsted for was dust in her mouth, like Dead Sea apples. She guessed that his little caresses and whispers had meant so much to her because she took them to be the symbols of so much more. Now she knew better, they were without meaning. And the measure of her disillusionment may be taken from the fact that independently of all that had happened, she was glad that there would be no chance of his coming to Brighton. She wanted him to love her, and failing that, she did not want the little tokens that had made her think he did. He might just remain in Bracebridge and dab away at Julia if he wished, provided only that he meant nothing whatever by it. She did not love him a whit the less, but just now she did not want him whose presence for these last six months had filled her with sunshine. She must go away into the dark, and see what the dark felt like. And poor Alice, sitting by the fire in her smart red dress, began to make the most extraordinary faces in efforts at self-control. But the convulsions in her throat threatened to master her completely, and with bitten, quivering lips she ran to her room, and burst into tears.

CHAPTER VIII

SPRING weather, languid and damp, with mild airs and pale suns, had set in early in March, and now for a fortnight the restlessness and effervescence of the vernal month had been busy in the world. The grass showed through the grayness of its winter foliage the up-thrusting of the fresh green spikes and spears: big gummy buds stood upon the chestnut trees, a sherbet of pink almond flowers clothed the shrubs all along the front gardens of Alfred Road, and daffodils, faithful for once to their Shakespearian calendar, were ready with a day or two more of sun, to take the winds of March with beauty. Birds chirruped in every bush and were busy with straws and twigs; there were tokens everywhere of the great renewal Then came three days of hot sun and tepid night showers and the sheaths of buds were loosed, and out of the swollen gummy lumps on the trees burst out the weak five-fingered chestnut leaves and the stiff varnished squibs of hawthorn.

It was many years since Keeling had given any notice at all to such unmarketable objects as chestnut-buds or building birds. Spring had a certain significance, of course, in the catering department, for early vegetables made their appearance, and soon there would arrive the demand for plovers' eggs: spring, in fact, was a phenomenon that stirred in his pocket rather than his heart. But this year it was full of hints to him, of delicate sensations too fugitive to be called emotions, of sudden little thrills of vague longings and unformulated desires. A surreptitious half-sheet lurked in the blotting-paper on his library table on which he scrawled the date of some new flower's epiphany, or the fact that a thrush was building in the heart of a syringa outside the window. It was characteristic of his business habits to tabulate those things: it was characteristic also that he should thrust the catalogue deep into the leaves of his blotting-paper, as if it held some guilty secret.

On this particular Sunday morning, he had not gone to Cathedral service at all, but after his wife and Alice had set forth in the victoria to St Thomas's, had walked out westwards along the road from The Cedars, to where half a mile away the last house was left behind and the billowing downs rolled away in open sea out of sight of the land of houses. In the main it was the sense of spring with its intimate stirrings that called him out, and the adventure was a remarkable one, for it was years since he had failed to attend Sunday morning service. But to-day he sought no stern omnipotent Presence, which his religion told him must be invoked among arches and altars: he sought maybe the same, under the guise of a smiling face, in windy temples. It was not that he consciously sought it: as far as any formulated expression went, he would have said that he 'chose' to go for a walk in the country, and would attend Cathedral service in the evening as usual. But as he walked he wondered whether Norah would come to The Cedars that morning to work in his library. He had not the slightest intention, however reserved and veiled from himself, of going back there to see; he meant to walk until his wife and daughter would certainly be back from church again, though probably this was among the last two or three mornings that Norah would come to The Cedars at all, for the catalogue was on the point of completion.

But he knew there was another disposition of events possible. She had told him yesterday that she was not sure whether she would work there that morning or not. All the week her hours in the office had been long, and she might spend the morning out of doors. He knew already that she loved the downs, and indeed it was she who had told him of this particular path which he was now taking as a favourite ramble of hers. Her brother almost invariably walked with her, and Keeling was quite innocent of contriving an accidental meeting with her alone. But somewhere floating about in his heart was the imagined possibility that she might be alone, and that he would meet her. He did not expect to meet her at all, but he knew he would love to see her, either with Charles or without, swinging along on this warm windy morning in the freedom of the country air and the great open spaces. They would suit her. . . . But primarily it was not she in any way that he sought: he wanted open space, and this wonderful sense of spring with its white bowlings of cloud along the blue, and its upthrusting of young grass. He wanted it untrammelled and wild, the tended daffodils and the buildings of birds so near house walls was not part of his mood.

He climbed quickly up the narrow chalky path, and at the top left it to tramp over the turf. Here he was on an eminence that commanded miles of open country, empty and yet brimful of this invasion of renewed life that combed through him like a swirl of sea-water through the thickets of subaqueous weed. His back was to the cup of hills round which Bracebridge clustered, and turning round he looked at it with a curious sense of detachment. There were the spires of the Cathedral, and hardly less prominent beside them the terra-cotta cupolas of the Stores. He wanted one as little as he wanted the other, and turned westwards, where the successive lines of downs stretched away like waves of a landless sea. Then he stopped again, for from a tussock of grass not fifty yards from him there shot up with throbbing throat and down-beating wings a solitary lark.

Somewhere in that tussock was the mate to whom it sang.

Quivering and tuneful it soared, now almost invisible against the blue, but easily seen again when a white cloud rolled up behind it, and the shadow preceding it turned the fresh emerald of the down grass to a dark purplish green. At that the delicate trembling hints of spring suddenly crystallised in Keeling's heart into strong definite emotion. It was young, it sang to its mate as it climbed into the sky. . . .

Soon it passed altogether out of his sight: it was just a sightless singing out of the winds of March. Then slowly descending it appeared again, and its song grew louder. Just before it dropped into its tussock of grass the song ceased.

Keeling waited quite still for a moment, and then came back into himself from the bright places into which he had aspired.

'God, there's no fool like an old fool,' he said to himself as he skirted with a wide berth past the tussock where larks were nesting.

The ridge on which he walked declined downwards into a hollow full of sunshine flecked with shadow. A few big oak-trees stood there, still leafless, and the narrow path, with mossy banks on each side, led through a copse of hazel which had been felled the year before. The ground was covered with the fern-like leaves of wood anemones and thickly tufted with the dark green spears, where in May the bluebells would seem like patches of fallen sky. It was sheltered here, and a brimstone butterfly flitted through the patches of sunlight. At the bottom of the hollow a runnel of water from some spring crossed the path, and babbled into a cup fringed with creeping ivy, and young crinkled primrose leaves. Then the path rose swiftly upwards again on the side of the next rolling billow of down, and coming towards him from it was the figure, tall and swiftly moving, of a girl. For a moment he resented the fact of any human presence here: the next he heard his heart creaking in his throat, for he saw who it was.

By the time he recognised her, he too was recognised, and half way up the climbing path they met. She was carrying her hat in her hand, and the sunlit sparks of fire in her brown bright hair, that the wind had disordered into a wildness that greatly became her and the spirit of the spring morning. Her brisk walking had kindled a glow in her cheeks, and she was a little out of breath, for she had run down the path from the crest of slope beyond. Standing a step or two above him on the steep slope their eyes were on a level; as straight as an arrow's flight hers looked into his.

'Not working at the catalogue, then, this morning?' he said. 'I wondered whether you would or not.'

'I meant to,' she said, 'until I smelt the wind. Then it was impossible. I should not care if every book in the world was burned, I think. And you, not at the Cathedral this morning?'

'And that might be burned too,' he said.

She laughed.

'I'm a Pagan to-day,' she said, 'and so it appears are you. Pan is sitting somewhere in this wood. Did you hear his flute?'

'No: only the wind and the song of a skylark.'

'Perhaps that was he. He's all over the place this morning.'

'You told me about Pan,' he said. 'I had never heard of him before.'

'Well, you heard him to-day. He was the wind and the skylark. He always is if you know how to listen. But I mustn't keep you. You are going farther.'

He looked at his watch, not deriving any impression from it, then back at her.

'No, I must turn too,' he said. 'Mayn't I walk with you?'

'Naturally till we get to the town, and then, as naturally, not. But we must wait in this hollow a little longer. It is brimful of spring. Look at the clumps of bluebell leaves. In a month there will be a thick blue carpet spread here.'

'Which are the bluebells?' he asked.

She pointed, and then bending down found in

the centre of one the bud from which the blossom would expand.

'I thought they were just some sort of grass,' he said. 'The woods are covered with them. Will you show them to me when they are all out?'

'Oh, Mr Keeling,' she said. 'You will surely be able to see them for yourself.'

'Not so well.'

She rose from her examination of the bud, her face still flushed.

'Yes, we'll see them together some Saturday afternoon then,' she said. 'I won't have any hand in your not going to Cathedral on Sunday morning. I suppose we must be getting back. What time was it when you looked at your watch just now?'

'I forget. I don't think I saw.'

She laughed.

'I do that so often when I'm working at the catalogue in the evening,' she said. 'I look to see if it is time to go to bed, and then go on working. There isn't any time so long as you are absorbed in anything.'

They mounted the steep ascent down which he had come a few minutes before. The wind was at their backs, ruthlessly blowing them towards Bracebridge.

'And there's the opening of the hospital wing to-morrow,' she said. 'I suppose you won't be at the office in the morning at all?'

'I shall just look in,' he said. 'Will you come

to the opening and to the lunch afterwards with your brother? There is a table for some dozen of my staff.'

'I am sure we should both like to. I love ceremonies and gold chains and personages. I've been visiting at the hospital, too, reading to patients.'

'Have you? You never told me that.'

'It wasn't particularly interesting. But I am so sorry for people in hospital. I shall take a basket of bluebells there one day. Only it makes me feel cheap to read for an hour on Saturday afternoon, or pick some flowers. It is so little, and yet what more can I do? If I were rich I would spend thousands on hospitals.'

He was silent a moment.

'Is that remark made to me?' he asked.

'I suppose it is just a little bit. It was very impertinent.'

'I do subscribe to it, you know,' he said.

'Oh, yes; I saw your name among the subscribers when I was there yesterday,' she said rather hurriedly

Keeling felt a keen and secret enjoyment over this. He knew quite well what she must have seen, namely the fact that he was a yearly subscriber of £10, as set forth on the subscription board. He had no temptation whatever to tell her who was the anonymous donor of the new wing. She would hear that to-morrow, and in the meantime would continue to consider him the donor of £10 a year. He liked that: he did not want any curtailment of it.

'And no one knows who the giver of the new wing is?' she asked.

'I fancy Lord Inverbroom does,' he replied, secretly praising himself for his remarkable ingenuity.

'I enjoyed that afternoon I spent there,' she said. 'They are kind, they are simple, and it is only simple people who count. I wonder if Lord Inverbroom gave the wing himself.'

'Ah, that had not occurred to me,' said Keeling.

This served his purpose. Clearly no suspicion of being tricked by an ingenious answer crossed the girl's mind, and she paused a moment shielding her eyes with her hand and looking towards Bracebridge. That shelter from the sun concealed all her face but her mouth, and looking at her he thought that if her mouth alone was visible of her, he could have picked it out as hers among a thousand others. The full upper lip was the slightest degree irregular; it drooped a little on the right, falling over the join with the lower lip: it was as if it was infinitesimally swollen there. For one second of stinging desire he longed to shut down her hand over her eyes, and kiss that corner of her mouth. It must have been that about which the skylark sang . . . .

They had come near to the end of the ridge where the steep descent on to the road began. Fifty yards in front, at present unnoticed by him, was the tussock out of which the bird had risen, and even as they paused, she looking at Bracebridge, and he at her, that carolling and jubilation began again. At once she put down her shielding hand, and laid it on his sleeve, as if he could not hear.

'There's your lark,' she whispered.

She did not move while the song continued, her hand still rested unconsciously on his sleeve, her eyes looked straight at him, demanding his companionship in that young joy of life that thrilled her no less than the bird. It was that in the main that possessed her, and yet, for that delicate intimate moment, she had instinctively (so instinctively that she was unaware of her choice) chosen him as her companion. She wanted to listen to the lark with him (or his coat) on her finger-tips. Her whole soul was steeped in the joyful hour, and it was with him she shared it: it was theirs, not hers alone.

The song grew faint and louder again, then ceased, and she took her hand off his arm.

'Thanks,' she said.

They made a wide circuit round that windy home of melody.

'And now which of us shall go first?' she said, 'for we must go alone now. Which of us naturally walks fastest? You, I expect. So I shall sit here for five minutes more and then follow.'

He agreed to this, and strode off down the steep descent. Just before he was out of sight he turned to wave a hand at her. Then she was alone on the great empty down, still hatless, still flushed with wind and walking, and just behind her the tussock where the lark lived.

He found a note for himself on the hall table, and with it in his hand walked into his wife's room to see if she had returned from church. She was already there, resting a little after the fatigue of worship, and extremely voluble.

'So you are back too, Thomas,' she said, 'and what a pity you did not get back sooner. Lord Inverbroom has just called, and left a note for you. I wonder you did not see him in the Cathedral, for he went to service there. I said you always took a walk on Sunday morning after service, so sooner than wait, he wrote a note for you. Oh, you have it in your hand. What a curious handwriting his is: I should have thought a spider from the ink-pot could have done better than that, but no doubt you will be able to make it out. Of course I asked him to stop to lunch, for whether we are alone or expect company, I'm sure my table is good enough for anybody. Alice will not be here: she has gone to lunch with Mr Silverdale.'

'Oh! Is that quite proper?'

'Not alone, my dear, what do you take me for? I hope I know what is proper and what is not. His sister has come to stay with him, a most lady-like sort of person, you might almost say distinguished. She and Alice made great friends instantly: I declare you would have thought they were sisters, instead of the two Silverdales. They were "my dear" to each other before they had talked for five minutes. I thought it quite an omen.'

'Of what?' asked he.

'Why of their becoming sisters. I am no match-maker, thank God, but really the way in which Mr Silverdale introduced his sister to Alice, why, I have never seen anything like it. "This is my Helper, Margaret," he said, or perhaps it was Martha: I could not quite catch the name. "This is my dear Helper (that was it) and I couldn't do without her." What do you say to that?'

'I don't say anything at all, my dear,' he said. 'Mr Silverdale has said it too often.'

'Ah, but the tone: there is so much in the tone,' said this excruciating lady. 'How very odd it would be to hear a clergyman give out his own banns.'

'I should think it remarkably odd if they were Alice's too,' said Keeling.

Well, and I dare say it won't be long before you are finely surprised then. Pray tell me what Lord

Inverbroom says. I am sure it is about the opening of the hospital to-morrow. I have practised my royal curtsey. I can get down and up quite easily, indeed Mamma thought it most graceful, and she does not praise without reason. Perhaps Lord Inverbroom wants me to come down to the bottom of the steps and make my curtsey there. If he insists, of course I will do it, for naturally he knows more about court etiquette than I do at present. I will certainly bow to his superior knowledge.'

Keeling stood there with his letter still unopened. Half an hour ago he had been with Norah, listening to the skylark on the downs. Now on the pink clock in front of him hung the quaint spider's web, which Jane had been most careful about. He felt as if he was caught there. . . .

'Or it may be about the bouquet,' continued his wife. 'Very likely he has found out that the princess has some favourite flower, in which case it would be only right to have it made of that instead of carnations and gypso-something, and I could say, "Your favourite flower, your Royal Highness," or something of the sort. Pray open your letter, Thomas, and see what it is.'

Keeling found no difficulty in deciphering the handwriting. There were three pages, and glancing through them, he moved towards the door.

'Nothing whatever about the ceremony to-morrow,' he said.

He went to his library and gave a more detailed perusal to what Lord Inverbroom had to say. It was a disagreeable letter to read, and he felt that the writing of it had been disagreeable to its author. It informed him that since Lord Inverbroom had put his name up for election into the County Club, he had become aware that there were a considerable number of members who would certainly vote against his election. Lord Inverbroom had spoken to various of these, but had not succeeded in mitigating their opposition and was afraid that his candidate would certainly not be elected. In these circumstances did Mr Keeling wish him to withdraw his name or not? He would be entirely guided by his wishes. He added a very simple and sincere expression of his regret at the course events had taken.

Keeling read this through once and once again before he passed to the consideration of the answer he would make to it. He found that it said very disagreeable things inoffensively, which seemed to him a feat, knowing that if he wrote a letter containing disagreeable news, the tone of his letter would be disagreeable also. He could not quite understand how it was done, but certainly he felt no kind of offence towards the writer.

But the contents were another matter, and they both annoyed him excessively, and kindled in him a blaze of defiance. He would much have liked to know who were these members for whom he was not good enough, and whose opposition Lord Inverbroom had been unable to mitigate. But as far as withdrawing his candidature went for fear of the result of the election, or acquainting Lord Inverbroom of the fact that as purchaser of the property he had the *ex officio* privilege of being a member, such craven notions never entered his head. If sufficient members to secure his rejection, objected to him, they should record their objections: he was not going to withdraw on the chance of their doing so. He had never yet abandoned a business proposition for fear of competition, and it seemed to him that to withdraw his name was somehow parallel to being frightened out of a deal. Judging from the purely business standpoint (and there was his mistake) he expected to find that a large quantity of this supposed opposition was bluff. Besides, before the election came on, it would be known who had given the new wing to the hospital, and pulled the committee out of a quagmire of rotten finance: it would be known too, that whether the County Club thought him a suitable occupant of the bow-window that looked on Alfred Street, his Sovereign thought him good enough to go into dinner before any of them except Lord Inverbroom. He was no snob himself, but he suspected that a good many other people were.

Accordingly even before the gong sounded for

lunch, he had finished a note in answer to Lord Inverbroom's as follows :—

'DEAR LORD INVERBROOM,—I am obliged for your favour just to hand, and regret I was out. I should be obliged if you would kindly fulfil the engagement you entered into with me, and put me up for election as agreed. I do not in the least fear the result of the election, and so trust you may be in error about it.

'Faithfully yours,

'THOMAS KEELING.'

This he read through before posting it. It was a sound business letter, saying just what it set out to say. But he wondered why it lacked that certain aroma of courtesy which distinguished the letter which it answered. He perceived that it was so, but no more knew how to remedy it than he knew how to fly. But he could walk pretty sturdily along the ground, and it required a stalwart push to upset him. And if the undesirable happened, and Lord Inverbroom's fears proved to be well founded, he knew he had a sound knock ready for the whole assembly of those who collectively thought he was not good enough for them.

'I'll find an answer that's good enough for them,' he said to himself, as he slipped the letter into his post-box.

In spite of her practice in the conduct of social functions as Lady Mayoress, and her natural aptitude for knowing how to behave suitably, Mrs Keeling had one moment of extremest terror when the Royal Princess came up the steps of the hospital next day, between Keeling and Lord Inverbroom, to where the Lady Mayoress awaited her. Her knees so trembled that though she felt that there would not be the smallest difficulty in sinking down in the curtsey, or indeed in sinking into the earth altogether, she much doubted her power of ever raising herself again, and the gysophila in the bouquet she was about to present shook so violently that it appeared to be but a gray mist among the daffodils which had been ascertained to be the Princess's favourite flower. She would have liked to run away, but there was nowhere to run to, and indeed the gorgeous heaviness of her satin gown rendered all active locomotion impossible. Then Her Royal Highness shook her hand, thanked her for the beautiful flowers and inhaled the perfume of the scentless daffodils before giving them to her lady-in-waiting to carry, and Mrs Keeling found herself able to say, 'Your favourite flowers, Your Royal Highness,' which broke the spell of her terror. Then followed the declaration that the new wing was open and the tour was made through the empty wards, while Mrs Keeling so swelled with pride and anticipation that she felt that it was she who had been the yet anonymous benefactor. Sometimes she talked to the Princess, sometimes only to Lord Inverbroom, or was even so mindful of her proper place as to drop a condescending word or two to the bishop, whose only *locus standi* there, so she considered, was that he would presently be permitted to say grace. Lining the big hall and in corridors were the 'common people' of Bracebridge, Mrs Fyson and that class of person, and naturally Mrs Keeling swept by them, as she had swept by the footmen on that pleasant domestic evening at Lady Inverbroom's.

Then came the lunch, in the town-hall near by, at which the bishop did his duty, and the guests theirs. There was a table and a raised dais for the principal of those, and on the floor of the hall a dozen others for the less distinguished. Close by against the wall were sitting those of Keeling's staff who had been bidden to the ceremony, and he had already satisfied himself that Norah was there. Then at the close of lunch came Lord Inverbroom's speech, and at the close of that the sentence for which Mrs Keeling had been waiting.

'Your Royal Highness,' he said, 'and ladies and gentlemen, I will now ask you to drink the health of the munificent benefactor whose name, by his express desire, has till now remained a secret. I ask you to drink the health of our most honoured Mayor, Mr Thomas Keeling.'

Then followed the usual acclamation, and it

was sweet to the donor's ears. But sweeter than it all to him was the moment when, as the guests sat down again and he rose to reply, he looked across at the table near the wall, and caught Norah's eye. Just perceptibly she shook her head at him as if to reproach him with his ingeniousness the day before, but all her face was alight. He had never met so radiant an encounter from her. . . .

Mrs Keeling was almost too superb to speak even to Lord Inverbroom in the interval after lunch, when presentations were made before the Princess drove to the station again. But she could not continue not to speak to anybody any more because of this great exaltation, and she was full of bright things as she went home with her husband.

'It really all passed off very tolerably,' she said; 'do you not think so, my dear? And was it not gratifying? Just as the dear Princess shook hands with me for the second time before she drove away, holding my hand quite a long time, she said, "And I hear your friends will not call you Mrs Keeling very much longer." Was not that delicately put? How common Lady Inverbroom looked beside her, but, after all, we can't all be princesses. I was told by the lady-in-waiting, who was a very civil sort of woman indeed, that Her Royal Highness was going to stay with the poor Inverbrooms next month. I can hardly believe that: I should not think it was at all a likely sort of thing to happen, but I felt I really ought to warn Mrs—

I did not quite catch her name—what a very poor sort of dinner her mistress would get, if she fared no better than we did. But we must keep our ears open next month to find out if it really does happen, though I dare say we shall be the first to know, for after to-day Lady Inverbroom could scarcely fail to ask us to dine and sleep again.'

'I cannot conceive why she should do any such thing,' remarked Keeling.

'My dear, you are too modest. You may be sure Lady Inverbroom would be only too glad to get somebody to interest and amuse the Princess, for she has no great fund of wit and ability herself. I saw the Princess laughing three times at something you said to her, and I dare say I missed other occasions. Did you see her pearls? Certainly they were very fine, and I'm sure we can take it for granted they were genuine, but I saw none among them, and I had a good look at them before and behind, that would match my pearl pendant.'

They drove on a little way in silence, for Mrs Keeling's utterance got a little choked up with pride and gratification, like a congested gutter, and in all her husband's mental equipment there was nothing that could be responsive to these futilities. They evoked nothing whatever in him; he had not the soil from which they sprang, which Mrs Keeling had carted into her own psychical garden in such abundance since she had become Lady Mayoress. Besides, for the present there was nothing real to him, not the lunch, not the public recognition, not the impending Club election, except that moment when he had fixed Norah's glance, drawn it to himself as on an imperishable thread across the crowded rooms, when he rose to reply. He almost wished his wife would go on talking again: her babble seemed to build a wall round him, which cutting him off by its inanity from other topics that might engage him, left him alone with Norah. Very soon his wish was fully gratified.

'How one frightens oneself for no reason,' she said. 'I declare when the Princess came up the steps, I was ready to run away. But it all passed in a moment, and by the time I had said, "Your favourite flowers, ma'am,"—did I tell you I said, "Your favourite flowers, ma'am?" and she gave me such a sweet smile, I felt as if I had known her for years. There are some sorts of people with whom I feel at home at once, and that was how I felt this morning. It must be very pleasant always to go about such people, and I declare I quite envied her lady-in-waiting, though if I was she I should certainly have something done to my teeth. I must run round and see Mamma this afternoon, and I should not wonder if I paid a few calls as well, for I am sure everybody will be pining to know what the Princess said all the time we were having a talk together over our coffee. I must try to recollect every word of that, though

I am sure I shall find difficulty in doing so, for we chattered away as if we had known each other all our lives.'

'I dare say you will recollect it very well, my dear,' said he, 'if you give your mind to it. And if you cannot remember you can make it up.'

'Well, if that isn't a rude speech! But perhaps you're tired, Thomas, with all this grandeur. For me, I never felt fresher in my life: it comes quite natural to me.'

'No, I am not the least tired,' he said. 'As soon as I have changed my clothes, I shall go down to my office.'

'Pray leave that for another day. I cannot bear to think of your demeaning yourself with business after what we have been doing: I do not think it is quite respectful to the Princess.'

Suddenly the babble that he had rather welcomed became intolerable. It had cut him off from the world, as if some thick swarm of flies had settled outside the window, utterly obscuring the outlook. Now, in a moment the window seemed to have been opened, and they swarmed in, buzzing about and settling on him.

'And where should we have been if I hadn't demeaned myself with business?' he asked. 'Didn't the new wing of the hospital and your pearl pendant, and your chatting like an old friend to a Princess all come out of my demeaning myself?'

Mrs Keeling paid no attention to this: she hardly heard.

And if she does come to stay with the Inverbrooms,' she said, 'I have no doubt she will express a wish to take lunch with us. We must see about getting a butler, Thomas. Parkinson is a good servant, but I should not like it to be known at court that I only kept a parlour maid.'

The carriage had stopped at the Gothic porch, and Keeling got out.

'I will promise to let you have twenty butlers on the day she lunches with us,' he said. 'Come, get out, Emmeline, and take care how you walk. There's something gone to your head. It may be champagne or it may be the Princess. I suspect it's the Princess, and you're intoxicated. Go indoors, and sleep it off, and let me find you sober at dinner-time. Take my arm.'

'My dear, what things you say! I am ashamed of you, though I know it's only your fun. The carriage must wait for me. I shall pay a call or two and then take a drive through the town. I think the citizens would feel it to be my duty to do that.'

Keeling found that Norah had got back to his office when he arrived, and was busy at the typewriting of the letters he had dictated to her that morning. She was in the little room opening off his, and the door was shut, but her presence was indicated by the muffled clacking of her machine. That sound was infinitely more real to him than what he thought of as 'the flummeries' of the day, and he was far more interested in how she would take the divulging of the donor's name than how all the rest of the town would take it. The significance which it held for him on account of the honour that would come to him, or on account of this matter of his election to the Club, mattered nothing in comparison to how she took it. He was determined to make no allusion to it himself, he would leave it to her to state the revision of her views about his support of the hospital.

While he waited for the completion of her work, he occupied himself with businesses that demanded his scrutiny, but all the while his ear was pricked to listen to the sound of her typewriting machine, or rather to listen for the silence of its cessation, for that would mean that Norah would presently come in with the letters for his signature. There was nothing in his work that demanded a close grip of his mind, and beneath the mechanical attention that he gave it, memory like some deep-water undertow was flowing on its own course past the hidden subaqueous landscape. There was a whole stretch of scenery there out of sight of the surface of his life. Till she had come into it, there was no man who possessed less of a secret history : he had his hobby of books as all the world knew, his blameless domestic conduct, his hard

Puritan morality and religion, his integrity and success in money-making and keen business faculty. That was all there was to him. But now he had dived below that, yet without making any break in the surface. All that he had done and been before continued its uninterrupted course; his life beneath the deep waters did not make itself known by as much as a bubble coming to the surface.

Gradually, while still his ear was alert to catch the silence next door which would show that Norah had finished her work, his surface-faculties moved more slowly and drowsily. The page he was reading, concerning some estimate, lay long unturned before him, and his eye ceased to travel along the lines that no longer conveyed any meaning to him. It was not the ceremony of to-day that occupied him, nor the moment when all Bracebridge knew that it was he who had made this munificent gift. Those things formed but the vaguest of backgrounds, in which too a veiled hatred of his wife was mingled: in front of that grey mist was the sunlit windy down, the skylark, the tufts of blue-bell foliage, and the companionship which gave them all their significance. And how significant, he now asked himself, were these same things to his companion? Did they mean anything to her because of him? True, she had silently and unconsciously taken him into her confidence when they listened together to the sky-lost song, but would not anybody else, her brother for instance, have done just as well? Did her heart want him? He had no answer to that.

And what, if it was possible to introduce the hard angles of practical issues into these suffused dimnesses, was to be the end or even the continuation of this critical yet completely uneventful history? All the conduct, the habit, the traditions of his life were in utter discord with it. If he looked at it, even as far as it had gone, in the hard dry light which hitherto had guided him in his life, he could hardly think it credible that it was the case of Thomas Keeling which was under his scrutiny. But even more unconjecturable was the outcome. He could see no path of any sort ahead. If by some chance momentous revelation he knew that she wanted him with that quality of wanting which was his, what would happen? His whole reasonable and upright self revolted from the idea of clandestine intrigue, and with hardly less emphasis did it reject the idea of an honest, open, and deplorable break-up of his well-earned reputation and respectability. He could not really contemplate either course, but of the two the first was a shade the farther away from the confines of possibility. And if some similar revelation told him that he was nothing to Norah beyond a kind, just employer with certain tastes and perceptions akin to her own? There was no path there either: he could not see how to proceed. . . . But he experienced no sense of self-censure in having got himself into this impossible place. It had not been his fault: only those who were quite ignorant of the nature of love could blame him for loving. A fish who did not need the air might as well say to a drowning man, 'It is quite unnecessary to breathe; you have only to make a determined effort, and convince yourself that you needn't breathe. Look at me: I don't breathe, and I swim about in the utmost comfort. It is very wrong to breathe!'

Then suddenly all surmise and speculation was expunged from his mind, for no longer the clack of the typewriting machine came from next door. He heard the stir of a chair pushed back, and the rattle of a door handle. Norah was coming; who was of greater concern than all his thoughts about her. . . . And he was going to give her no quarter: she would have to introduce the subject of her feelings with regard to his niggardly hospital-subscription herself. He knew something of her pride from the affair of the book-plate, and he longed to see her take that armour off.

He looked rather grimly at his watch.

'You are rather late,' he said.

Apparently the breast-plate was not to be taken off just yet. She answered him as she had not answered him for many weeks.

'I am afraid I am, sir,' she said. 'But you kindly invited me to go to the luncheon and the opening of the new wing. I have been working ever since.'

He delighted in her, in the astonishing irony of her calling him 'sir' again. He had deserved it too, for he had spoken to her with the old office manner.

'Have you them ready for me now?' he asked, keeping the farce up.

'Yes, sir. They only want your signature.'

He drew the sheets towards him, and began signing in silence, wondering when she proposed to say how sorry she was for misjudging him about his generosity. Surely he could not have misinterpreted that radiant glance she gave him when he rose to reply to the toast of his health.

She had gone back for a moment into her room to fetch the pile of directed envelopes which she had forgotten. Most injudiciously he allowed himself a swift glance at her as she re-entered, and saw beyond doubt that the corners of her mouth were twitching, that her eyes danced with some merriment that she could not completely control. His own face was better in command, and he knew he wore his grimmest aspect as he continued glancing through her typed letters and scrawling his name at the foot. As usual, she took each sheet from him, blotted it, and put it into its envelope. She always refused to use the little piece of damped sponge for the gumming of the envelopes, but employed the tip of her tongue.

'Is that all?' he said, when he had gone through the pile.

'Yes, sir.'

He rose. Had he been wrong about the glance he had got from her? If so, he might have been wrong in everything that concerned her from the first day of her appearance here.

'I shall be getting home then,' he said.

At the door he turned back again. Once more she had beaten him.

'Look here, Miss Propert,' he said. 'There's enough of this.'

She laughed straight out.

'Oh, I am so glad you said that,' she said. 'I was going to let you turn the door-handle before I spoke.'

He put down his hat again.

'Oh, you were, were you?' he said. 'Well, what were you going to say when I did turn the door-handle?'

'I think you are rather brutal,' she said. 'You don't help me out at all.'

'Not an atom,' he said.

'You know quite well. First I was going to apologise for all the thoughts that had ever been in my mind about you and the hospital. I was an utter fool not to have known that you were the most generous——'

He interrupted her.

'Never mind that.'

'But I do mind that. It was idiotic of me, and it was ungrateful of me. I should have known you better than that.'

She came a step closer.

'Will you forgive me?' she said. 'I adored that moment when your name was announced. I felt so proud of serving you.'

He held out his hand.

'That is very friendly of you,' he said. 'But we are friends, aren't we?'

And again she looked at him with that brightness and radiance in her face that he had seen once before only.

CHAPTER IX

It is perhaps hardly necessary to state that Mrs Keeling on the eve of the ceremony for the opening of the Keeling wing had subscribed to a press cutting agency which would furnish her with innumerable accounts of all she knew so well. But print was an even more substantial joy than memory, and there appeared in the local press the most gratifying panegyrics on her husband. These were delightful enough, but most of all she loved the account of herself at that monumental moment when she presented the Princess with the bouquet of daffodils and gypsophila. She was never tired of the perusal of this, nor of the snapshot which some fortunate photographer had taken of her in the very middle of her royal curtsey, as she was actually handing the bouquet. This was reproduced several times: she framed one copy and kept all the rest, with the exception of one with regard to which she screwed herself up to the point of generosity that was necessary before she could prevail on herself to send it to her mother.

Then, while still the industrious press-cutters had not yet come to the end of those appetising morsels, the packets on her breakfast table swelled in size again, and she was privileged to read over and over again that the honour of a baronetcy had been conferred on her husband. She did not mind how often she read this; all the London papers reproduced the gratifying intelligence, and though the wording in most of these was absolutely identical, repetition never caused the sweet savour to cloy on her palate. She was like a girl revelling in chocolate-drops; though they all tasted precisely alike, each tasted delicious, and she felt she could go on eating them for ever. Even better than those stately clippings from the great London luminaries were the more detailed coruscations of the local press. They gave biographies of her husband, magnanimously suppressing the fish-shop, and dwelling only on the enterprise which had made and the success which had crowned the Stores, and many (these were the sweetest of all) gave details about herself and her parentage and the number of her children. She was not habitually a great reader, only using books as a soporific till they tumbled from her drowsy grasp, but now she became a wakeful and enthusiastic student. The whole range of literature, since the days of primeval epics, had never roused in her one tithe of the emotion that those clippings afforded.

Keeling himself had no such craving to see in print all that he was perfectly well aware of, and even looked undazzled at the cards which his wife had ordered, on one set of which he appeared alone as 'Sir Thomas Keeling, Bart.,' to differentiate him from mere knights, whilst on the other the Bart. appeared in conjunction with her. But the events themselves filled him with a good deal of solid satisfaction, due largely to their bearing on the approaching election at the County Club. Never from a business point of view had there been a more successful 'timing' of an enterprise: it was as if on the very day of his getting out his summer fashions, summer had come, with floods of hot sunshine that made irresistible to the ladies of Bracebridge the muslins and organdies and foulards that floated diaphanously in the freshly dressed windows. The summer of his munificence and his honours had just burst on the town, and, in spite of Lord Inverbroom's warning, he felt, as he walked down to his office on the morning of the day on which the election took place, that every member of the Club would be, so to speak, a customer for his presence in future in those staid bow-windows. During these months of his Mayoralty, he had come into contact with, and had been at civic functions the host of a quantity of members of the County Club whose suffrages he sought to-day, and there was none among them who had not shown him courtesy and even deference. That no doubt was largely due to his position as mayor, but this Thomas Keeling who was a candidate for the Club was the mayor, he who had given the new wing to the hospital, thereby averting a very unpleasant financial mess, he, too, whom his King had delighted to honour. To the business mind nothing could have happened more opportunely, and the business mind was his mind. He could not see how he could fail, after this bouquet of benefits and honours, to be 'an attractive proposition' to any club. As he walked down to his office that morning he swept the cobweb of Lord Inverbroom's apprehensions away, and wondered at himself for having allowed them to infect him with a moment's uneasiness, or to make him consider, even at the very back of his brain, what he should do if he were not elected. This morning he did not consider that at all: he was sure that the contingency for which he had provided would not arrive. The provision was filed away, and with it, shut up in the dusty volume, was the suggestion his agent had made that he might quite reasonably raise the rent that the Club paid for the premises which were now his property. That business was just concluded; he proposed to inform Lord Inverbroom at once of the fact that he was now the landlord of the County Club, and that the question of a rise in the rental might be considered as shelved. Lord Inverbroom would be in Bracebridge this morning, since he would be presiding at the election at the Club at twelve o'clock, and had promised to communicate the result at once. Very likely Keeling would drop in at the club to have a bit of lunch there, and he could get a chat with Lord Inverbroom then. . . . But as he slid upwards in the droning lift that took him to the floor where his office was, the Club, the election, and all connected with it, vanished from his brain like the dispersing mists on a summer morning, for a few steps would take him along the corridor to the room where Norah was opening his letters.

That moment of his entry had become to him a matter of daily excitement and expectation. Sometimes the soft furrow would be ruled between her eyebrows, and she would give him but the glance of a stranger and a chilly 'Good-morning,' and instantly turn her attention to her work again. Sometimes she would show such a face as she had shown him that Sunday morning on the downs when they had listened to the skylark together, a face of childhood and the possession of spring, sometimes (and it was this that gave the grizzled elderly man the tremulous excitement of a boy when his hand opened the door) she would give him that look which had shot across the town-hall like the launching of a silver spear and transfixed him. But if he did not get it then, sometime during the morning, in some pause in the work, or perhaps even in the middle of his dictation, he would receive it from her, just that one look which made him know, so long as it lasted, that there was no bar or impediment between himself and her. 'There was neither speech nor language,' but her essential self spoke, revealing, affirming to him its existence. Then without pause she would drop her eyes to her work again, and her busy pencil scooped and dabbed over the paper, and he heard in some secret place of his brain, while his lips pronounced sharp business-like sentences, the words, 'And thou beside me singing in the wilderness.' . . . In the afternoon, when he came to read over her typewritten transcription of the dictation, he always knew at what point in some peremptory letter out of all the sheaf that moment of the clear glance had come. He was always on the look-out for it, but he could never induce it: she gave it him, so it had begun to seem, not in answer to him, but just when she could withhold it no longer.

This morning the correspondence was both heavy and complicated. A whole series of widely scattered dates had to be turned up, in order to trace some question of the payment of carriage on a certain consignment. It was a tiresome job, which Norah recommended him to leave for verification to the clerk downstairs whose business it was, and probably for that very reason Sir Thomas insisted on doing it himself. He was fractious, he was obstinately determined to have the matter settled here and now, and like a child, cross with hunger, he wanted the clear look she had not yet given him. The furrow, that soft smudge, had long been marked on Norah's forehead, as she turned up letter after letter that failed to deal with the point, and she spent what she considered a wasted half hour over it. She was still rather irritated when she found what she had been looking for, unclipped the communciation from the spring that fastened it into its place and passed it him.

'I think that's what you are wanting, Sir Thomas,' she said.

He took it from her, and noticing the rather incisive politeness of her tone, looked up at her. The furrow was still there, very impatiently ruled, but the clear glance was there also: radiantly it shone on him, quite undisturbed by the superficial agitation. It concerned not the surface of her, but the depths.

He did not look at the paper she handed him, on which his unconscious fingers had closed. He was not going to miss one infinitesimal fraction of the moment that she had at last given him. She frowned still, but that was the property of her tiresome search: it was neither his nor hers, as he or she 'mattered.'

'You will find it on the third line from the end,' she said. 'Messrs Hampden are perfectly right about it.'

And then the moment was over, except that in the secret place of his brain the voice sang in the wilderness, and he looked at the letter she had given him. The words danced and swam; presently they steadied themselves.

'I see,' he said. 'Well then, Miss Propert, you must cross out what I have dictated to you about it. Please read the letter through. . . . Yes, cross out from the sentence beginning, "Re the payment for carriage of goods." Dear me, it is nearly one: what a lot of time we have spent over that. The booking-clerk would have done it much more quickly.'

The frown cleared, but the clear look did not return. It was over: it seemed she had satisfied herself.

'I think we should have saved time,' she said.

'Yes, you were quite right. You like being right, don't you?'

He got a smile for that, the sort of smile that anybody might have had from her.

'I suppose I do,' she said. 'Certainly I hate being wrong.'

'But I was wrong this time,' he said. 'I gave you a lot of trouble in consequence.'

That again was no use: he but got another smile and a friendly look of the sort he no longer wanted.

'Is that all, then?' he asked.

'No, Sir Thomas, there are half a dozen more letters yet.'

He had just taken the next, when there came a tap at the door, and a boy entered. He was not one of the messenger-boys of the Stores, with peaked cap and brass buttons, but Keeling had an impression of having seen him before. Then he recollected: he often lounged at the door of the County Club.

'A note from Lord Inverbroom, sir,' he said. 'His lordship told me to give it you personally.'

'Wait and see if there is an answer,' said Keeling.

He tore open the envelope: it was already after one, and probably there would be no answer, since he would see Lord Inverbroom at the Club, where he proposed to have lunch. The note was quite short.

'DEAR SIR THOMAS,—I promised to let you know the result of the election. The meeting is just over, and I am sorry to say you have not been elected. Please allow me to express my sincere regrets.

'Yours truly,

'INVERBROOM.'

Keeling had one moment of sheer surprise: he had been perfectly sure of being elected. Then without any conscious feeling of rancour or disappointment, his mind passed direct to what he had already determined to do if this contingency, which since the opening of the hospital-wing he had thought impossible, actually occurred.

'Wait a moment,' he said to the messenger.

'There will be an answer for you to take back to Lord Inverbroom.'

He turned to Norah.

'Please take this down direct on your typewriter,' he said, 'with a carbon copy to file.'

Norah put the two sheets on the roller, dated the paper, and waited.

Keeling thought for half a minute, drumming with his fingers on the table.

'Are you ready?' he said, and dictated.

'DEAR LORD INVERBROOM,—Yours to hand re the election at the County Club to-day of which I note the contents.

'I wish also to acquaint you as President with the fact that I have lately bought the freehold of your premises. I see that there is a break in your lease at Midsummer this year on both tenants' and landlord's side, and therefore beg to give you this formal notice that I do not intend to renew the lease hitherto held by your Club, as I shall be using the premises for some other purpose.

'Yours faithfully,

'Read it over please Miss Propert,' he said, 'and I will sign it. File this note of Lord Inverbroom's with your carbon copy, and docket them.'

Norah brought him over the typed letter.

'What docket shall I put on them?' she asked.

'Non-election to County Club. Notice of termination of Club's lease.'

He signed the letter to Lord Inverbroom and sent the boy back with it.

'Now we will go on with the rest of the shorthand,' he said.

Norah came back to the table, took up her pencil and then laid it down again. The frown was heavily creased in her forehead.

'May I just say something to you before we begin?' she said. 'You may think it a great impertinence, but it is not meant impertinently.'

'What is it?' he said.

'I beg you to call the boy back, and not send that note,' she said. 'I hate to think of your doing that. It isn't the act of——'

She stopped suddenly. He easily supplied the rest of her sentence.

'It isn't the act of a gentleman,' he said. 'But they've just told me that I'm not one, or they would have elected me. They will like to know how right they are.'

He paused a moment.

'I am sure you did not mean an impertinence, Miss Propert,' he added, 'but I think you have committed one.'

'I am very sorry then,' said she.

'Yes. We will get on with the shorthand, please.'

Keeling seldom wasted thought or energy on

irremediable mischances: if a business proposition turned out badly he cut his loss on it, and dismissed it from his mind. But it was equally characteristic of him to strike, and strike hard, if opportunity offered at any firm which had let him in for his loss, and, in this case, since the Club had hit at him, he felt it was but fair that he should return the blow with precise and instantaneous vigour. That was right and proper, and his rejoinder to Norah that the Club who did not consider him sufficient of a gentleman to enter their doors should have the pleasure of knowing how right they were, had at least as much sober truth as irony about it. The opportunity to hit back was ready to hand; it would have been singular indeed, and in flat contradiction to his habits, if he had not taken it. But when once he had done that, he was satisfied; they did not want him as a member, and he did not want them as tenants, and there was the end of it. Yet, like some fermenting focus in his brain, minute as yet, but with the potentiality of leaven in it, was the fact that Norah had implored him not to send his answer to Lord Inverbroom. He still considered her interference an impertinence, but what stuck in his mind and began faintly to suggest other trains of thought was the equally undeniable fact that she had not meant it as an impertinence. In intention it had been a friendly speech inspired by the good-will of a friend. But he shrugged his shoulders at it: she did not understand business, or, possibly, he did not understand clubs. So be it then: he did not want to understand them.

It was with a mixture of curiosity and annoyance that he saw Lord Inverbroom walking towards him along Alfred Road when he left the Stores that afternoon. The curiosity was due to the desire to see how Lord Inverbroom would behave, whether he would cross the street or cut him dead; the annoyance arose from the fact that he could not determine how to behave himself at this awkward encounter. But when he observed that there was to be no cutting or crossing the street at all, but perfect cordiality and an outstretched hand, it faintly and pleasantly occurred to him that, owing to his letter, there might be forthcoming another election at the Club, with a request that he would submit himself to a further suffrage. That would certainly have pleased him, for he had sufficient revengefulness in his character to decline such a proposition with thanks.

No such proposition was submitted to him.

'I was just going to leave this note at your office, Sir Thomas,' said Lord Inverbroom. 'May I give it you instead and save myself a further walk? It is just the acknowledgment of your letter about the termination of our lease. Perhaps you will glance at it, to see that it is in order.'

Keeling felt, in spite of his business-like habits,

that this was unnecessary. True, this was a matter of business, and he should have verified the correctness of Lord Inverbroom's information. But instead he merely put it into his pocket.

'That is all right,' he said.

'Are you going home?' asked the other. 'My wife, I know, is calling on Lady Keeling, and she will pick me up there. If she has not been so fortunate as to find Lady Keeling in, she will wait for me in the motor. May we not walk down there together?'

'I shall be delighted,' said Keeling. He still did not know how to behave, but was gradually becoming aware that no 'behaviour' was necessary. 'Behaviour,' as such, did not seem to exist for his companion, and he could not help wondering what took its place.

'My wife is furious with me,' Lord Inverbroom went on. 'I have succumbed to the Leonardo book, instead of having the dining-room ceiling whitewashed. She has a materialistic mind, preferring whitewash to Leonardo. Besides, as I told her, she never looks at the ceiling, and I shall often look at my book. Have you come across anything lately which life is not worth living without? Perhaps you had better not tell me if you have, or I shall practise some further domestic economy.'

'I shall be very pleased to show you anything I've got,' said Keeling. 'We will have a cup of tea in my library unless Lady Inverbroom is waiting in your motor.'

'Ah, that would be a great treat. Let us do that, in any case, Sir Thomas. Surely we can go in some back way so as to escape my wife's notice if she is really waiting outside. It will do her good to wait: she is very impatient.'

Keeling was completely puzzled: if he had ventured to speak in this sense of Lady Keeling, he knew he would have made a sad mess of it. In his mouth, the same material would have merely expressed itself in a rude light. He tried rather mistakenly to copy the manner that was no manner at all.

'Ah, I should get a good scolding if I treated Lady Keeling like that,' he said.

It did not sound right as he said it; he had the perception of that. He perceived, too, that Lord Inverbroom did not pursue the style. Then, presently arriving, they found that the waiting motor contained no impatient Lady Inverbroom, and they stole into the library, at her husband's desire, so that no news of his coming should reach her, until he had had a quarter of an hour there with his host. Then perhaps she might be told, if Sir Thomas would have the goodness. . . .

Lord Inverbroom sauntered about in the grazing, ambulatory fashion of the book-lover; and when his quarter of an hour was already more than spent, he put the volume he was examining back into its place again with a certain air of decision.

'I should like to express to you by actual word of mouth, Sir Thomas,' he said, 'my regret at what happened to-day. I am all the more sorry for it, because I notice that in our rules the landlord of the club is *ex officio* a member of it. If you only had told me that you had become our landlord, I could have informed you of that, and spared you this annoyance.'

There was no mistaking the sincerity of this, the good feeling of it. Keeling was moved to be equally sincere.

'I knew that already,' he said.

Lord Inverbroom looked completely puzzled.

'Then will you pardon me for asking why you did not take advantage of it, and become a member of the club without any further bother?'

'Because I wished to know that I was acceptable as a member of the club to the other members,' said Keeling. 'They have told me that I am not.'

There was a good deal of dignity in this reply: it sprang from a feeling that Lord Inverbroom was perfectly competent to appreciate.

'I understand,' he said. 'And what you have said much increases my regret at the election going as it did.' He paused a moment, evidently thinking, and Keeling, had an opportunity to wager been offered him, would have bet that his next words would convey, however delicately, the hope that Keeling would reconsider his letter of the morning, announcing the termination of the Club's lease. He was not prepared to do anything of the sort, and hoped, indeed, that the suggestion would not be made. But that he should have thought that the suggestion was going to be made showed very precisely how unintelligible to him was the whole nature of the class which Lord Inverbroom represented. No such suggestion was made, any more than half an hour ago any idea of a fresh election being held was mooted.

'I had the pleasure of speaking very warmly in your favour, Sir Thomas,' said Lord Inverbroom, at length, 'and, of course, of voting for you. I may tell you that I am now considering, in consequence of the election, whether I shall not resign the presidency of the Club. It is an unusual proceeding to reject the president's candidate; I think your rejection reflects upon me.'

Keeling was being insensibly affected by his companion's simplicity. 'Behaviour' seemed a very easy matter to Lord Inverbroom: it was a mere matter of being simple . . .

'I should be very sorry to have been the cause of that,' he said, 'and I don't think it would be logical of you. You urged me to withdraw, which was the most you could do after you had promised to propose me.'

Lord Inverbroom's sense of being puzzled increased. Here was a man who had written a letter this morning turning the Club out of their premises merely because he had been blackballed, who yet showed, both by the fact of his seeking election in the ordinary way instead of claiming it *ex officio*, and by this delicate unbusiness-like appreciation of his own position, all those instincts which his letter of this morning so flatly contradicted.

'Yes, I urged you not to stand,' he said, 'and that is the only reason why I hesitate about resigning. I should like you to know that if I remain in my post, that is the cause of my doing so. Otherwise I should resign.'

The other side of the question presented itself to Keeling. It would be a rare stroke to deprive the Club not only of its premises but of its president. Though he had just said that he hoped Lord Inverbroom would not resign, he felt it would be an extreme personal pleasure if he did. And then a further scheme came into his head, another nail in the coffin of the County Club, and with that all his inherent caddishness rose paramount over such indications of feelings as Lord Inverbroom understood and appreciated.

'Perhaps if you left the County Club,' he said, 'you would do us the honour to join the Town Club. I am the president of that: I would think it, however, an honour to resign my post if you would consent to take it. I'll warrant you there'll be no mischance over that election.'

Lord Inverbroom suddenly stiffened.

'You are very good to suggest that,' he said. 'But it would be utterly out of the question. Well, Sir Thomas, I envy you your library. And here, I see, is your new catalogue. Miss Propert told me she was working at it. May I look at it? Yes, indeed, that is admirably done. Author and title of the book and illustrator as well, all entered. Her father was a great friend of mine. She may have told you that very tragic story.'

'She has never mentioned her father to me. Was he—well, the sort of man whom the County Club would not have blackballed?'

Perhaps that was the worst thing he had said yet, though, indeed, he meant but a grimly humourous observation, not perceiving nor being able to perceive in how odious a position he put his guest. But Lord Inverbroom's impenetrable armour of effortless good breeding could turn even that aside. He laughed.

'Well, after what the Club has done to-day,' he said, 'there is no telling whom they would blackball. But certainly I should have have been, at one time, very happy to propose him.'

Keeling's preoccupation with the Club suddenly ceased. He wanted so much more to know anything that concerned Norah.

'Perhaps you would tell me something about him,' he said.

'Ah, that would not be quite right, would it?'

said Lord Inverbroom, still unperturbed, 'if Miss Propert has not cared to speak to you of him.'

Keeling found himself alternately envying and detesting this impenetrable armour. There was no joint in it, it was abominably complete. And even while he hated it, he appreciated and coveted it.

'I understand,' he said. 'No telling tales out of school.'

'Quite so. And now will you take me to find my wife? Let us be in a conspiracy, and not mention that we have been in the house half an hour already. I should dearly like another half-hour, but all the time Lady Keeling is bearing the infliction of a prodigiously long call.'

'Lady Keeling will be only too gratified,' said her husband.

'That is very kind of her. But, indeed, I think we had better go.'

Gratification was certainly not too strong a term to employ with regard to Lady Keeling's feelings, nor, indeed, too strong to apply to Lady Inverbroom's when her call was brought to an end. The sublimity of Princesses was not to be had every day, and the fortnight that had elapsed since that memorable visit, with the return of the routine of undistinguished Bracebridge, had caused so prolonged a visit from a peeress to mount into Lady Keeling's head like an hour's steady drinking of strong wine.

'Well, I've never enjoyed an hour's chat more,' she said, as Keeling returned after seeing their guests off, 'and it seemed no more than five minutes. She was all affability, wasn't she, Alice? and so full of admiration for all my—what did she call them? Some French word.'

'Bibelots,' suggested Alice.

'Biblos; that was it. And she never seemed to think how time was flying, for she never once alluded to her husband's being so late. To be sure she might have; she might perhaps have said she was afraid she was keeping me from my occupations, for I could have assured her very handsomely that I was more than pleased to sit and talk to her. And it is all quite true, Thomas, about the Princess's visit next month. You may be sure I asked about that. She is coming down to spend three days with them, very quietly, Lady Inverbroom said; yes, she said that twice now I come to think of it, though I caught it perfectly the first time. But I shall be very much surprised if I don't get a note asking us to dine and sleep, with Alice as well perhaps, for I said what a pleasure it would be to Alice to see her beautiful house and grounds some day. But I shall quite understand after what she said about the visit being very quiet, why there will be no party. After all, it was a very pleasant evening we spent there before when there were no guests at all. I said how much we enjoyed quiet visits with no ceremony.'

'Did you ask for any more invitations?' said Keeling, as his wife paused for breath.

'My dear Thomas, you quite misunderstand me. I asked for nothing, except that I might take Mamma some day for a drive through their park. I hope I know how to behave better than that. Another thing, too: Miss Propert has been there twice, once to tea and once to lunch. I hope she will not have her head turned, for it seems that she did not take her meals in the housekeeper's room, but upstairs. But that is none of my business: I am sure Lady Inverbroom may give her lunch on the top of the church-steeple if she wishes, and I said very distinctly that I had always found her a very well-behaved young woman, and mentioned nothing about her bouncing in in the middle of my dinner-party, nor when she spent Sunday morning in your library. Bygones are bygones. That's what I always say, and act on, too.'

This certainly appeared to have been the case: Lady Keeling's miscroscopic mind seemed to have diverted its minute gaze altogether from Norah. To Keeling that was a miscroscopic relief, but no more, for it seemed to him to matter very little what his wife thought about Norah.

'Lord Inverbroom was a great friend of Miss Propert's father at one time,' he said. 'He told me so only to-day.'

'Oh, indeed. Very likely in the sense that a

man may call his butler an old friend of the family. I should be quite pleased to speak of Parkinson like that. I am all for equality. We are all equal in the sight of Heaven, as Mr Silverdale says. Dear me, I wish I was his equal in energy: next month he holds a mission down at Easton Haven among all those ruffians at the docks, in addition to all his parish work.'

'He is doing far too much,' said Alice excitedly, 'but he won't listen. He is so naughty: he promises me he will be good, and not wear himself out, but he goes on just the same as ever, except that he gets worse and worse.'

Keeling listened to this with a mixture of pity and grim amusement. He felt sure that his poor Alice was in love with the man, and was sorry for Alice in that regard, but what grimly amused him was the utter impotence of Alice to keep her condition to herself. He was puzzled also, for all this spring Alice seemed to have remained as much in love with him as ever, but not to have got either worse or better. Silverdale filled her with some frantic and wholly maidenly excitement. It was like the love of some antique spinster for her lap-dog, intense and deplorable and sexless. He could even joke in a discreet manner with poor Alice about it, and gratify her by so doing.

'Well, all you ladies who are so much in love with him ought to be able to manage him,' he said.

Alice bent over her work (she had eventually

induced Mr Silverdale to sanction the creation of a pair of slippers) with a pleased, lop-sided smile.

'Father, you don't know him,' she said. 'He's quite, quite unmanageable. You never saw any one so naughty.'

'Punish him by not giving him his slippers. Give them me instead, and I'll wear them when he comes to dinner.'

Alice looked almost shocked at the notion of such unhallowed feet being thrust into these hardly less than sacred embroideries: it was as if her mother had suggested making a skirt out of the parrots and pomegranates that adorned the 'smart' altar-cloth. But she divined that, in spite of her father's inexplicable want of reverence for the Master (they had become Master and Helper, and sometimes she called him 'sir,' much as Norah had called her father, but for antipodal reasons), there lurked behind his rather unseemly jokes a kindly intention towards herself. He might laugh at her, but somehow below that she felt (and she knew not how) that a part of him understood, and did not laugh. It was as if he knew what it meant to be in love, to thirst and to be unslaked, to be hungry and not to be fed.

She gave him a quick glance out of her short-sighted eyes, a glance that deprecated and yet eagerly sought for the sympathy which she knew was somewhere about. And then Lady Keeling put in more of her wrecking and shattering remarks, which so unerringly spoiled all the hints and lurking colours in human intercourse.

'Well, that would be a funny notion for Sir Thomas Keeling to wear slippers at dinner,' she said. 'What a going-back to old days! I might as well wear some high-necked merino gown. But what your father says is quite true, Alice. We might really take Mr Silverdale in hand, and tell him that's the last he'll see of us all, unless he takes more care of himself. I saw him coming out of the County Club to-day, looking so tired that I almost stopped my carriage and told him to go home to bed. And talking of the County Club, Thomas, doesn't your election come on soon? You must be sure to take me to have lunch in the ladies' room one of these days. Lady Inverbroom told me she was lunching there to-day, and had quite a clean good sort of meal. Nothing very choice, I expect, but I dare say she doesn't care much what she eats. I shall never forget what a tough pheasant we had when we dined there. If I'd been told I was eating a bit of leather, I should have believed it. Perhaps some day when Lord and Lady Inverbroom are in Bracebridge again, we might all have lunch together there.'

For the last six months Keeling had been obliged to keep a hand on himself when he was with his wife, for either she had developed an amazing talent for putting him on edge, or he a suscepti-bility for being irritated by her. Both causes probably contributed, for since her accession to greatness, her condescension had vastly increased, while he on his side had certainly grown more sensitive to her pretentiousness. It was with the utmost difficulty that he restrained himself from snapping at her.

'No, I'm afraid that can't be, Emmeline,' he said. 'The election came off to-day, and the Club has settled it can do without me.'

'Well, I never heard of such a thing! They haven't elected you, do you mean, the Mayor of Bracebridge, and to say nothing of your being a baronet? Who are those purse-proud people, I should like to know? My dear Thomas, I have an idea. I should not wonder if Lord Inverbroom was in it. He has been quite cock of the walk, as you may say, up till now, and he doesn't want any rival. What are you going to do? I hope you'll serve them out well for it somehow.'

'I have done so already. I bought the freehold of the Club not so long ago, and I have given them notice that I shall not renew their lease in the summer.'

Lady Keeling clapped her soft fat hands together.

'That's the right sort of way to treat them,' she said, in great glee. 'That will pay them out. I never heard of such a thing as not electing a baronet. Who do they think they are? What fun it will be to see all their great sofas being bundled into the street. And they bought all their furniture at your Stores, did they not? That is the cream of it to my mind. I should not wonder if they want to sell it all back to you, second-hand. That would be a fine joke.'

For the first time, now that his wife so lavishly applauded his action, Keeling began to be not so satisfied with it. The fact that it commended itself to her type of mind, was an argument against it: her praise disgusted him: it was at least as impertinent as Norah's disapprobation.

Alice fixed her faint eyes on her father.

'Oh, I wish you hadn't done that!' she said. 'Does Lord Inverbroom know that?'

'Mark my words,' said his wife, 'Lord Inverbroom's at the bottom of it all.'

'Nothing of the kind, Emmeline,' he said sharply. 'Lord Inverbroom proposed me.'

Then he turned to Alice.

'Yes, he knows,' he said. 'I gave notice to him. And why do you wish I hadn't done it? I declare I'm getting like Mr Silverdale. All the ladies are concerning themselves with me. There's your mother saying I've done right, and you and Miss Propert saying I've done wrong. There's no pleasing you all.'

'And what has Miss Propert got to do with it,' asked Lady Keeling, 'that she disapproves of what you've done? She'll be wanting to run your Stores for you next, and just because she's been to lunch with Lord Inverbroom. I never heard of such impertinence as Miss Propert giving her opinion. You'll have trouble with your Miss Propert. You ought to give her one of your good snubs, or dismiss her altogether. That would be far the best.'

Keeling felt as some practitioner of *sortes Virgilianæ* might do when he had opened at some strangely apposite text. To consult his wife about anything was like opening a book at random, a wholly irrational proceeding, but he could not but be impressed by the sudden applicability of this. His wife did not know the situation, any more than did the musty volume, but he wondered if she had not answered with a strange wisdom, wholly foreign to her.

'Now you have given your opinion, Emmeline,' he said, 'and you must allow somebody else to talk. I want to know why Alice disapproves.'

Alice stitched violently at the slipper.

'Mr Silverdale will be so sorry,' she said. 'He drops in there sometimes for a rubber of bridge, for he thinks that it is such a good thing to show that a clergyman can be a man of the world too.'

Keeling rose: this was altogether too much for him.

'Well, we've wasted enough time talking about it all,' he said, 'if that's all the reason I'm to hear.'

'But it isn't,' said Alice. 'I can't express it, but I can feel it. I know I should agree with Miss

Propert and Lord Inverbroom about it. What did Miss Propert say?'

'Well, talking of waste of time,' observed Lady Keeling indignantly, 'I can't think of any worse waste than caring to know what Miss Propert said.'

Keeling turned to her.

'Perhaps you can't,' he said, 'and you'd better have your nap. That won't be waste of time. You're tired with talking, and I'm sure I am too.'

He left the room without more words, and Lady Keeling settled another cushion against what must be called the small of her back.

'Your father's served them out well,' she said. 'That's the way to get on. To think of their not considering him good enough for their Club. He has shown his spirit very properly. But the idea of Miss Propert telling him what's right and what isn't, on twenty-five shillings a week.'

'I can't bear to think of Mr Silverdale not having his rubber of bridge now and then,' said Alice. 'It was such a refreshment to him.'

Keeling had intended to pass an hour among his books to wash off the scum, so to speak, of this atrocious conversation, but when he got to his library, and had taken down his new edition of Omar Khayyam, which Charles Propert had induced him to buy, he found it could give him very little emotion. He was aware of the exquisite type, of the strange sensuous wood-cuts that somehow affected him like a subtle odour, of the beautiful binding, and not least of the text itself, but all these perfections were no more than presented to him; they did not penetrate. He could not rid himself of the scum; the odiousness of his wife's approbation would not be washed off. And what made it cling was the fact that she had divined him correctly, had rejoiced at his 'serving the Club out.' It was just that which Norah deprecated, and he felt that Lord Inverbroom's complete silence on the point, his forbearance to hint ever so faintly that perhaps Keeling would reconsider his action, expressed disapprobation as eloquently as Norah's phrase, which he had finished for her, had done. It was a caddish act, that was what they both thought about it, and Alice, when she had finished her nonsense about Mr Silverdale's rubber of bridge, had a similar protest in her mind. He did not rate poor Alice's mind at any high figure; it was but the fact that she was allied to the other two, and opposed to her mother, that added a little weight to her opinion.

He wanted to be considered a gentleman, and when others declined to receive him as such, he had but justified their verdict by behaving like a cad. . . . He was a cad, here was the truth of it, as it struck him now, and that was why he had behaved like one.

He shut his meaningless book, now intensely disliking the step he had taken, which at the time had seemed so smart a rejoinder. Probably if at this moment Lord Inverbroom had appeared, asking him to cancel it, he would have done so. But that was exactly what it was certain Lord Inverbroom would not do. There remained Norah; he wondered whether Norah would refer to it again. Probably not: he had made clear that he thought the offering of her opinion was a great impertinence. And now to his annoyance he remembered that his wife had also considered it as such. Again she agreed with him, and again the fact of her concurrence made him lose confidence in the justice of his own view. He had instantly acquitted Norah of deliberate impertinence; now he reconsidered whether it had been an impertinence at all. . . . What if it was the simple desire of a friend to save a friend from a blunder, an unworthiness?

He had grown to detest the time after dinner passed in the plushy, painted drawing-room. Hitherto, in all these years of increasing prosperity, during which the conscious effort of his brain had been directed to business and money-making, he had not objected after the work of the day to pass a quiescent hour or two before his early bed-time giving half an ear to his wife's babble, which, with her brain thickened with refreshment, always reached its flood-tide of voluble incoherence now, giving half an eye to Alice with her industrious needle. All the time a vague simmer of mercantile meditation gently occupied him; his mind, like some kitchen fire with the damper pushed in, kept itself just alight, smouldered and burned low, and Alice's needle was but like the bars of the grate, and his wife's prattle the mild rumble of water in the boiler. It was all domestic and normal, in accordance with the general destiny of prosperous men in middle age. Indeed, he was luckier in some respects than the average, for there had always been for him his secret garden, the *hortus inclusus*, into which neither his family nor his business interests ever entered. Now even that had been invaded, Norah's catalogue had become to him the most precious of his books: she was like sunshine in his secret garden or like a bitter wind, something, anyhow, that got between him and his garden beds, while here in the drawing-room in the domestic hour after dinner the fact of her made itself even more insistently felt, for she turned Lady Keeling's vapidities, to which hitherto he had been impervious, into an active stinging irritation, and even poor Alice's industrious needle and the ever-growing pattern of Maltese crosses on Mr Silverdale's slippers was like some monotonous recurring drip of water that set his nerves on edge. This was a pretty state of mind, he told himself, for a hardheaded business man of fifty, and yet even as with all the force of resolution that was in him he tried to find something in his wife's remarks that could awake a relevant reasonable reply, some rebellious consciousness in his brain would only concern itself with counting on the pink clock the hours that lay between the present moment and nine o'clock next morning. And then the pink clock melodiously announced on the Westminster chime that it was half past ten, and Alice put her needle into the middle of the last Maltese cross, and Lady Keeling waddled across the room and tapped the barometer, which a marble Diana held in her chaste hand, to see if the weather promised well for the bazaar to-morrow. The evening was over, and there would not be another for the next twenty-four hours.

He was always punctual at his office; lately he had been before his time there, and had begun to open letters before Norah arrived. This happened next morning, and among others that he had laid on his desk was Lord Inverbroom's acknowledgment of his notice to terminate the County Club's lease. Norah, when she came, finished this business for him, and in due course handed him the completed pile. Then, as usual, she took her place opposite him for the dictation of answers. She wore at her breast a couple of daffodils, and he noticed that, as she breathed, the faint yellow reflection they cast on her chin stirred upwards and downwards. No word had passed between them since she had expressed regret for what he considered her impertinence the day before, and this morning she did not once meet his eye. Probably she considered herself in disgrace, and it maddened him to see her quiet acceptance of it, which struck him as contemptuous. She was like some noble slave, working, because she must work, for a master she despised. Well, if that was her attitude, so be it. She might despise, but he was master. At his request she read out a letter she had just taken down. In the middle he stopped her.

'No, you have got that wrong,' he said. 'What I said was this,'—and he repeated it—'please attend more closely.'

She made no reply, and two minutes afterwards he again found her at fault. And the brutality, the desire to make the beloved suffer, which in very ugly fashion often lies in wait close to the open high road of love, became more active.

'You are wasting your time and mine, Miss Propert,' he said, 'if you do not listen.'

Again he waited for some reply, some expression of regret which she undoubtedly owed him, but none came. Then, looking up, while her pencil was busy, he saw that she did not reply because she could not. The reflection of the daffodils trembled violently on her chin, and her lower teeth were fast clenched on her upper lip to stifle the surrender of her mouth. And when he saw that, all his brutality, all the impulse that bade him hurt the thing he loved, drained out of him, and left him hateful to himself.

He paused, leaving unfinished the sentence he was dictating, and sat there silent, not daring to look at her. He still felt she despised him, and now with additional reason; he resented the fact that any one should do that, his pride choked him, and yet he was ashamed. But oh, the contrast between this very uncomfortable moment, and the comfortable evenings with Emmeline!

But he could not bring himself to apologise, and presently he resumed his dictation. Norah, it appeared, had recovered control of herself, and when that letter was finished, she read it over to him quite steadily. The next she handed him was Lord Inverbroom's acknowledgment, which he had himself placed among the rest of the morning's correspondence.

'Is that just to be filed?' she said, 'or is there any answer?'

He took it up.

'Yes, there's an answer,' he said, and dictated.

'DEAR LORD INVERBROOM,—Re lease of premises of County Club. If you will allow me I should like to cancel the notice of termination of said lease which I sent you yesterday, if this would be any convenience to the Club. I should like also to express to you personally my regret for my action.'

He paused.

'I think that's all I need say, Miss Propert, isn't it?' he asked.

And then there came for him the direct glance, a little dim yet, with the 'clear shining after rain' beaming through it.

'Oh, I am so glad,' she said. 'And if it's not impertinent may I suggest something?'

Never had the clear glance lasted so long. He expanded and throve in it.

'Well, go on; but take care,' he said.

'It's only that you should write it yourself,' she said. 'It would be more—more complete.'

'And that will satisfy you?'

'Quite. You will have done yourself justice.'

He pushed back his chair.

'I don't see why you should care,' he said. 'I've treated you like a brute all morning.'

'I know you have. I cared about that too.'

'Would you like me to apologise?' he asked.

She shook her head and pointed at the letter.

'Not again,' she said. 'You've sent me a lovely apology already, addressed to Lord Inverbroom.'

'Have I, indeed? You must have everything your own way. And how are the bluebells getting on?'

'Quite well. They'll all be out in a fortnight, I think. I went to look again yesterday. The buds, fat little buttons, do you remember, have got tall stalks now. And the lark is still singing.'

'May we go there then on Saturday week?' he asked.

She looked down a moment.

'Yes,' she said softly, raising her eyes again. 'And now shall we get on with the letters, Sir Thomas. There are still a good many not answered.'

'I would sooner talk to you,' he said.

'You shall dictate. That will be talking. And I will try to listen very attentively.'

'Now don't be mean, Miss Propert,' said he.

For the second time that morning she let the clear glance shine on him. It brightened like dawn, filling the space between them. And it smote on his heart, stupefyingly sweet.

CHAPTER X

KEELING had ten days to wait for the Saturday when he and Norah were to visit the bluebells together. He knew with that certainty of the heart which utterly transcends the soundest conclusions of reason and logic that she loved him; it seemed, too, that it was tacitly agreed between them that some confession, some mutual revelation would then take place. That was to be the hour of their own, away from the office and the typewriting, and all those things which, though they brought them together, essentially sundered them. What should be said then, what solution could possibly come out of it all, he could form no notion. He ceased even to puzzle over it. Perhaps there was no solution: perhaps this relationship was just static.

Outwardly the days passed precisely as usual. They had made their appointment, and no further allusion or reminder was necessary. Each evening brought nearer the hour of azure in that hollow among the empty downs, and he desired neither to shorten nor to lengthen out the days that separated him from it. But to him everything, except that moment, regular but rarely recurring, when her eye sought his with need and love in it, seemed dream-like and unsubstantial. Nothing had power either to vex or please him. He was, as always, busy all day, and transacted his own or municipal business with all his usual thoroughness and acute judgment. But it all went on outside him; the terra-cotta cupolas which his industry had reared in the market-place were as unreal as the new system of drainage in the lower part of the town, which he had exerted all his influence to get carried through the obdurate conservatism that pointed to the low-death rate of Bracebridge under the old conditions. He got his way; all his life he had been accustomed to dominate and command and organise. Then when his day's work was done, and he returned home for dinner and the ensuing hours, which lately had been so intolerable, he found they irritated him no longer, and the fatuous drip of his wife's conversation was no more to him than some gutter that discharged not into his house but into the street outside. Simply he cared nothing for it, nor, when his failure to get elected to the County Club occurred to him, did he care: it appeared to have happened, but it must have happened to some stranger. Sometimes, before the pink clock announced that it was half-past ten, he would leave the drawing-room and go to his library, to see whether in his books there was to be found anything that stimulated his reactions towards life. But they had no message: they were dumb or he was deaf. Even the catalogue showed no sign of life: it was Norah's work, of course, but it was not Norah.

The day before their tryst out among the downs, this stupefied stagnation of emotion suddenly left him. All morning and through half the afternoon a succession of Spring showers had flung themselves in mad torrents against the plate-glass windows of his office, and more than once he had seen Norah look up, and knew as well as if she had spoken that she was speculating on the likelihood of another drenching afternoon to-morrow. But she said nothing, and again he knew that neither storm nor tempest would keep her back from their appointment, any more than it would keep him. The thing had to be: it was arranged so, and though they should find all the bluebells blackened and battered, and the thunder bellowed round them, that meeting in the bluebell wood was as certain as the rising of the sun. . . . And then the clock on his chimney-piece chimed five, and with a rush of reawakened perception, a change as swift and illuminating as the return of consciousness after an anaesthetic, he realised that by this time to-morrow their meeting would be over, and they would know, each of them, what they were to become to each other. The week's incurious torpor, broken once and sometimes twice a day by her glance, rolled away from him: the world and all that it contained started into vividness again. Simultaneously with the chiming clock, she got up, and brought him the finished type-written letters for his signature. To-day there were but a dozen of them, and the work of reading and signing and bestowal in their envelopes was soon finished. But an intolerable sense of restraint and discomfort surrounded these proceedings: he did not look at her, nor she at him, and though both were hugely conscious of each other, it was as if they were strangers or enemies even under some truce. That feeling increased and intensified: once in handing a letter to him a finger of hers touched his, and both drew their hands quickly away. She hurried over her reading, he scrawled his name; they wanted to get away from each other as soon as was possible. Then the thought that they would have to sit here again together all morning to-morrow occurred to him, and that to him at least was unfaceable. In this reawakened vividness to the crisis that now impended in less than the space of a day and a night, he felt he could not meet her again over common tasks.

It had happened before occasionally that he had given her a holiday on Saturday morning from the half-day's work, and he seized at this, as she handed him the last of the batch to be signed.

'I don't think you need come down to-morrow morning, Miss Propert,' he said. 'You can take the half-day off.'

He did not look up, but heard her give a little sigh of relief, and knew that once again he had found the pulse in her that beat with his own.

'Yes,' she said, and dropped the letters into his post-box.

She had been working that day at the table in his big room and stood there tidying it. Then she went back into the small room adjoining, and he heard her rustle into her mackintosh. Then returning she stood at the door of it a moment and from underneath his half raised eyes, he saw that she looked slowly all round his room, as if, perhaps, searching for something, or as if rather committing it to her memory. Then without another word to him she went out, and he heard her steps tapping along the cement-floored corridor to the lift. Once they paused, and he half-longed, half-dreaded that she was coming back. They began again, and stopped, and immediately afterwards he heard the clang of the grille, and the faint rumble of the descending lift. He had one overpowering impulse that brought him to his feet, to dash downstairs, and see her go out, or if she was gone already to follow her into the street, just for the sake of setting eyes on her once more, but it took him no further than that, and presently he sat down again.

That intense vividness of perception that had been lit within him when, half an hour ago, the clock on his chimney-piece chimed, still blazed.

He noticed a hundred minute details in the room, his ear separated the hum of the street below into its component ingredients: there was a boy whistling, there was a motor standing with its engines still working, there was a street-cry concerning daffodils, another concerning evening papers. Memory was similarly awake: he remembered that his wife was giving a little dinner-party this evening, that Silverdale, who was setting out on his mission to the docks next day, was to be among the guests, and that Alice expected that the slippers of Maltese crosses would be back from being made up, in time for him to take them with him. He recalled, out of the well of years, how in the early days of his married life Emmeline had made him a pair of slippers which did not fit, and in the same breath remembered the exact look of her face this very morning when a message had come from her cook saying that she could not get a bit of salmon anywhere. And as each impression registered itself on eye and ear and memory, he hated it. But nothing concerning Norah came into his mind: sometimes for a moment a blank floated across it, behind which perhaps was Norah, but she produced no image on it. He could not even recollect her face: he did not know what she was like. There was the horror of it all: everything in the world but she had the vividness of nightmare, and she, the only thing that did not belong to nightmare, had gone from him.

He sat there, alone in the darkening room, doing nothing as far as definite effort went, and yet conscious of an intense internal activity in just looking at the myriads of images that this magic lantern of the mind presented to him. Now for a little it seemed to him that he contemplated a series of pictures that concerned the life which had once been his, and was now finished and rolled up, done with for ever. Now again for a little it seemed that all that was thus presented to him was the life that was going to be his, until for him all life was over. Alice would always be sewing slippers, his wife would always be ordering a bit of salmon, he would always be sitting in an empty office. For a few weeks there had passed across those eternal reiterations somebody whose very face he could not now recall, and when he tried to imagine her, he could see nothing but a blank, a black strip where words had been erased. To-morrow by this time he would know which of those two aspects was the true one: either the salmon and the slippers and this lonely meditation would be his no longer, or they would be all that he could call his. He felt, too, that it was already settled which it was to be: fate had already written in the inexorable book, and had closed it again. To-morrow the page would be shown him, he would read what was inscribed there. No effort on his part, no imposition of his will, no power of his to organise and build up would alter it. Though the crisis was yet to come, its issue was already determined.

He struggled against this nightmare sense of impotence. All his life he had designed his own career, in bold firm strokes, and fate had builded as he had planned. Fate was not a predetermined thing: the book of destiny was written by the resolute and strong for themselves, they had a hand on the pen, and made destiny write what they willed. It should be so to-morrow: he had but to determine what he chose should be, and this was the hour of his choice. . . .

Suddenly into the blanks, into the black erasures, there stole the images which just now he had tried in vain to recall. All else was erased, and Norah filled the empty spaces. Her presence, voice and gesture and form pervaded his whole consciousness: there was room for nothing else. They loved each other, and to each other they constituted the sum of all that was real. There was nothing for it but to accept that, to go away together, and let all the unrealities of life, The Cedars, the salmon, the slippers, pass out of focus, be dissolved, disintegrated. . . . And yet, and yet he knew that he did not make the choice with his whole self. Deep down in him, the very foundation on which his character was built, was that hidden rock of his integrity, of his stern Puritanism, of the morality of which his religion was made. He was willing to blow that up, he searched for the explosive that would shatter it, he hacked and hammered at it, as if in experiment to see if he had the power to shatter it. It could hardly be that his character was stronger than himself: that seemed a contradiction in terms.

And yet all else in the world was hateful to him; he could contemplate life neither without Norah nor with her in continuance of their present relations. This afternoon he had longed for her to go away, and when she had gone he had been on the point of hurrying down like a madman into the street only to set eyes on her again. He could not imagine sitting here all day with her week after week, dictating letters, hearing her typing them, getting the clear glance from her now and again (and that would be the most intolerable of all), saying 'good-evening' to her when the day's work was done, and 'good-morning' to her when it was beginning. Something must happen, and whatever that was, was already written in the book. There was no escape.

The clock chimed again, and his room had grown so dark that he had to turn on the electric light to see what the hour was. He went downstairs and through the show rooms, blazing with lights and still populous with customers, into the square. The toneless blue of night had already advanced far past the zenith; in the west a band of orange marked where the sun had set, and just above it was a space of delicate pale green on the upper edge of which a faint star twinkled. As he passed between the hornbeam hedges in the disused graveyard, the odour of the spring night, of dew on the path, of the green growth on the trees, was alert in the air. The mysterious rapture of the renewal of life tingled round him, the summons to expand, to blossom, to love was echoed and re-echoed from the bushes, where mated birds were still chirruping. As he walked through the gathering dusk thick with the choruses of spring, the years fell from him like withered leaves long-lingering, and his step quickened into the pace of youth, though it only bore him to The Cedars, and the amazing futility of one of Lady Keeling's smaller dinner-parties.

Two very auspicious pieces of news awaited him when he got home, and found his wife and Alice just about to go upstairs to dress. Alice's slippers had come back from the shoe-maker's, and could be presented to Mr Silverdale to-night, while, as by a miracle, a bit of salmon had been procured also. Lady Keeling had been driving by that little fishmonger's in Drury Place, and there on the marble slab was quite a nice bit of salmon. She had brought it home herself on the box of the victoria, for fear of there being any mischance as to its delivery. Alice was even more excited, for nobody else had ever been permitted to work Master a pair of slippers, and Julia Fyson was coming to dinner, who, with eyes green with jealousy, would see the presentation made. They were to be brought into the dining-room at the end of dinner, when Lady Keeling gave two short pressures to the electric bell that stood by her on the table, by the boy covered with buttons, wrapped round with endless swathings of paper. He was to present this bale to Mr Silverdale, saying that it was immediate and asking if there was any answer. Would it not be fun to see the astonished Master take off all those wrappings, and find the Maltese crosses within?

This entertaining scheme succeeded admirably. Alice showed a remarkable sense of dramatic by-play, and talked very eagerly to her neighbour, while Mr Silverdale stripped off layer after layer of paper, as if she was quite unaware that anything unusual was happening, and it was not till an unmistakable shape of slippers began to reveal itself in the core, that Master guessed.

'It's my Helper,' he cried, 'my sly little Helper.' Then pushing back his chair, he took off his evening shoes, and putting on the slippers went solemnly round the table, saying to each of his hosts and fellow-guests, 'May I introduce you to my slippers?' But when he came to Alice he said, 'I think you and my slippers have met before.' There was never anything so deliciously playful. . . . But when he had padded back to his place, Keeling saw poor Alice's eye go wandering, looking at every one in turn round that festive table except

Master. Finally, for one half second, her eye rested on him, and Keeling, as one of those who run, could read, and his heart went out to poor Alice. She was prodigiously silly, yet that one self-revealing glance decorated her. She loved, and that distinguished and dignified her.

After the guests had gone, Lady Keeling launched forth into her usual comments on the success of her dinner-party.

'Well, I'm sure I should be puzzled to name a pleasanter evening,' she said. 'I thought it all quite brilliant, though I'm sure I claim no share in its success except that I do think I gave you all a very good dinner. I'm sure I never tasted a better bit of spring salmon than that. Was it not lucky it caught my eye this afternoon. And the slippers, too, Alice! It was quite a little comedy: I am sure I have seen many less amusing scenes in a play. To introduce everybody to his slippers! That was a good idea, and it must have been quite *ex tempore*, for I am certain he did not know what was inside the packet till he came to the last wrappings.'

. . . Perhaps this was the last time that Keeling would ever listen to those maunderings. That would be determined in the bluebell wood. Perhaps to-morrow evening . . .

'And then saying to Alice, "I think you and my slippers have met before!" That was fun, was it not? I saw you enjoyed that, Thomas, and when you are pleased, I'm sure the joke is good enough for anybody. I wish I had asked Lord and Lady Inverbroom to dine to-night. They would have enjoyed it too, though perhaps he would feel a little shy of meeting you after that snub you gave him and his Club in taking their premises away from them.'

. . . Would the bluebells reflect their colour on to her face, as the daffodils she wore one day had done? By the way, no word had been said about the hour at which they should meet. But it did not matter: he would be there and she . . .

'I have cancelled the notice I gave them,' he said. 'You will not have the pleasure of seeing the club furniture coming out into the street.'

'Well, indeed! You are much too kind to them after what they did to you, Thomas. I am sorry you did that; they deserved a good slap to serve them out.'

An awful spirit of raillery seized the unfortunate woman. She would say something lightly and humorously, just to show she had nothing but goodwill towards Miss Propert; it should be quite in that felicitous comedy-style which had made the business of the slippers such a success.

'Ah, but now I remember that Miss Propert did not want you to give them notice,' she said. 'Now we can guess why you took it back again. Oh, not a word more. I am discretion itself.'

Even this did not hurt him. He was rather amused than otherwise.

'Trust you for hitting the nail on the head, Emmeline,' he said. 'That was why.'

Lady Keeling rose in great good humour. Once, she remembered, her husband had been very rude when she made a little joke about his regard for Miss Propert. She had hit the nail on the head then, too, for no doubt there was something (ever so little) of truth in what she said, and it had 'touched him up.' But now he did not mind: that showed that there was no truth in it at all now. She had never thought there was anything serious, for Thomas was not that sort of man (and who should know better than she?), but perhaps he had been a little attracted. She was delighted to think that it was certainly all over.

'Ah, I knew I had guessed,' she said. 'And perhaps Miss Propert's right, for it is always best to be friendly with everybody even if they do behave shabbily. I have always found Miss Propert very sensible and well-behaved, and if she and her brother are coming to see your books on Sunday afternoon, Thomas, and you like to bring them in to tea, you will find me most civil and pleasant to them both. There! And now I think Alice and I will be getting to bed. Dear me, it's after eleven already. Time flies so, when you are enjoying yourself.'

She gave him a cheerful kiss, she tapped the

barometer, and, taking Alice in tow, she left him. Their cheerful voices, talking about the slippers, died away as they went upstairs.

It was not one lark but many that were carolling specks against the blue, as Keeling walked along the ridge of the down next day, to where after an upland mile it dipped into the hollow where he and Norah had met before, and where they would meet again now. The afternoon was warm and windless, and the squalls and showers of yesterday had been translated into the vivider green that clothed the slopes. But all this epiphany of spring that had so kindled his heart before, passed by him to-day quite unobserved: he saw only the tops of the trees, which, climbing up on the sides of the hollow for which he was bound, fringed the edge of the ridge. Soon he had reached that, the track dipped over down the slope, and on each side, between the oak-trunks, and the stumps of the felled hazels, there was spread one continuous sheet of azure, as if the sky had flooded the ground with itself. But he hardly saw that even, for sitting on the bank, where, at the bottom of the hollow, the stream crossed the track, was Norah.

She had watched him come down the path, and when he was some ten paces from her, she rose. She had no word, it would seem, for him, nor he for her, and they stood in silence opposite each other. But the clear glance shone on him, steady and quiet and complete. Then, as by some common impulse, her hands and his were clasped together.

'Just Norah,' he said.

The grave smile with which she had welcomed him grew a shade graver, a shade more tender.

'Do you know how I love you?' he asked.

'Yes, I know. And—and I give you all you bring me. You know that, don't you?'

Again by some common impulse they moved off the path, still with hands clasped. They walked through the fallen sky of bluebells, not seeing it, and came to where a fallen trunk, lopped of its branches, lay on the ground.

'We will sit here a little, shall we?' she said. 'It mustn't be long.'

'Why not for ever?' he asked.

'You know that, too,' she said.

At that moment there was nothing in the world for him but she.

'I know nothing of the sort,' he said. 'We belong to each other. That's all I know. I have you now: you needn't think I shall let you go. You will leave that damned place this evening with me. That's the only reason why we mustn't be long here.'

She raised her eyes to his, and without speaking shook her head.

'But it is to be so,' he cried. 'There's no other

way out. We've found each other: do you think I am going to let us lose each other? There is no other way.'

Even as he spoke, that silent inexorable tug, that irresistible tide of character which sweeps up against all counter-streams of impulse which do not flow with it, began to move within him. He meant all he said, and yet he knew that it was not to be. And as he looked at her, he saw in her eyes that fathomless eternal pity, which is as much a part of love as is desire.

'There is no way out there,' she said. 'Look into yourself and tell me if you really believe there is. The way is barred. You yourself bar it. How could I then pass over it?'

'If you loved me——' he began.

'Ah, hush; don't say that. It is nonsense, wicked nonsense. Isn't it?'

'Yes,' he said.

She was infinitely stronger than he: a dozen times in details she had proved that. Now, when there was no detail, but a vital issue at stake, she could show all her strength, instead of but sparring with him.

'Well, then, listen,' she said. 'We are honest folk, my dear, both you and I. You are under certain obligations; you have a wife and children. And since I love you, I am under the same obligations. They are yours, and therefore they are mine. If it weren't for them—but it is no use thinking of that.'

'But I repudiate them,' he said. 'They have become meaningless. You are the only thing which means anything to me. Norah! Norah! Thou beside me singing in the wilderness! What else is there? What else?'

His passion had lifted him upon his feet: he stood there before her, strong and masterful. He was accustomed always to get his way: he would get it now in spite of the swift-flowing tide against which his impulse struggled, in spite of her who was sailing up on the tide.

'There is nothing else,' she said. 'But there is not that.'

He knelt down on the ground by her.

'But, my darling,' he said, 'it is not our fault. It happened like that. God gave us hearts, did He not, and are we just to disobey what our hearts tell us? We belong to each other. What else can we do? Are we to eat our hearts out, you on one side of the table in that hell upstairs, I on the other? Don't tell me that is the way out!'

She raised her hands and let them lie with strong pressure on his shoulders.

'No, there is no way out there,' she said. 'I couldn't stand that, nor could you. But there is a way out, and you and I are going to take it.'

Again the infinite pity of her strength welled up and dimmed her eyes.

'I am going away,' she said. 'I shall leave Bracebridge to-night. It's all settled.'

He shook himself free of her hands.

'We go together then,' he said, but there was no conviction in his voice. It was but a despairing, drowning cry.

She made a little gesture with her head.

'Come back here,' she said. 'Let me put my hands on your shoulders again. Yes, just like that. It is all settled. Charles agrees. He knows enough: I think he guesses the rest. I shall go back to London, and get work there. I shall find it perfectly easy to do that. If you will give me a little testimonial, it would help me. You mustn't come to see me. You mustn't write to me. I won't say anything so foolish as to tell you to forget me. You can't, to begin with, and also I don't want you to. I want you to remember me always, with love and with honour——'

She stopped for a moment, smiling at him through her tears.

'You made me cry two mornings ago,' she said, 'and I felt so ashamed of myself. I don't feel ashamed of myself now. I—I am rather proud of myself, and I want you to be proud of me.'

Her voice broke utterly, and she sat with her head in her hands, sobbing her heart out. Presently with one hand she felt for his, and sat thus clasping it.

'Sit by me,' she said at length, 'and very soon we must walk back over the down, and when we come to the skylark's nest you shall go on and

I will follow after a few minutes. Let's go through these few months, as if pasting them into our memories. We must each have the same remembrance as the other. I hated you at first, do you know? I hated working for you. The books began to bring us together, the mischievous things. Then there came the wood-block for your book-plate, but you apologised. And then came the catalogue, was not that it? By that time I had got to love working for you, though I did not guess at once what was the matter with me. Then came the spring day, that first day of real spring, and I knew. And there is one thing I want to ask you. Did Lord Inverbroom ever tell you about my people?'

'No, never.'

'Well, you might like to know. My father was a great friend of his at one time. But he went off with another woman, deserting my mother. That was another reason why we have settled our affairs as we have settled them. I thought I would like to tell you that. We can't bring on others the misery they brought.'

She put her hand through the crook of his arm.

'Look,' she said. 'We came to see the bluebells, and we have never noticed them till now. Did I not say they would be a carpet spread under the trees. Shall we pick some? I should like to leave a bunch at the hospital on my way home.'

Very soon her hands were full of them, and she tied her handkerchief round their juicy stems.

'We must go,' she said. 'But there will be bluebells in my heart all my life.'

They walked together up the slope on to the down, and along the ridge. As they got near to the end of it, where it plunged down again towards Bracebridge, their pace grew slower, and at last they stopped altogether.

'It is good-bye,' she said, and quite simply like a child she raised her face to his.

He went on alone after that, and she sat down on the turf to wait, as she had done before, with her bunch of bluebells beside her. She kept her eyes on his receding figure, and just before it passed downwards out of sight he turned, as she knew he would do. A moment afterwards he had disappeared.

Late that night he was sitting alone in his library. The evening had passed precisely as it always did when he and his wife and Alice were by themselves. Lady Keeling had been neither more nor less fatuous than usual, Alice, the slippers being off her mind, had played a couple of games of backgammon with him, and had shown herself as futile an adversary as ever.

Norah had gone: that fact was indelibly imprinted on his mind, but as yet it aroused no emotion. It had produced no sense of desolation in him: all the strainings of doubt and desire which had racked him before were dead. The suspense was over, his love would enjoy no fruition, and he had been all evening exactly as is the man who has been condemned to be hung, and now, though he has passed a month of sleeplessness or nightmare, has no anxiety to torture him, and for that first night after his trial is over, can rest in the certainty of the worst and the uttermost. Several times this evening Keeling had probed into his own heart, pricking it with the reminder of the knowledge that she had left him, but no response, no wail or cry of pain had come from it. His heart knew it, and there was no use in repeating the news. His heart had received it, and lay there beating quietly and steadily. Meantime all his surface-perceptions went on with no less vividness than was their wont. There was Alice making her usual mistakes over the moves of the pieces, there was Lady Keeling alternating between drowsiness and volubility. Her fat face wrinkled and bulged on one side when her head fell a little crooked as she dozed; it became symmetrical again when she recovered herself, and talked on her invariable topics, Lord Inverbroom, dinner, her engagements as Lady Mayoress, Mr Silverdale, and so forth. She alluded again to her husband's magnanimity in not turning out the County Club from their premises, she even introduced Norah's name, and endorsed her expressed intention to be polite to her if she came in to tea on Sunday. When necessary he replied, 'Quite so, my dear,' but nothing reached him. It was perfectly easy now to be polite and patient. He was locked up somewhere inside himself, and sparrows were twittering in the bushes far outside.

This absolute numbness came with him into his library, where he went when his wife and daughter, on the warning of the pink clock, proceeded upstairs, after the usual kisses. He did not want to wake his sensibilities up, simply because he did not want anything. Even here, in his secret garden, all he saw round him was meaningless: his library was a big pleasant room and he wondered why he had kept it so sacredly remote from his wife and Alice. There were some books in it, of course. Hugh had got a mercantile idea from one, Alice had been a little shy of an illustration in another, and for some reason he had felt that these attitudes were not tuned to the spirit he found here. But to-night there was no spirit of any kind here, and Alice might be shocked if she chose, Hugh might pick up hints for the printing of advertisements, his wife might put the Leonardo volume in her chair if she did not find it high enough, and if that did not give her the desirable position in which to doze most comfortably, there was the catalogue ready to make her a footstool. Books, books? . . . They were all strange and silly. In some there were pictures over which he had pored, in others there were verses that had haunted his memory as with magic, and all had a certain perfection about them, whether in print or page or binding or picture, that had once satisfied and intoxicated a certain desire for beauty that he had once felt. There they were on their shelves, there was the catalogue that described them, and the shelves were full of corpses, and the catalogue was like a column of deaths in the daily paper, of some remote individuals that concerned him no more than the victims of a plague in Ethiopia.

It was hot in here : except in summer a fire was always lit in the evening to keep damp out, unless he counter-ordered it, and he drew up the blind and opened the French window that gave on to the garden. An oblong of light cast itself outside, and in it he saw a row of daffodils that bordered the lawn across the gravel path, nodding in the night wind. They were very yellow : they would cast yellow reflections on anything near them. . . .

Then awoke hunger in his heart, and it screamed out to him, starving. Perhaps she had not gone : perhaps she, like himself, had experienced a numbness of the heart, that made her feel that she did not care. He had been stupid and tongue-tied this afternoon, he had not shown her the depth of his passion, he had not *made* her listen to him. He had not done that : it was that she was waiting for, eager to be overmastered, to be made unable to resist. Surely she had not gone. . . .

He let himself out of the front-door, remembering how, but a few months ago, he had done just that, on a night of snow. Now, as then, he wanted to be sure that she was safe at home, but now, not as then, he would not content himself with seeing the light behind the blind. He must see her, he must make her understand that they only existed for each other. Certainly she had not gone away . . . certainly she was waiting exactly for this. She would be there still, he would make her feel the impossibility of any solution but this. She would bow to his indomitable force; she would recognise it, and consent, with her whole heart, to endorse it, to come away with him and cut the knot, and find all that God meant them to be to each other.

The empty sparsely-lit streets streamed by him, and it seemed that the earth seemed to be swiftly spinning below him; he just marked time as it turned. The night-wind of spring both cooled and intoxicated him, he felt surer and surer of the success of his errand as he went, and at the same time practical considerations occurred to him. Her brother would be in the house; it was still not late, and probably they would be together. Charles understood enough, so she had told him, to make him sanction her departure; now, when Keeling had seen her, he would understand more. Charles perhaps would open the door to him, for their two servants would have gone to bed, or be out for Saturday night, and Keeling would say to him, 'I must see your sister.' That was what he would say; and Charles, understanding enough, would see the justice of that demand of love.

He came opposite the house, and his heart leaped, for there was a light behind her window-blind. He had known there would be, and he almost shouted for exultation at the fulfilment of his anticipation. Of course she had not gone: she was waiting just for this.

Swiftly and jubilantly he crossed the road: at the sight of that lit blind all the awakening pangs of his heart had passed from him, even as at the sight of the nodding daffodils had passed the apathy that encompassed it before. His intolerance of his wife, the dreaminess of his purposeless existence ceased to be: on the other hand his secret garden, now that the gardener who had made it sacred was waiting for him, bloomed again in an everlasting spring. In answer to his ring, which he heard faintly tinkling inside, there came steps on the stairs, and the dark fan-light over the door leaped into brightness, as some one turned on the switch. Then the door opened, and, as he had expected, there was Charles.

'Sir Thomas?' he said. 'Won't you come in? I answered the door myself, the servants have gone to bed. What can I do for you, sir?'

It was all happening exactly as Keeling had

anticipated, and he laughed for joy, as he stepped inside.

'I want to see your sister for a minute,' he said. 'We did not quite finish our talk this afternoon.'

Charles looked at him rather curiously, and Keeling wondered whether some doubt as to his sobriety had crossed the young man's mind. The idea amused him.

'But my sister has gone, sir,' he said. 'Surely you know that.'

Keeling closed the front-door into the street.

'Ah, yes, and left her room lit,' he said, joking with him out of sheer happiness.

'I was in her room,' said Charles. 'I was packing some things which she had not time enough to pack herself.'

For a moment it seemed to Keeling that the light and the walls and the floor quivered.

'Nonsense, Propert,' he said, and his voice quivered too.

'Perhaps you would like to come up and see for yourself, sir,' said Charles.

Keeling looked at him with perfectly blank eyes.

'Do you really mean she has gone?' he asked.

'Yes, sir. I felt sure you understood that. She said she had told you.'

He had grasped the back of a chair that stood near him, and leaned on it heavily. Then recovering his steadiness he spoke again.

'Kindly give me her address then,' he said.

'She wanted me to write her a testimonial, which I am happy to do. She was a very efficient secretary; I have nothing but praise for her. I will send it her to-morrow.'

'She spoke to me of that,' said Charles, 'and asked that you would send it to me, to forward to her. But I can't give you her address without her express permission.'

'But what nonsense this is,' said Keeling angrily. 'As if I couldn't find her in a week for myself.'

'I trust you will attempt to do no such thing, sir,' said Charles.

'And do you presume to dictate to me what I shall do and what I shall not?' asked he.

Charles looked at him with some shadow of the pity he had seen to-day in Norah's eyes.

'I don't dictate to you at all,' he said. 'I only remind you of Norah's wishes.'

'And do you agree with them? Do you approve of her mad freak in running off like this?'

'Yes, sir; as far as I understand what has happened I do approve. I think it was the only honest course left her.'

Suddenly Keeling's anger evaporated, leaving only a sore throbbing place where it had burned.

'I hope she's not—not very unhappy,' he said. He could not help saying that: he had to speak of her to somebody.

'She is utterly miserable,' said Charles. 'It

couldn't be otherwise, could it? And you are miserable too, sir. I am—I am awfully sorry for you both. But I suppose that has got to be. Norah could do nothing else than what she has done.'

Keeling sank down in the chair on which he had been leaning. He felt completely tired out.

'Do you think she will allow me to see her or write to her?' he asked.

'Not for a long time. But—there is no harm in my telling you this—she wants me to tell her how you are. She hopes, sir, that you will make yourself very busy. That's the best thing to do, isn't it?'

Keeling had no reply to this. The apathy of intense fatigue, of an excitement and anticipation suddenly nullified, was blunting the sharp edges of his misery. For a little while he sat there with his head in his hands, then slowly and stiffly he got up, looking bent and old.

'I am sorry that I asked you for her address,' he said; 'I will be going home, and you must get back to your packing. Good-night, Propert.'

The world had ceased spinning for him as he walked back. He lifted heavy feet, as if he was going up some steep interminable hill. . . .

CHAPTER XI

KEELING went to his office on the following Monday morning, with his mind already made up about the extension of his business. He had an option on a big building site at the neighbouring manufacturing town of Nalesborough, and this he determined to exercise at once, and have put in hand, without delay, the erection of his new premises. His trade seemed to have reached its high-water mark here in Bracebridge, but the creation of a similar business elsewhere would occupy him for a dozen years yet, and what was more to his immediate purpose, give him a piece of critically important work now. Last summer he had more than half resolved to turn the Bracebridge Stores into a company, and, leaving Hugh as the director, himself retire from business, and enjoy among his books the leisure of which all his life he had had so little. Now his one desire was to set this new enterprise going, and thereby gain for himself not the leisure that lately he coveted, but the absorption which he hoped the work of organisation would bring him. It would be an immense task, and that was why he undertook it, for he had no desire any more for unoccupied hours, in which he could browse in the pastures of his secret garden. What he wanted was work, work of the kind that kept him so busy all day, that he had no further energy left for thought. He proposed to continue directing the course of his Bracebridge business also: with these two to superintend, he surely would find stupefaction for those bees of the brain whose bitter honey-making he had no use for.

He had made an excursion into fairy land—that was how he framed the matter to himself. There had been The Cedars and work for him before, there would be work and The Cedars for him afterwards. Those who have drunk of the metheglin never perhaps afterwards are wholly free from the reminiscence of the sweet draught brewed magically from the heather and the honey, but they go back after their sojourn among the little people, and behave like ordinary mortals again, and eat the home-brewed bread, and move about their appointed ways. But the nights and days they have spent in the secret places of the earth will, till they die, be more vivid to them than all the actual experiences that they go through afterwards and went through before they penetrated the enchanted glen; the remembrance will colour their idle moments with the ensanguined hue of dream; that baseless fabric, that vision of hidden doors thrown open and the things that lurk within, is more rich, just because to them it is more real than the sober tonelessness of their profession or pursuit. Therefore if they are wise, the best thing they can do is, like Prospero, to drown the magic book beneath the waters of absorbing employment. Often it will float up again to the surface, and each time it must be prodded back with averted eyes. So, for Keeling, a love that could not be realised once crowned the hill-tops of his nature; now that citadel and the very hill-tops themselves had been shaken down and strewn over the plains. He had now one paramount need—that of forgetting, and, since he could not forget, the need resolved itself into the effort to remember as little as possible, to use up in other ways the energy which was his, and the leisure that he could command if he chose.

He let himself into his office, where his letters were already being opened by the girl he had sent for to take over Norah's work. On the little table by the window there still stood Norah's typewriting machine, which it appeared she had altogether forgotten: her brother must be asked to take it away. By it was the pile of letters which dealt with businesses not yet concluded: all were in order with dockets of the affairs contained in them. Probably, before she quitted the office for the last time on Friday afternoon, she had foreseen that she would not return, and had left everything so that her successor might take up the work without difficulty. Nothing was omitted or left vague; she had finished everything with the most meticulous care. He searched through these papers to see if there was any private word for him. But there was nothing: this was office work, and such private words as she had for him had all been said in the bluebell wood.

Her successor, a rasping young woman with strong knuckles, proved herself very efficient, and before long she retired to the small room adjoining with her sheaf of shorthand notes. Her typewriting machine was already installed there, and soon the clack of the keys proclaimed her a swift worker. For a few minutes only the sound worried him: there was a new touch, a new note, (one that meant nothing to him except that it told him that his work was going forward) to get accustomed to. But very soon he was absorbed in the mass of affairs which his new venture brought with it. There was twelve years' work before him: here he was in the first hour of it. It stretched endlessly away, but he gave no attention to the enormous perspective. All he desired was to attend to the immediate foreground; he would progress inch by inch, detail by detail, till the perspective began to grow. He would look neither forwards nor backwards.

He left his office late that night after a long day's uninterrupted work, and, still busy with some problem, took without thinking the path through the Cathedral graveyard, which farther on led past the house where Norah had lived. But before he got there, he remembered, and turned off so as to avoid it. And then he paused, and retraced his steps again. Was it weak to avoid it, or was it weak to let himself walk by it? Perhaps the stronger course was just to get used to it. Sometime, perhaps, he would be able to go by it without noticing. . . .

It was already the dinner-hour when he arrived home, and he went into his wife's boudoir to tell her to begin without waiting for him. To his astonishment he found her not yet dressed, and as he entered, she hastily picked up her handkerchief, which was on the floor, and applied it to her eyes.

'Why, Emmeline, what's the matter?' he said.

She did not seem to him to be actually crying, but the ritual of crying was there, and had to be respected.

'Oh, my dear Thomas, you haven't heard the terrible news then?' she said. 'I thought you would be sure to have seen it placarded somewhere. Alice went straight to her room, and I haven't seen her since, though I repeatedly knocked at the door, which she has locked on the inside, and I'm sure it's most unnatural of her not to let her own mother comfort her. It all happened in a moment: I have always said those great motor-cars shouldn't be allowed to career about the streets, especially when they are all paved with cobbles as they are at Easton Haven, which are so slippery when it's wet. He slipped, and it went over him in a moment.'

'Will you please tell me whom it went over?' asked Keeling, as his wife paused for a second.

'Why, poor Mr Silverdale, and to think that it was only last Friday that we had such fun over the slippers. I declare I shall never want to see a slipper again. He was crushed to a jelly, and I'm sure I hope the driver will be well hung for it, though they are certain to prove that it wasn't his fault, which is so easy now that poor Mr Silverdale can't give his account of the matter. It was all over in a moment, though I know quite well you didn't like him, and said many sarcastic things about him and the young ladies whom he inspired. I'm sure I never said a hard thing about him, nor thought it either, though he didn't ask Alice to be his wife. But I am convinced he would have if he had been spared, that's one comfort. If only he had, all this might have been avoided, for they would be on their honeymoon now, let me see, February, March, April, or if they had come back, he wouldn't have wanted to set out on this mission just yet, and so the van wouldn't have been there. And what are we all to do now?'

These pathetic reflections had the effect of really working on Lady Keeling's feelings, and her throat tied itself into knots.

'His shepherd's crook!' she said. 'All his delightful ways, though, as I say, you never liked him. The muffins he has eaten sitting on the floor before this very fire! The way he used to run, like a boy! The Gregorian chants which he used to call so ripping! All that beautiful music! I declare I shall never want to go to church again. And pray what are we to do now? What's to happen to Alice, if she won't unlock her door.'

'The best thing we can do is to leave Alice alone for the present,' he said. 'I'll go up to her after dinner.'

'She won't see you,' said Lady Keeling confidently. 'She wouldn't see me, who have always been so sympathetic about Mr Silverdale, so what chance is there of her seeing you?'

'That is what I shall find out. Now it's late already; I have been detained at the office, so let us go into dinner as we are.'

Lady Keeling sighed.

'I couldn't eat a morsel,' she said, 'though I know it is the duty of all of us to keep our strength up. There is hare soup too: he was so fond of hare soup. But I must run upstairs first, and put on a black *fichu* or something. I could not sit down to table without some little token of respect like that.'

Lady Keeling performed this duty of keeping her strength up with her usual conscientiousness, and after dinner her husband sent a note up to Alice, saying that he would be alone in his library if she would like to come down. While they were still in the dining-room over coffee, the answer came back that she would do so, and presently he went in there, while Lady Keeling, in a great state of mystification as to how Alice could want to see her father, went back in what may be called dudgeon to the plush and mirrors of the drawing-room. It seemed to her very unnatural conduct on Alice's part, but no doubt the poor girl's head was so 'turned' with grief that she hardly knew what she was doing. Her mother could think of no other possible explanation. She indulged in a variety of conjectures about the funeral, and presently, exhausted by these imaginative efforts, fell asleep.

Keeling, when he went into his library, found Alice already there, sitting limply in front of the fire. She turned round when her father entered, and fixed on him a perfectly vacant and meaningless stare. Till then he had no notion what he should say to her: now when he saw that blank tragic gaze, he knew there was no necessity to think at all. He understood her completely, for he knew what it was to lose everything that his soul desired. And his heart went out to her in a manner it had never done before. She sat there helpless with her grief, and only some one like himself, helpless also, could reach her. Her silliness, her excited fussinesses had been stripped off her, and he saw the simplicity of her desolation.

From him had fallen his hardness, and in him she divined a man who, for some reason, could reach her and be with her. Before he had walked across the room to her, her expression changed: there came some sort of human gleam behind the blankness of her eyes, and she rose.

'Father,' she said, and then she ran to him, stumbling over her dress, and put her hands on his shoulders.

That grim mouth, which she had always thought so forbidding and unsympathetic, suddenly wore to her a perfectly new aspect: it was strong and tender.

'My dear,' he said, 'I am so glad you have let me come to you. You are in deep waters, poor girl.'

'I loved him,' she said.

'I know you did. That's why you're right to come to me. I can understand. I can't do anything for you except understand. I've loved too: I've lost too. I know what it's like.'

'I felt you did: I don't know why,' she said.

'Well, you felt right. We're together, my dear.'

Since she had heard the news, she had sat dry-eyed and motionless in her bedroom. Now in the sense of a companionship that comprehended, the relief of tears came, and with head buried on his shoulder, she clung to him while the storm raged. He just let her feel the pressure of his arm, and for the rest stood there braced and firm in body and steadfast soul. There was none who could help him, but comfortless himself he could comfort, and he waited with that live and infinite patience which is the gift only of the strong and masterful.

'There, my dear,' he said at length, 'you have cried enough, and you're better for it. Now you're going to be very good and dry your eyes, and sit down again by the fire, while I fetch you something to eat. You've had nothing.'

'I couldn't eat,' she said.

'Oh, yes, you could. Now do just as I tell you, Alice. When you've eaten, we'll talk again.'

Quietly and firmly he disengaged her arm from his, and putting her into her chair again, he presently returned, bringing a tray for her. Then, gently insisting, he made her eat and drink.

'Ought I to see mother?' she asked at length.

'Just wish her good-night when you go upstairs. I'm going to pack you off to bed in half an hour.'

'But she won't talk and cry—and—and not understand?' asked Alice.

'No, she shan't talk and cry. I'll take care of that. I'll act policeman. But I can't promise you that she'll understand. I should think nothing more unlikely.'

Alice had a faint smile for this.

'I never knew you before to-night, father,' she said.

'No, but we must try to be friends now.'

Alice moved aside the table which carried her

tray. 'You never liked him,' she said. 'How is it you can help me like this? How can you understand, if you didn't like him?'

'I know you did. That is all that concerns me.'

'Yes, but you thought him silly, and you thought me silly.'

He smiled at her.

'Yes, I often thought you both extraordinarily silly, if you will have it so,' he said. 'But I respect love.'

Alice's face began slowly to get misshapen and knotted. He spoke to her rather firmly.

'Don't begin crying again, Alice,' he said. 'You've had your cry.'

'But it's all so hopeless. There's nothing left for me. All the things we planned together——'

He interrupted.

'You've got to carry them out alone. Set yourself to do them, my dear. Don't leave out one. That's the thing. Make yourself busy: occupy yourself.'

He got up, speaking to himself as much as to her.

'That's what we have both got to do,' he said. 'We've got to work instead of snivelling, we've got to set our teeth and go ahead. I'm going to be busier than I've been for years. I'm going to start a new Stores in Nalesborough, and see after them and the Stores here myself.'

'But you were thinking of giving up your business altogether,' said she.

'I was, but I have reconsidered that. I'm going to be busier than ever: let us see which of us can be the busiest. I can't forget, nor can you, but we can leave as little time as possible for remembering.'

Suddenly their rôles were reversed, and she found herself in the position of sympathiser, if not comforter.

'But I thought you were so full of energy and happiness,' she said. 'What has happened?'

'Nothing that I can tell you,' he said. 'I didn't mean to speak of myself.'

She got up too.

'Poor father,' she said. 'I'm sorry, whatever it is.'

'Thank you, my dear. Don't try to guess. And now I'll take you in to your mother, just to say good-night. She shan't bother you. And we've got to bite on the bullet, Alice.'

A few minutes later he returned alone to his library. All round him were the shelves, now packed from floor to ceiling with book cases half filled projecting into the room, and on the table lay the three volumes of the catalogue. From all round thoughts and associations and memories gathered and swarmed, and, forming into a wave of pent-up bitterness, they roared over him. Everything he cared about had crumbled and disappeared. Here was his secret garden, which from boyhood he had tended and cultivated with ever-increasing care, and now each shelf was to him only a reminder of Norah, propping open the door he was resolved to shut. He had dreamed of leisure hours here, free from the sound of the grinding millstone of business, and now he only wanted to get back into the roar and thump of the wheels. He had wanted the society and companionship of men who would appreciate and sympathise, now they had shown that they did not want him, and indeed he wanted them no longer; his contractors and wholesale merchants and dealers would supply all the society he had any use for for years to come. He had let himself seek love, and he had found love, and just because it was love and no mere sensual gratification that he had sought, it had, with the full consent of all in him that was worthy of it, been plucked from him. And with its vanishing his secret garden had blossomed with bitter herbs, rosemary for rose and rue. Perhaps if he had looked he might find dim violets for remembrance, and if he waited and was patient there might spring up pansies for thoughts. But that at present was beyond the region of his desire: were he to seek for flowers, he would but seek poppies for forgetfulness.

The room was intolerable to him, he stifled and struggled in its air of bitter longings. His dreams had built a pavilion in his garden, and hung it with tapestries, and fate, terrible as an army with banners, had torn them down and trampled upon them in its relentless march. He could at least refuse to look on the ruins any more.

He turned to leave the room, looking round it once more, even as last Friday Norah had looked round his office, knowing that she would not see it again. There was nothing here that belonged to the life that stretched in front of him: all was part of the past. The most he could do was to exercise the fortitude he had enjoined on Alice, and banish from sight the material things round which, close as the tendrils of ivy, were twined the associations of what he had missed. All that his books had to say to him was pitched in the tones of the voice that he must remember as little as possible, for now if he opened one and read, it was Norah whom he heard reading. She filled the room. . . .

It was late: a long day's work was behind him, another lay in front of him, and he went out turning the key in the lock. He hung it on one of the chamois-horns tipped with brass, that formed the hat-rack.